"The woman," the earl said softly.

"I beg your pardon?" the Frenchman replied.

"You may wager the woman," Dare said.

"Mrs. Carstairs?" Bonnet asked, his voice astounded. "But this is England, my lord. Not…" The Frenchman's voice faltered, as if he could not think of a location where one might wager a human being.

"Indeed, it is," Dare agreed. With one finger he touched the enormous pile of notes on the table between them. "And these are the coins of the realm. Quite a lot of them, as a matter of fact. I'll wager them all, Mr. Bonnet, on one game. All of this for the woman."

Bonnet's eyes had followed the movement of the earl's hand as it reached out and touched the money. And then they rose again, considering his opponent's face. "One game?"

"Winner take all," Dare said softly. "And the only stake you must put up is Mrs. Carstairs."

Dear Reader,

Much of the beauty of romance novels is that most are written by women for women, and feature strong and passionate heroines. We have some stellar authors this month who bring to life those intrepid women we love as they engage in relationships with the men we also love!

We are very proud of Gayle Wilson, who has won awards for several of her Harlequin Historicals novels, as well as her contemporary romances for Harlequin Intrigue. Known for her gripping and original stories, Gayle's latest book, *My Lady's Dare,* is no exception. This Regency-set tale will grab you and not let go as the Earl of Dare becomes fascinated by another man's mistress, Elizabeth Carstairs. Nothing is as it seems in this dangerous game of espionage that turns into an even more dangerous game of love!

In *Bandera's Bride,* the talented Mary McBride gives her Southern belle heroine some serious chutzpah when, pregnant and alone, she travels to Texas to propose marriage to her pen pal of six years, a half-breed who's been signing his partner's name! And don't miss Susan Amarillas's new Western, *Molly's Hero,* a story of forbidden love between a—married?—female rancher and the handsome railroad builder who desperately needs her land.

Jacqueline Navin rounds out the month with *The Viking's Heart,* the sensational story of a fierce Viking who vows to save a proud noblewoman from a loveless arranged marriage.

Enjoy! And come back again next month for four more choices of the best in historical romance.

Sincerely,

Tracy Farrell,
Senior Editor

MY LADY'S DARE

GAYLE WILSON

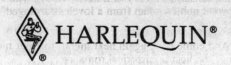

HARLEQUIN®

TORONTO • NEW YORK • LONDON
AMSTERDAM • PARIS • SYDNEY • HAMBURG
STOCKHOLM • ATHENS • TOKYO • MILAN • MADRID
PRAGUE • WARSAW • BUDAPEST • AUCKLAND

ISBN 0-373-29116-7

MY LADY'S DARE

Copyright © 2000 by Mona Gay Thomas

This edition published by arrangement with Harlequin Books S.A.

® and TM are trademarks of the publisher. Trademarks indicated with
® are registered in the United States Patent and Trademark Office, the
Canadian Trade Marks Office and in other countries.

Visit us at www.eHarlequin.com

Printed in U.S.A.

Please address questions and book requests to:
Harlequin Reader Service
U.S.: 3010 Walden Ave., P.O. Box 1325, Buffalo, NY 14269
Canadian: P.O. Box 609, Fort Erie, Ont. L2A 5X3

For my cousin Elizabeth—the pretty one

Prologue

Paris, 1813

The edge of the blade sliced through the skin of the Earl of Dare's neck as its point thudded into the scarred wood at his back. Only a reflexive jerk of his head to the side had prevented the tip from piercing his throat instead of the door behind him.

With a lightning shift of balance, Dare thrust his own sword forward and into the chest of the man whose blade was momentarily useless, its tip embedded in the wood. When Dare pulled back his arm, the hiss of escaping air and the gush of blood that followed told him this fight was at an end.

The dying man slumped against him, and the earl supported the body with his sword hand while he sought for the latch of the door behind him with his other. Just as he found it, a cry went up from the courtyard in front of the house where he was hiding.

He didn't know how the French had found him. It made no difference now. What was important was getting out without being seen or heard by the soldiers in the street. He opened the door, making as little noise as possible, and stepped out, pulling the body of the dead man with him into the concealing darkness of the night.

Dare tried to execute his missions when no moon rode the night sky. During those expeditions, which put him within the very heart of the enemy's strongholds, he needed every advantage he and nature could devise. But with the relentless manhunt now being carried out through the winding Parisian streets, he would need more of those advantages than ever before.

The earl eased the body he'd been supporting into the shadows cast by the wide eves and pulled the door closed behind him. Then he leaned back against it as, breathing suspended, he strained to follow by sound alone the progress of the search.

The shouted commands and the noise of the milling horses all seemed to be coming from the crooked lanes that ran in front of the house. He could hear no movement here along the river, except for the occasional lap of water against one of the rotting piers that serviced the shops and houses that had been built along this embankment.

Using his teeth, the earl pulled the thin leather glove off his left hand and put his bare fingers against the wound on his neck. The cut had begun to burn, and he found it was bleeding more profusely than he would have liked, the blood warm and thick against the chill of his trembling fingertips.

He took his hand away, holding it by force of habit in front of him. The Stygian blackness of the alleyway, an odoriferous cobblestoned ribbon which followed the left bank of the Seine, prevented him from being able to see either blood or fingers.

Wiping the moisture on his cloak, Dare pulled the glove back on, again using his teeth to finish the job. He was still listening to the sounds of the hunt, ready to spring to action if his pursuers approached. He tugged his cravat higher around his throat, hoping it would catch the blood.

Eventually the searchers would bring torches to try to find any trace of their prey as the hunt fanned out along the riverbank. He couldn't afford to leave a telltale trail of blood by which they could track him. Although he himself might be back in England by the time those droplets were discovered, the man in whose house he would take shelter tonight would not be.

And the Earl of Dare had a hard-earned reputation for protecting his associates. Anyone who didn't wouldn't last long in this business. The line of the earl's mouth slanted suddenly. Despite his predicament, he was amused by that thought. Actually, *no one* lasted long in his business, no matter the care he took.

He had certainly been pushing his luck tonight. Of course, that was something he had always done. His brother Ian accused him of needing the thrill this dangerous game gave him. The narrow escapes. The occasional pursuit. Perhaps his brother was right, he admitted, his lips tilting again. After all, Ian usually was. Especially about his siblings.

Dare stepped away from the shadows of the building, moving with the graceful stealth of a hunting cat, the hilt of his sword still clutched in his hand. He carried a loaded pistol as well, but it was the blade that had saved his life tonight. As it had on more than one occasion. The sound of a shot in a Parisian street would undoubtedly be investigated by the authorities, but the whisper of a rapier, as quick and deadly as an adder's strike, had never given away his location.

Once he had put some distance between himself and the yard of the house where he had left the dead man, the earl began to hurry. He moved almost soundlessly, his booted feet running lightly over the rough and broken stones. His eyes examined every patch of darkness that loomed ahead, but gradually the noise of the soldiers faded away behind him.

It wouldn't be long before they found the body of the man he had killed, however. And when they did, he had no doubt that they would redouble their efforts. If only his famous luck would hold a little longer, he thought, recognizing that he was nearing his destination. Then the French would again be disappointed in their efforts to capture him.

Eventually, the earl slipped into a low stone doorway, ducking his head to accommodate his height to an entrance that had been constructed three centuries before. This area was one of the oldest in the city, the buildings still partially enclosed by the medieval wall.

Even without light, it was obvious he was in the right place. The scent in the low room was so strong it was almost taste. Dare stood a moment, his nose raised like a hound's, breathing in the thick air, richly pungent with hops and malt.

"Running late are you, my lord?" a voice asked. The accent was English, broadened by the speaker's obvious Yorkshire heritage. "I was beginning to get worried."

"Someone tried to slice my gullet," Dare explained, closing the heavy door by which he had just entered and throwing the iron bolt across it. "I was forced to…dissuade him."

As soon as the lock shot home, he heard the sound of a flint, and the pale, wavering thread of fire it had produced gradually became a glow. Then slowly, out of the shadows beside the strengthening light, a face, Mephistophelianlike, floated into view.

Unlike the voice that had preceded them, its features were nondescript, as easily French or Italian as British: dark eyes, an undistinguished jut of nose, a wide, generous mouth, arranged in a grin. And all of them surmounted by mouse-brown hair, which had been tied back in a neat queue.

"Oh, you ain't gone and bloodied your linen, have you, my lord?" the earl's valet asked plaintively. "You've no idea what a time I have with bloodstains. And you would be wearing one of our new cravats."

"I've almost been beheaded, Ned, and all you can worry about is the state of my cravat," the earl said, laughing. He slipped the woolen cloak off his shoulders and threw it carelessly over a convenient cask.

"It's not just the linen that's the problem," Ned Harper said. "It's the lace as well. Hard to come by now that Nappy's got the continent tied up."

"Perhaps we might shop for a yard or two before we leave Paris," Dare suggested politely.

He crossed the room to where his valet was standing and took the brimming mug held out to him. The earl raised the cup and drank down its contents in one long quaff, then lowered it to look into his servant's eyes.

"He wasn't there," Dare said softly, and watched the laughter fade from Ned Harper's face.

"Damn," the smaller man said feelingly.

"Bloody right," agreed the earl. "He wasn't there, and the gendarmes were."

There was a long silence as his valet considered the information. "Someone told them you were coming."

"There was only one man who knew that."

"He'd never talk," Harper declared with conviction.

"*Anyone* can be made to talk," the earl said softly. "There are things which may be done to a man…." The words faded, and again the Earl of Dare's eyes met those of his friend. "Anyone can be made to talk," he finished simply.

Harper nodded, his gaze still locked on the earl's classically handsome face. The grin with which he had greeted his master was gone. Perhaps he was thinking, as Dare was, of the terrible things that were done to prisoners in France today. The same unspeakable tortures that had once, a long time ago, been carried out in the bowels of England's own dungeons.

"Then…we have to get him out," Harper said. "Out of Paris. Out of the country."

"Indeed," the earl said, his eyes, made sapphire by the lamplight, were no longer focused on his valet's face. They were gazing instead, unseeing, into the heart of the flame.

"What will you do?" Harper asked.

"First, we shall have to find him. Which may take some time." The earl's voice faltered again as his imagination visited the prison where his friend would be held while his enemies tried to extract information from him. Information about his contacts in espionage, such as the earl himself.

"And time, Ned…" Dare continued after a long silence, his voice very soft. "Time is now a luxury we no longer have."

Chapter One

London, three nights later

"If all goes according to plan, my dear, we shall have a very special guest tonight," Henri Bonnet said, smiling with undisguised satisfaction. "One to whom I wish you to be especially attentive."

Elizabeth Carstairs' eyes lifted to the reflection of her employer's in the mirror above her dressing table. She said nothing, however, and after a moment she returned her attention to the task of darkening the pale lashes above her blue eyes.

The Frenchman strode angrily across the room and caught her chin in his fingers, roughly turning her to face him. "A *very* special guest," he said again, each word sharp and distinct. "Do you understand me, Elizabeth?"

"Of course," the Englishwoman said. Neither her face nor her voice expressed dismay at the gambler's treatment of her.

For the past two years, Elizabeth Carstairs had had little control over any aspect of her life except her

demeanor. And she had decided from the beginning
that Henri Bonnet would never be allowed to know
what she was thinking. Or feeling.

Still gripping her chin painfully, Bonnet turned her
face toward the light of the lamp on her dressing table.
He examined it critically before he dipped one finger
into a pot of rouge, which was standing open on the
dresser. He added more color to her lips and then to
her cheeks, blending the rouge into the small amount
she had already applied.

He stepped back, his head tilted, still assessing.
Then he touched the sleeve of the blue gown she was
wearing, flicking its edging of lace dismissingly. "And
wear the red, I think, rather than this. We are entertaining someone important, Elizabeth. Someone very
important. And I'm counting on you, of course, to do
your part," he added softly.

Without waiting to see if she would obey his command to change—because he knew that she would—
the gambler turned, leaving her alone in her bedroom.
Her eyes returned to the reflection in the mirror. She
watched her lips tighten in anger, and then using the
tips of her fingers, she scrubbed at the rouge, trying
to remove it from her cheeks.

After a moment, the movement of her fingers
stopped, and she leaned forward, staring intently into
the eyes of the woman in glass. Slowly she shook her
head, a single negative movement. Then she rose, her
fingers working over the buttons down the back of her
bodice, preparing to put on the dress the gambler had
instructed her to wear. Her lips were set, her eyes cold,
and after she had changed, she never looked again into
the mirror.

* * *

"So good of you to honor us with your company, my Lord Dare," Henri Bonnet said.

The Frenchman bowed from the waist. His left hand, graced by a brilliantly faceted emerald ring, made a sweeping gesture toward a large gaming table, which had been set up in one of the private salons of his elegant London hell.

There were two empty chairs at the table. The other four were occupied by gentlemen of the earl's acquaintance, who had obviously been awaiting his arrival. Dare's gaze skimmed almost insultingly over his host, not even acknowledging his bow. He considered the group at the table, his eyes resting briefly on the face of each man.

"I believe you know everyone," the Frenchman added, his tone expressing no displeasure that the earl had failed to respond to his effusive greeting. However rude the earl might be, they all knew the gambler couldn't afford to offend so wealthy a patron.

All conversation at the table had come to a halt with the earl's arrival, and every eye was focused on the figure poised in the doorway. Despite the fact that he had reached his London town house less than an hour ago, Dare knew there was nothing to criticize in his appearance. With Harper's assistance, and according to the reassuring reflection in his mirror, he had again achieved the sartorial elegance for which Valentine Sinclair, the Earl of Dare was justly famous. Or perhaps justly *infamous,* he thought, mocking his own carefully constructed reputation.

It was said that some of the younger members of the *beau monde* had once tried to estimate the cost of the clothing Dare had worn to some court occasion, even going so far as to place wagers on the amount in the betting books. Despite the fact that he was known for indulging his expensive taste to the utmost, the sums Dare heard mentioned in that incident hadn't even approached the amount he had actually spent.

And spent for a good cause, he acknowledged, bowing formally toward the Duke of Pendlebrooke, the only man present who outranked him. Dare's attention to fashion was part of his ongoing masquerade. As were most of his excesses, including the one he would engage in tonight.

"Gentlemen," Dare said, inclining his head to the men at the table, "I bid you good evening. And offer my abject apologies to have kept you waiting. My man was singularly inept tonight."

Forgive me, Ned, Dare thought, as he made that ridiculous statement. Harper's reputation rivaled Dare's own among the fops of the ton, and they laughed together about the secret offers the valet received, attempting to lure him away from his employer.

"I throw myself on your mercy and beg your forgiveness for my tardiness," Dare finished with the slightest bend of his upper body. His tone somehow made it obvious that he didn't really give a tinker's damn whether or not they forgave him.

As he bowed, Dare's fingers unobtrusively touched the heavily starched cravat around his throat, tied tonight in an intricate style that bore his name. He eased the cloth upward, although Harper had assured him the gash was completely covered.

Adjusting his clothing once he had left his dressing room was something that Dare, like Brummel, ordinarily would never have done. However, revealing that he bore a sword cut on his neck would be a far more serious *faux pas.* A wound of that nature would be totally out of character for the Earl of Dare that London believed she knew.

Despite his apology for being late, Dare crossed the room as unhurriedly as if he were strolling along the shop windows on Bond Street. With impeccable timing, Bonnet's servant pulled out the empty chair on the nearer side just as Dare reached the table. Gracefully adjusting the tail of his coat, the earl sat down, blue eyes again considering the men who were very shortly to become his opponents.

Although he had rather be almost anywhere else on earth than here, Dare's face reflected nothing of that feeling. Only a languid boredom was allowed to play across his features. The expression appeared to be habitual and, like his clothing, was frequently aped by aspiring dandies, who hoped to achieve this same air of elegantly detached ennui.

The earl was not, however, suffering from boredom. He was grief-stricken and furious, exhausted from a more than forty-eight hour lack of sleep, and sickened by the events of the three days he had just spent in France.

He had kept this engagement tonight only because *not* appearing might have called into question his whereabouts during those days. And the fact that a dear friend had died in his arms today would not have served as an excuse for his absence. After all, given Dare's reputation, most people would be surprised had he claimed to possess a friend. Certainly not one who had been willing to give his own life to protect the earl's.

Remembering that sacrifice, Dare's lips flattened, almost imperceptibly. Emotion was something he

could not allow, of course, so deliberately he forced
from his mind the image of the broken body he had
held. He could not afford to let his failure in France
interfere with his purposes here, which were perhaps
as important as the ones which had taken him to the
continent.

Henri Bonnet entertained the most influential men
in the British capital, including those who ran the
Horse Guards and those who sat in the House of Lords
and occupied positions of authority within the current
government. Talk of politics and war flowed as freely
at these tables as did the Frenchman's wine, which
made this house an excellent source of information.

Bonnet was openly contemptuous of the Corsican
upstart who occupied the throne of France. Reportedly
the descendent of a family prominent in the *ancien
régime,* Bonnet had come to England at the height of
the Revolution. With no skills and little money, the
former aristocrat had opened a small gaming house
where, he had proclaimed, there would never be a betting limit.

His establishment had become the most popular
gaming hell in the city and was now housed in this
magnificent Palladian town house. And there was still
no limit on what could be staked on the turn of a card
or the spin of the wheel.

"Would you care for wine, my lord?" Bonnet
asked.

Looking up, Dare realized that the servant who
seated him had disappeared. A woman now stood beside his chair, holding a silver tray on which stood a
decanter of claret and a single goblet. The light from
the candles which illuminated the room was refracted
from the crystal, turning the wine a rich ruby red.

The woman's gown, expertly fashioned from a heavy satin of almost that same hue, was cut straight across and very low over the swell of her breasts. In contrast to the jewellike tones of the fabric, her skin was luminous as pearl, shaded with gold by the flattering candlelight.

Looking up into her eyes, Dare realized they were as blue as his own. As she waited, they rested on his face with a patent disinterest. Dare's features had evoked a myriad of responses from women through the years. Disinterest, however, had never been one of them, and it intrigued him.

To his very experienced eyes, it was apparent her face had been painted, although it had been done with an expert hand. The use of cosmetics, which no respectable Englishwomen of his class wore, of course, told the earl a great deal. Her hair, silver-gilt in the candlelight, was dressed very simply in a style that any hostess of the ton might have worn. Loose curls, tumbling artlessly above the flawless oval of her face, had been threaded with a single strand of what appeared to be genuine rubies.

"My lord?" she inquired softly. One fair eyebrow arched with her question.

"Of course," Dare said, realizing that in his fascination he had never answered Bonnet. Even to his own ears, his voice as he did sounded unnatural, almost husky, touched with emotion.

Surprisingly, he found himself still watching the woman as she handed the tray to the manservant. She removed the decanter with a graceful economy of motion and poured wine into the goblet, which she had set on the table. She never looked at Dare during the process.

As she bent over him, however, the earl was suddenly surrounded by the subtle scent she wore. Not the familiar rose or lavender waters favored by the women of his set. This was something darker, heady with musk, sensually evocative, and almost certainly French.

When the woman straightened and began to turn to put the decanter back on the tray, Dare spoke, his accent deliberately no better than the average Englishman's, although he had been fluent in French since childhood. *"Merci, mademoiselle."*

"But Mrs. Carstairs is a countrywoman of *yours,* my lord," Bonnet corrected, his tone verging on amusement.

"Indeed," Dare said, pretending to study her features as if her nationality might somehow be revealed by them. "I'm sure I should never have guessed. My compliments, madam."

At his words, she turned back, the decanter still in her hands. From the look in her eyes, the earl could not be perfectly certain she wasn't about to throw it at his head.

"Your...compliments, my lord?" she asked.

"For being English, of course," the earl said, his lips tilting. "Why, whatever did you think I meant, Mrs. Carstairs?"

"I thought you were complimenting me that I didn't *appear* to be English." Her eyes challenged him a moment before she added, her tone conciliatory, as befitted someone in her position. "Obviously, I was mistaken. Pray forgive me, my lord."

"Had I meant *that,* madam," Dare said smoothly, "then *I* should be the one to beg *your* forgiveness."

"There is no need for your apologies here, Lord

Dare," Bonnet said laughing. "*Whatever* your meaning. Elizabeth is here to serve you. If there is anything you should require during your visit, anything at all…" The Frenchman paused and again gestured expansively, this time seeming to include the woman and the servant behind her, who was still holding the tray. "Please don't hesitate to make your wishes known. *Any* of my servants will be pleased to accommodate so welcome a guest. In any way you desire," he added, his voice soft, and his eyes on the woman.

There had been an obvious undercurrent in the suggestive words, and Dare found himself interested in Elizabeth Carstairs' reaction. Her eyes met Bonnet's. Dare was unable to see what was in them, but there was no doubt about the rush of color that ran beneath the translucent skin of her throat and spread upward into her cheeks, far more pronounced than the rouge.

The intent of Bonnet's offer had probably been clear to everyone. Mrs. Carstairs' "services" were available to the Earl of Dare, and perhaps even to the rest of them. Given the character of women who were usually employed in a gaming hell, there had been nothing particularly startling about the Frenchman's offer. What *had* been surprising was Mrs. Carstairs' response. Seldom had the earl encountered a *demimondaine* who had the capacity to blush. Or, he admitted admiringly, the courage to parry wits so openly with one of her employer's guests.

"You are too kind, sir," Dare said, inclining his head.

The gambler had introduced her as *Mrs.* Carstairs, but that title was almost certainly a sop to convention. In England, any unmarried woman living under a man's protection was referred to in such a way. It was a ridiculous pretense, but then much about the conventions of their society was ridiculous.

At Dare's expression of gratitude, Elizabeth Carstairs had turned her head. Her eyes met his. In them, quite clear, was rage. And beneath that unspoken anger was pain, an agony perhaps as deep as that which he had seen in the eyes of the man whose tortured body he had held today as he drew his last breath. For a moment the force of her anguish was so strong and communicated to him so forcefully that it literally took his breath.

It had not been an appeal. He had no doubt that the revelation had been unintended. Perhaps if he had not had so recent an experience with suffering, he might not even have recognized what he had seen.

Breaking the contact that had briefly flared between them, Elizabeth Carstairs turned, calmly replacing the decanter on the tray and stepping away from the table. Dare heard the fabric of her gown whisper as she moved, and the hint of her perfume lingered in the air, but he could no longer see her face.

And he found he really wanted to. A discovery that was almost as shocking to the Earl of Dare as Elizabeth Carstairs' unexpected reaction to Bonnet's offer had been.

"Gentlemen," the Frenchman said, "shall we begin?"

It was almost dawn. A thin, watery daylight was beginning to creep between the folds of the thick velvet curtains that had been pulled to keep it out. A pall of smoke, floating a few inches off the floor, hung over the Turkish carpets. Several of the candles had guttered and gone out, and there was no more conversation.

No one had yet left the table, although now only two men were playing. And it was obvious that very soon one of those two would be the victor.

The heap of notes piled carelessly before the Earl of Dare had steadily grown during the last few hours. The stack that stood before Bonnet had conversely shrunk until only a handful of what had been there at the beginning of the evening was left. And the fickle cards, like a woman enamored with one gallant, continued to favor the earl.

"*Capet,*" Dare said. "Forty points, *and* my game, I believe."

There was no tally sheet beside his long-fingered hands that rested, totally relaxed, against the surface of the table. The totals were kept in his head, and in every instance Dare's calculations had matched those announced by Elizabeth Carstairs, who stood slightly to the right and behind Bonnet's chair.

The kind of score keeping she had done was little more than a parlor trick, and one Dare had certainly seen before. One of the German casinos employed a dwarf to do the same thing. And in Paris, during the short respite from the hostilities provided by the Peace of Amiens, Dare had once seen a small, brown-skinned boy, dressed like an Indian rajah in a turban and a striped silk tunic, keeping up with the points.

All it took was concentration on the cards and a head for sums. It was unusual to find those abilities in a woman, certainly, and the novelty was almost sure to appeal to the jaded gentleman of London's ton. Dare suspected, however, that Mrs. Carstairs' physical attributes were far more important in drawing visitors to Bonnet's rooms than was her head for numbers.

Throughout the long hours of the night, with the lift of her brow or the tilt of her chin she had directed the Frenchman's servants to refill the wineglasses or light the gentlemen's cigars. And when he and Bonnet had switched to *piquet,* she had kept their points in order. However, since her challenge to the earl's comment at the beginning of the evening, she had said almost nothing, except to answer Bonnet's demand for the score.

Once or twice, when Dare had raised his eyes from his cards, he had found hers resting on his face. Her gaze would then move to consider the face of another of the players, without haste and with no indication of discomfort at having been caught looking at him. Each time that happened, the earl had allowed his amusement to show, smiling as he followed her eyes, watching the gambler's woman deliberately not look at him.

''Elizabeth?'' Bonnet's tone this time was sharper and more demanding than it had been before. The strain the Frenchman was feeling as his losses mounted had gradually become apparent.

That was hardly surprising, however, since an enormous amount of money had changed hands tonight. The earl had raised the stakes with each game. And it was by now obvious to everyone, including Bonnet, that Dare seemed out to ruin the house.

''His lordship's total is correct,'' Mrs. Carstairs said. ''The game is his.''

Her eyes considered the man seated across the table from her master, and this time they remained on his face, even when he lifted his own to meet them. He inclined his head, silently acknowledging her agreement.

"Another game," the earl suggested to his opponent, his gaze still on Elizabeth Carstairs' face.

All night, his mind only partially engaged by the cards, he had found himself trying to imagine what would bring a woman like her to this place. It had been merely an intellectual exercise, perhaps, designed to prevent his having to think about what had happened today—yesterday, he amended—in France.

The Frenchman's lips tightened angrily at Dare's suggestion, but there was no doubt what he would say. As long as a guest wished to play, Henri Bonnet's tables were open. No matter the elegance of its furnishings, this was, after all, a gaming house. Gentlemen came here for only one reason; they wanted to gamble. And usually the Frenchman wanted that, as well. Tonight, however, luck had deserted him. The cards had fallen Dare's way, and he had won with stunning regularity.

Without speaking, Bonnet reluctantly pushed his remaining notes to the center of the table. The stone in the ring he wore flashed green fire with the movement, just as it had with every turn of the cards. At the last it had seemed almost an omen of the Frenchman's ill fortune.

Bonnet's gaze lifted from that diminished stack of notes in front of him to the earl's face. His lips pursed again, and then, reluctantly, he began to remove the emerald ring, twisting and turning until the thick gold band slipped over his knuckle. He placed it on top of the money.

"This wager is agreeable to you, my lord?"

Dare's eyes examined the ring as it lay among the

scattered notes. Finally, he picked it up, and holding the band between his thumb and forefinger, lifted the jewel to the light. After a few seconds, he tossed the ring carelessly onto the table.

"An exceptional stone," he said. The Frenchman smiled, his relief was almost palpable, until Dare added, "Except that it is badly flawed."

He raised his eyes once more to Elizabeth Carstairs' face. Her posture was as erect as it had been when the evening began, her head high, her hands at her waist, one resting within the other. The earl's gaze traveled slowly down and then back up her slender figure, clearly revealed by the narrow cut of her gown.

"A piece not worth half as much as it appears on first glance," Dare said softly.

His voice was pleasant. There was no hint of accusation in its deep timbre. It was obvious to everyone, however, that Dare's words were a thinly veiled metaphor for the woman standing behind the Frenchman's chair.

"I had been informed that the emerald is a gem of exceptional value," Bonnet said stiffly.

There was a small and deadly silence as everyone waited for Dare to respond. He chose not to, his eyes now on Bonnet's reddened face, his own expressionless. He displayed no anger at the Frenchman's denial. And he made no defense of his statement. The silence grew.

"However," Bonnet said finally, "I bow to your lordship's undoubtedly superior knowledge of such things. I had no idea the stone was flawed when I offered it."

"I was sure that was the case," the earl said, "which is why I felt I could do no less than point it out to you. A shame you were hoodwinked. Did you take it as a wager?'' Dare asked, his eyes again lifting to the woman's face.

The same flood of color which had invaded her cheeks when Bonnet offered her ''services'' to his guest had again begun to edge her throat. Nothing else about her face had changed. She appeared undisturbed by either the earl's eyes or by his words, her features tranquil and composed.

''I took it as payment of a debt,'' Bonnet said.

''Pity,'' Dare replied, the boredom in his tone dismissing the ring as an object unworthy of further discussion.

He pushed the huge, untidy pile of notes which had been lying in front of him into the center of the table. It represented the bulk of everything that had been wagered tonight, and its size dwarfed the small stack the gambler had offered. Then the earl waited. And the silence grew once more.

Across the room a candle sputtered and died. A whiff of white smoke trailed from it, drifting upward into the darkness. After a moment, Bonnet picked up the ring and pushed it almost violently back onto his finger.

''This house,'' the Frenchman said, his words clipped. ''I give you my word, my lord, that it is unencumbered by debt.''

The earl's eyes examined the room as if he had not been sitting within it all night. Then he inclined his head to Bonnet. ''May I offer my congratulations on the excellence of your property.''

The gambler's lips flattened at the mockery before he gathered control and said, his voice clearly furious,

"I believe its value to be more than equal to your current wager."

"Ah," Dare said, as if in sudden understanding. "You wish to put the house up as your stake."

"That *was* my intent, my lord."

"Forgive my slow wits. I thought you were merely making conversation. Your house against..." Dare's eyes fell to consider the notes he had pushed to the center of the table only a moment before. He began pushing through them with one long finger as if he were counting. "Then it seems that I must add something to my own stake. Something to sweeten the pot, so to speak. Something to make my wager as valuable as yours."

Bonnet bowed. "I believe you are correct, my lord."

"And do *you* believe I am correct, Mrs. Carstairs?" Dare asked. When she didn't answer, he raised his eyes from the pile of notes. The color had drained from her face, leaving it milk-white. Her eyes met his.

"I do, my lord," she said, her voice calm and controlled.

For almost the first time, Bonnet looked up, his gaze fastening on Mrs. Carstairs' profile. His eyes narrowed when he found her oblivious to his examination, her gaze locked on Dare's. Then the gambler looked at the English nobleman, whose mouth was arranged in an enigmatic half smile. Bonnet's eyes came back to the woman standing just to the right of his chair.

Suddenly, with a violence that was totally unexpected, given the politeness which had veiled the accusations implied in the recent exchange, the Frenchman stood. He moved so suddenly that the heavy chair he had been sitting in tilted and fell over.

Startled, Elizabeth Carstairs' gaze flew from Dare's face to Bonnet. Without speaking, the Frenchman grasped her upper arm, his fingers digging into the soft flesh just above her elbow. Automatically, she flinched from the pain and tried to pull away, but his grip was brutal.

"Perhaps my luck might change if you weren't here," he said in French, adding a very idiomatic appellation, a gutter term which one might more appropriately expect to hear in a Parisian brothel. The words were almost inaudible, muttered under the gambler's breath, and Bonnet had already begun to pull Elizabeth away from the table when he said them.

The Earl of Dare's hearing, however, was acute. He had heard them, half rising from his chair in response. His own iron control had already reasserted itself, however, when the gambler's eyes were drawn back to the table by that movement.

"No offense to *you*, my lord," Bonnet said, his fingers still gripping his employee's arm.

Elizabeth had by that time ceased to struggle. She did not look again at the earl, and her face was once more coldly composed, the blue eyes shuttered and emotionless. It was obvious she didn't expect Dare or any of the others to mount a rescue. She was Bonnet's property. He might therefore do with her as he wished. She understood that, it seemed, as did they.

Dare didn't glance toward the woman Bonnet was holding. His gaze was fastened instead on the Frenchman's face.

"Gamblers are a superstitious brotherhood," Bonnet continued. "When our luck is in, we wish everything to remain the same. When our luck is out, however—" The Frenchman turned to look at Elizabeth.

"We make changes," he said softly, the words, and the threat, obvious.

Then he turned back to the table, smiling at his guests. "More wine, gentlemen?" He gestured imperiously to the servant across the room, the emerald again flashing, before he added, "We shall resume our game, Lord Dare, as soon as I return."

His fingers tightened, provoking another involuntary recoil from his victim. The gambler stalked to a small private door at the other side of the room, propelling Mrs. Carstairs along with him. With her free hand, she had gathered the long, straight fall of her gown to keep from stumbling over it.

When the two of them had disappeared through the door, which Bonnet slammed behind them, none of the Englishmen at the table said a word. Pendlebrooke signaled again for more wine, and this time the Frenchman's servant hurried forward to fill their glasses. When he had finished, he passed around more of Bonnet's cigars. Most of the men accepted, and as the familiar ritual of lighting them ensued, no one proposed any conversation to end the unnatural silence.

They had been as aware of the implication of what Bonnet had done, Dare imagined, as he had been. Bonnet might claim to be concerned about the effect the woman was having on his luck, but his action in taking her out of the room had suggested there was a more sinister explanation for Dare's good fortune.

The gambler had skirted very close to accusing the earl of cheating, implying that he had been receiving signals from the woman who stood behind the Frenchman's chair—in a perfect position to see his cards. Many of the hotheaded young coxcombs of the ton, ever careful of their honor, might well have challenged

Bonnet, ignoring his stated reason for banishing Mrs. Carstairs from the room. Dare's reputation, however, was not as someone who went off half-cocked. He was considered coldly controlled, almost dispassionate.

And so he appeared to be now. No one was aware of the surge of rage that had engulfed him as he had watched Bonnet humiliate and then physically mistreat Elizabeth Carstairs. It had brought back too vividly to his mind a torture far more brutal, but almost certainly as casually done. And to a victim who had been as helpless to prevent it as Bonnet's victim had been.

When the Frenchman reentered the room, he was pulling down his cuffs as he came through the door. Their costly lace fell over his hands as he walked back to the table. He nodded to his guests and waited as one of the servants hurried to restore his chair, which was still lying overturned on the thick carpet.

When he was seated, Bonnet raised his eyes to the earl. "I believe we were discussing the terms of your wager, my lord?"

Gradually, the smile began to fade as Dare said nothing, his eyes on the gambler's face. It disappeared completely when the earl spoke.

"What if your house, like your emerald, *monsieur,* has some hidden flaw? One may examine a stone, but it would be difficult to verify your claim of a free and clear title tonight."

"Do you doubt my word, my lord?"

"You didn't know the stone was flawed," Dare reminded him, his voice free of inflection. "Perhaps there is some…impediment to your title that you are also unaware of? How should I know if that were the case?"

"I possess nothing else of value, Lord Dare. My

assets are, at the moment, all tied up in this establishment. It is a recent purchase and needed a great deal of refurbishing. I'm afraid I have nothing else. If you are unwilling to accept my stake…''

He shrugged, the gesture eloquent and dismissive at the same time, neatly lobbing the ball back into Dare's court. It seemed that the earl's reluctance might offer Bonnet an escape.

"The woman," the earl said softly.

"I beg your pardon?" the Frenchman said.

"You may wager the woman," Dare said.

Again the silence in the room was complete. No one protested, although what Dare was proposing was unheard-of. Perhaps at one time women had been chattel, which might be won or lost on a hand of cards, but that was not the case today.

"Mrs. Carstairs?" Bonnet asked, his voice astounded.

"Mrs. Carstairs," the earl agreed, his voice expressing amusement at that astonishment.

"Mrs. Carstairs is…"

"Yes?" Dare questioned after there had been a pause of several long heartbeats.

"This is England, my lord. Not…" Again the Frenchman's voice faltered, as if he could not think of a location where one might wager a human being.

"Indeed it is," Dare agreed. With one finger he touched the enormous pile of notes on the table between them. "And these are the coins of the realm. Quite a lot of them, as a matter of fact. I'll wager them all, Monsieur Bonnet, on one game. All of this for the woman."

Bonnet's eyes had followed the movement of the earl's hand as it reached out and touched the money.

And then they lifted again, considering his opponent's face. "One game?"

"Winner take all," Dare said softly. The corners of his mouth tilted. "And the only stake you must put up is Mrs. Carstairs."

"My lord, I'm afraid that I really must—"

"We are all gentlemen here," Dare continued, almost as if the gambler hadn't protested. "This will go no further. I can assure you that what happens here tonight will never be spoken of again by any of these gentlemen."

His eyes traveled slowly over the faces of each of the men at the table. They were all inveterate gamblers, well-known for their habits. What Dare saw in their eyes satisfied him that what he had said was indeed the truth. A wager legitimately made and agreed to by both parties was sacrosanct. Finally his gaze came back to the Frenchman.

"You needn't be afraid," Dare said. "No one will ever hear of this from any of us. Certainly not the authorities. After all, we would have as much, if not more, to lose than you if this were brought to their attention."

That was true, of course. There was no reason for the Frenchman not to accede to the earl's wishes. Dare might easily have demanded Bonnet put up the house, and if he had lost, the Frenchman would have been ruined. If he lost now, however...

"All right," Bonnet said.

Apparently, once the decision had been reached, his reluctance disappeared. He picked up the cards and began to shuffle them with a practiced proficiency. They flew through his fingers in a blur. When he had finished, he placed the deck face down on the table for Dare to cut.

"Your stake?" the earl asked.

Surprised, the French gambler looked up from the cards.

"The lady should be present," Dare said.

There was a long hesitation. "Superstition, my lord. I believe I explained my reluctance to you."

"If her proximity to you bothers you, she may stand behind my chair."

After another long delay, the gambler said, "I believe Mrs. Carstairs has already retired."

"Send for her."

"I'm afraid…that is, I believe she is…indisposed."

"Send for her, please," Dare said again, his voice very low. A command rather than a request.

Bonnet held the earl's eyes a moment, his mouth tightening with unexpressed anger, and then he raised his hand and gestured to the servant who had refilled the wineglasses. When the man approached his chair, the Frenchman drew him close and whispered in his ear. The man nodded and walked across the room, disappearing through the same doorway out of which Bonnet had dragged Elizabeth Carstairs only moments before.

For the next ten minutes there was almost no sound in the salon. Occasionally, one of the gentlemen pulled deeply on his cigar and audibly expelled the smoke. Finally, the door through which the servant had departed opened again. He entered and then stepped aside, holding it for the woman.

Elizabeth Carstairs hesitated in the doorway, her eyes first seeking Bonnet's and then touching briefly on the Earl of Dare's face before they came back to her master's. She was dressed in the same dress, but the rubies that had been entwined in her hair were gone. Apparently the curls they had held had been hastily repinned when she was summoned. A few unsecured tendrils floated around her temples and along her throat.

"Monsieur Bonnet feels, perhaps with some justification, that you have brought him ill fortune," the Earl of Dare said, speaking directly to her. "However, considering my own run of good luck, I have asked that you be allowed to rejoin us. If you would be so kind," he added politely.

She didn't move, her eyes again tracking from his face to the gambler's. Dare rose, walking across the room toward her. When he was near enough, he could see that he had been right in his suspicions. The imprint on her cheek, made by the Frenchman's palm, was quite clear.

The blow had reddened the delicate skin, leaving the distinct impression of each separate finger. There was a small spot of blood at the corner of her mouth, where it had cut against her teeth.

When Dare met her eyes again, he could see within them doubt and perhaps even a trace of fear. She was uncertain of his motives. He couldn't blame her for being wary. After all, he had not protested when Bonnet dragged her from this room. None of the English gentlemen had. And so, Elizabeth Carstairs had no reason to believe that he intended to befriend her.

Dare himself could not explain why he had embarked on this crusade. It was out of keeping with the persona he had adopted years ago, and that made it dangerous, of course. As well as ridiculously quixotic, he acknowledged.

Without further comment, Dare held out his arm, wrist upward. He did not offer to take her hand. His gesture was far more formal, the same one he might have used to offer his escort to any lady of his acquaintance onto the dance floor perhaps or to be introduced to his friend, the Prince Regent.

As he watched Elizabeth Carstairs' slightly widened eyes come up to his, he knew that he had not been mistaken in his assessment of her. After a second or two, she placed her hand in the proper position on top of his wrist.

Despite her outward composure, he could feel her fingers tremble. They were cool against the heat of his own skin, and his body reacted to the feel of them there, the sudden rush of blood to his groin strong and hot.

And potentially embarrassing. *Like a bloody schoolboy,* Dare thought in amazement, exerting a control he had not been called upon to use in years. He allowed the images of his friend's face to reform in his mind, images he had fought all evening. Even Elizabeth Carstairs' undeniable attractions were not proof against that horror.

When they reached the table, the illogical aversion he had taken to Bonnet was stronger than it had been before. He almost regretted not having required the house be a part of this wager. But of course, this whole thing was now about something more than his dislike for the gambler. It was now about this woman, and that, Dare admitted, was even more illogical than the other.

Chapter Two

When they reached the table, Elizabeth removed her hand from the Earl of Dare's arm and took her place behind his chair. The apprehension that had begun when Bonnet sent for her again was unabated. She wasn't sure why she was here. Although she had questioned the servant, he could tell her little beyond the fact that Monsieur Bonnet required that she come back downstairs.

Since she had been made very much aware of the gambler's displeasure when she left the salon, she had been surprised by his summons to return. She had already removed her dress, but it had been a matter of a few seconds to pull it back on again. She had then gathered her hair atop her head, hurriedly securing the curls with a few hairpins from the top of her dressing table.

Despite the fact that she knew she had done nothing to deserve his anger, she was mortified to be seen with the mark of Bonnet's hand still livid on her cheek. It wasn't the first time the gambler had struck her. Once he had even used his fists, but the resulting bruises had been too difficult to hide. She had missed several nights in attendance at the tables, and so, thankfully, he had never done that again.

The blow tonight had been painful, but not disfiguring. Based on experience, she knew the mark would hardly be noticeable tomorrow. At least it wouldn't have been, she amended, had she been allowed to remain in her bedroom with a cold compress pressed to her cheek. Now, however...

The man seated in the chair beside her reached across the table and cut the deck of cards that lay face down upon it. Unlike her own, his fingers were perfectly steady—long and dark and somehow elegant. Her eyes had followed their movements all evening.

The Earl of Dare. Elizabeth tried to think what she had heard about the man who bore that title, but she could remember almost nothing beyond the family name, which was Sinclair. She wasn't sure why that had stuck in her memory.

She looked down at the man seated beside her, desperately trying to determine his age. Only the midnight-black hair and a narrow portion of his profile were visible from where she stood. She wished she had studied his face more closely when she had had the chance. Instead, she had determinedly fought the impulse to look at him all evening.

That was something that never happened to her before. Usually she avoided eye contact with the men who came to play at Bonnet's tables. It was safer that way. Her greatest fear had been that she might encounter a familiar face.

Dare's had not been, but still, there had been something about it that had drawn her. She tried to re-create his features in her mind's eye, even while her attention, like everyone else's, was seemingly locked on the cards.

His nose was almost aquiline, she remembered, the bridge high and finely shaped. As were his lips. And there was a small cleft in the center of his chin. His skin was dark, more in keeping with the raven-blackness of his hair than with the remarkable blue eyes. Of course, she admitted, those were made even more noticeable by the sweep of long, thick lashes that surrounded them.

His high forehead was softened by the fashionable curls that were arranged to fall over it. All in all, it was a memorable face, the austere planes and angles suggesting a purpose and discipline that his manner throughout the evening had not.

There was a touch of gray at his temples, she noticed now, examining his profile. And a minute fan of lines radiated from the corner of the eye she could see. Which meant he was older than Jeremy, she decided in relief. Older by perhaps as much as five years, a difference great enough that Dare had probably not known him. She drew a deep, infinitely grateful breath.

That was not, then, why he had had Bonnet send for her. Not because he recognized her. Maybe it really had been only what he said. Maybe he really did believe she had brought him luck. Something obviously had, considering the size of the wager that lay in the center of the table.

And with that her mind came back to the cards. She found that despite her inattention, she could remember every trick that had been played, every card that had fallen. She had done this so often now that it required almost no conscious thought, allowing her mind to range freely, unencumbered by her present circumstances.

Her father had taught her sums when she was only a child. He had been a mathematician and an amateur astronomer. For him, as for her, mathematics had been an avocation. A joy. And now, even that had been perverted. Again, out of necessity this time, she compelled her mind to concentrate on the cards. Thinking of her father was forbidden. Almost as forbidden as the other.

"More wine, my lord?" Bonnet asked softly.

She glanced at the gambler, and realized he was smiling, his eyes almost gloating. There was a satisfaction in his voice which she had heard there before. He believed he would win. Perhaps he had been right about her presence behind his chair bringing him bad luck. God knew that if she could possibly have arranged ill fortune for the Frenchman, she would have.

"Thank you, no," the earl said. His eyes had lifted to his opponent's face, and the corner of his mouth that was visible to her had also lifted. "The clearer one's head, you know."

There was nothing in the deep voice that she could read. Certainly not anxiety, despite the fortune that rested on the table, riding on the turn of the cards. Whatever Bonnet believed about his own hand, the man beside her, the man who claimed she had brought him luck, had not yet conceded defeat. And for some reason, she was comforted by his unspoken confidence.

In the end, the margin was very narrow, only a few points separating the totals, but Bonnet had won the first hand.

"I believe your luck may indeed have changed,"

Dare said. He was smiling. Of course, the Frenchman's victory in this hand had not been so great that it could not be overcome on the next.

"I think you're right, my lord," Bonnet said.

His eyes found Elizabeth's face. She schooled her features to indifference, but in truth, she knew she should be glad the Frenchman was winning. Life would be far easier for her if he were in a better mood.

Judging by his attire and by the deference with which Bonnet had treated him, the Earl of Dare could afford to lose. He could bear this loss, and if he did, then she might not have to bear the brunt of the Frenchman's anger.

As the game unfolded, however, the lead went back and forth, the narrow margin that separated the two opponents making it impossible to predict a final victory for one or the other. It was full day now, and several of the gentlemen had indicated by the impatience of their postures, if by nothing else, that it was past time to leave. Everyone was reluctant, however, to cause any loss of concentration by the players at this critical juncture. And then suddenly, as so often happened with the fickle cards, it was over.

"My hand," the Earl of Dare said again. "The game as well, I believe. An unfortunate discard brought you down, I'm afraid, Monsieur Bonnet. But then, knowing what to discard and when to do so is often tricky."

Bonnet's eyes rose to Elizabeth, and believing he wanted verification of the nobleman's calculation, she gave it.

"The earl's hand by thirty points. And the game," she said.

"It seems the lady has indeed brought you good fortune, my lord," Bonnet said.

Elizabeth was surprised by the equanimity with which the gambler was dealing with his loss. She had expected rage. She knew that what he had told the earl was the truth. Everything Bonnet had was tied up in this house. And now…

"I wish you well of her," the Frenchman added.

The phrase reverberated strangely in Elizabeth's consciousness. It made no sense in the context of his congratulations. Why would he wish Dare "well of her"?

"And good riddance," the gambler added softly in French, his eyes meeting hers. And then his tone changed, as did his language. "Gentlemen," he said, speaking to his guests in English, "it has, as always, been a pleasure to entertain you. I hope you will all return tomorrow night. Since the earl has been so kind as to leave me my house, play will resume then. And I especially look forward to the opportunity of another encounter with you, my Lord Dare."

The earl had risen. He gathered the notes that lay scattered across the table and stacked them together before he shoved the thick wad into the pocket of his coat.

"The pleasure was mine," Dare said. "And as for a return engagement…" His eyes found Elizabeth's face. "Anything is possible, of course, but I believe I've won already the best your house has to offer."

"I wish you joy of her, my lord. Be warned. She's headstrong and occasionally needs a firm hand."

"Indeed?" Dare said, his eyes still on her face. "Such as the one you applied?" he asked softly.

Slowly realization began to dawn for Elizabeth. They were talking about her as if...

The Earl of Dare presented his arm. She stared at him, her mind racing. "Madam?" he said.

"What does this mean?" she asked, breathless with anxiety.

"I have won you. I trust you have no objections."

"Won me?" she repeated. "I'm not a *thing* that might be won, my lord."

"It was my understanding from Monsieur Bonnet that you are. And as a result of that understanding, I have just...won you."

"No," she said softly, appealing to the Frenchman. "Tell him, Henri, that he is—"

"A long-standing rule of the house, my dear," the Frenchman interrupted. "Whatever a gentleman wishes to wager is allowed—if the value is deemed appropriate. Apparently the earl believed your value to be...appropriate."

"You wagered me?" she asked, her voice incredulous.

"You were the stake Lord Dare required."

"But surely you can't mean..." she began, and then her voice faltered, the words dying away. She didn't understand what Bonnet was up to, but she knew him well enough by now to know there was more to this than appeared on the surface. And the less she said that might endanger his plans the better it would be for her.

"Come, Mrs. Carstairs. I'm not usually considered to be such an ogre as all this," Dare said lazily.

His eyes again examined the place where Bonnet had struck her. By now, she supposed her cheek would have begun to discolor. Her mouth was very sore where the flesh had cut against her teeth.

Then the earl's eyes fastened once more on hers. In them was a question. He believed he was offering her escape. A way to leave Bonnet's cruelty behind. And he was naturally curious as to why she wasn't more eager to accept it.

"The unknown is always more frightening than the known, my lord," she said very softly, "no matter how…unpleasant the known may be."

"Frightening?" he repeated, his beautifully shaped lips tilting at the corners. "I'm quite sure that I have never before been considered *frightening*. And I promise I shall endeavor to make your stay with me at least as pleasant as your 'service' has been here."

It was the same word Bonnet had used at the beginning of the evening. Her *service*. Never before had the gambler made that offer, and when he had done so tonight, her fury had almost escaped her control. In her situation, she could never afford to let that happen.

"I'm sure the earl will treat you with every consideration, my dear," Bonnet said. "I wish you well."

And with those words, it seemed she would have to be content, her own questions unanswered. At least for tonight.

Dare was still looking at her. She turned her head, and he smiled at her again, his blue eyes full of curiosity. Perhaps even kindness.

Elizabeth Carstairs, however, no longer believed in kindness. Or in men who acted from altruistic motives. She knew very well what had prompted the Earl of Dare to demand that Bonnet make her his stake tonight. Therefore, she knew exactly what to expect from him. And she also knew there was nothing she could do except acquiesce. Not if this was what Bonnet wanted.

"Come, Mrs. Carstairs," the earl said again.

The smile was gone, and although the words were soft, they were obviously a command. And so she placed her hand on the Earl of Dare's arm, and this time, despite her dread, she was pleased to find that, through an enormous act of will, it did not tremble.

Dare had expected Elizabeth Carstairs to be grateful for his rescue, and instead she was clearly dismayed by the prospect of coming home with him. He might be suffering from wounded vanity, he supposed, smiling at the notion in the concealing dimness of the carriage's interior. He had not really been anticipating any particularly favorable reaction to him. Nothing except a little gratitude, perhaps.

It seemed, however, that she didn't plan to offer him even that. She hadn't spoken since he'd handed her into the carriage. Through the window on her side of the closed coach, she had examined the London streets, which were just coming to life, as if she had never seen them before.

Maybe she hadn't. At least not at this hour. Dare had, usually when coming home from an all-night gaming session such as they had just left. Or when returning from his mistress's.

"I shall send for your things," he said, more to solicit a response than because he was concerned about whatever possessions she had left behind. Those could be easily replaced.

"Thank you," she said.

She turned to face him finally. In the sunlight, the cosmetics, even artfully applied, were jarring. There was something about them that was blatantly out of place. They simply didn't fit. Not with her speech or with her manner. Of course, that shouldn't be too surprising. Almost nothing he now knew about her fit with those.

"How long have you worked for Bonnet?" he asked.

There was a moment's hesitation, and then she said, "Almost two years, my lord."

"And before that?"

"Surely my past can be of no concern to you, Lord Dare," she said softly, her eyes almost defiant.

"I'm simply curious," he said. "Indulge me."

He *was* curious, of course, but that wasn't why he was pressing the issue. He wanted her to talk. She was obviously hiding something, and the sooner he discovered what it was, the sooner he could put this entire quixotic episode behind him. After all, there were other things he should be doing today, far more important than trying to unravel the mystery of the Frenchman's whore.

The word jolted, annoyingly, almost painfully, just as the rouge was jarring against the clear purity of her skin. But she probably *is* a whore, he reminded himself. Before his admittedly romantic nature managed to transform her into something else, Dare knew he needed to engrave that fact on his consciousness.

"The story of my life isn't particularly interesting," she said. "Or unusual. I'm sure you would quickly become bored if I attempted to tell it to you."

"Why don't you let me make that determination."

"Because it doesn't matter. What I did before I came to Bonnet's has nothing to do with the present. And certainly nothing to do with now."

And nothing to do with you, her tone suggested.

"Be warned, Mrs. Carstairs. Mystery piques my interest. Forbidden fruit, I suppose."

"There is no mystery. If you must hear it, mine's an ordinary enough story. My husband died, leaving a number of debts. Many of those were owed to Monsieur Bonnet. He made an offer of employment, and I accepted it."

"You had no family to turn to, of course," Dare suggested, his lips quirking. "Nor did your husband. Neatly done, my dear. My compliments, but…no starving children? Or perhaps we are to pick them up on the way."

"Are you mocking me?"

"Are you lying to me?" he countered.

There was a long pause, and then she said, "If I am, what can it possibly matter to you?"

"I told you. I'm curious."

She held his eyes a moment more, and then she turned her head again, looking out the window. The carriage had entered Mayfair and, in the morning sun, the facades of the town houses swept by in a panorama of architectural elegance. Servants busily polished brass plates and the bells on their front doors or washed marks of the previous day's traffic from broad, shallow steps. Phaetons stood patiently before their entrances, waiting for the inhabitants to embark on rounds of morning calls or on business in the city.

"And what was the late Mr. Carstairs' occupation?" the earl asked politely, almost as if the sharpness that had ended the last exchange had not occurred.

Again she turned to face him. "Are we to continue to play games, my lord? If so, perhaps I should tell you that my imagination is not great. I have no gift for storytelling.''

"Only a gift for numbers,'' he said, the subtle movement of his mouth not quite a smile. "Where did you learn to do that? What you do for Bonnet?''

She didn't answer, but she didn't turn away.

"Forbidden as well? Then what would you like to talk about, Mrs. Carstairs?''

"I should like to know what you want from me,'' she said bluntly, her eyes cold.

"The pleasure of your company?'' he suggested, his tone lightly mocking. "Your wit. The scintillating sparkle of your conversation.''

"My...conversation, my lord?'' she repeated, her tone equally caustic.

"Of course,'' he said softly. "What did you think I wanted from you, Mrs. Carstairs?''

The carriage drew to a halt, preventing her from having to formulate an answer. The footmen rushed forward to open the door and to lower the steps. The earl descended, and then, playing the perfect gentleman, a role he had been trained for from birth, he held out his hand, palm upward. Elizabeth Carstairs gathered her skirts and put her fingers into his.

They were trembling again, Dare realized. If she was accustomed to being offered to Bonnet's guests for their pleasure, like his wine or his excellent cigars, then why would the thought of entering his town house cause this reaction?

After all, what he had told her before was the truth. Dare was unaccustomed to being considered an ogre. Not by women. And certainly not an object of fear and trembling. If anything, he had the opposite effect on the fairer sex.

Of course, he had decided a long time ago that their favorable reception might more properly be attributed to his wealth and position than to his person. However, those considerations aside, he had never had a complaint from a woman about his attentions. The thought was almost comforting in the face of her unspoken distress.

"I'm not going to eat you, you know," he said sotto voce, as he escorted her toward the front door.

His servants were too well-trained to gawk, but he could imagine what they were thinking, despite their perfectly correct expressions. Dare had never even brought his mistress, who did *not* paint her face, to his home. He had certainly never before introduced a whore into its environs.

Even as he thought the word, using it deliberately and for all the good reasons he had determined in the carriage, he could feel the childlike softness of her hand in his, trembling as strongly as if she were in the grip of an ague.

"I can assure you, my lord, that I never once envisioned *that* as being my fate," Elizabeth said.

Despite her shaking hand, her chin was tilted upward, her posture as correct as if she were walking into court. When the footman opened the door, Dare released her hand and watched her sweep through the entrance to his home like a duchess.

Whatever else Elizabeth Carstairs might be, the earl acknowledged in amusement, she was a consummate actress. And despite her earlier disclaimer, he definitely wasn't bored.

"Mrs. Hendricks is my housekeeper," the earl said. "She will look after you. Mrs. Carstairs will be my guest for…an as yet unspecified visit,'' he continued, speaking to the woman he had summoned as soon as they entered the town house.

Again he had managed to surprise her, Elizabeth acknowledged. She had been steeling herself for something quite different, something far more unpleasant than facing the clear disdain in the housekeeper's eyes. Quite different, she thought, glancing at the earl's face.

He looked tired. Exhausted, actually. Of course, they had both been up all night. That was not unusual for her, but perhaps Lord Dare didn't normally keep the same irregular hours she was so accustomed to.

''Very good, my lord,'' Mrs. Hendricks said stiffly.

Her eyes said that she saw nothing *good* about this at all, but she wasn't about to admit that to her employer. She might indicate her true feelings when she and Elizabeth were alone, but she obviously didn't want to anger the earl. And having spent the past two years in Bonnet's employ, Elizabeth could sympathize with her reluctance to incur her employer's wrath.

''If you'll follow me, miss,'' the housekeeper said. Her face was as starchy with disapproval as her housemaids' aprons would be. She had barely avoided adding an accompanying sniff when she issued the invitation.

''Mrs.,'' the earl corrected softly. ''Mrs. Carstairs.''

The housekeeper's eyes focused on his face, evidently hearing the unspoken admonition in his voice. ''I beg your pardon, Mrs. Carstairs.''

''Please don't,'' Elizabeth said. ''I understand perfectly.''

The housekeeper looked at her then, almost for the first time, her eyes widening a little at the sympathetic tone.

"I shall see you at dinner tonight, Mrs. Carstairs," the earl said.

At dinner, Elizabeth thought. Tonight. Night. Was that when he planned...?

She tried to analyze the earl's tone. Of course, since she had been unable to since she had met him, she didn't know why she was attempting to do so now. His face was equally expressionless. There was no leer, no innuendo, no hint in his manner that she should expect more from this *dinner* engagement with him than what was usually conveyed by the word.

"I have nothing to wear to dinner," Elizabeth said, refusing to look down on the garish, too-revealing gown in which she was attired.

The Earl of Dare laughed, and when he did, she could feel the rush of blood into her cheeks. Did his laughter mean—

"Do you know that's the first completely feminine thing I have heard you say," Dare said. "I can't tell you how reassuring it is."

With that, he turned and began to climb the enormous staircase that dominated the entrance hall. He took the steps two at a time, silk knee britches stretching with the play of muscles in his thighs. Much more strongly defined muscles than she would have believed a wealthy gentleman of the ton might possess, Elizabeth thought, and then realized, a little startled, how inappropriate her contemplation of the Earl of Dare's posterior really was.

"This way, then, Mrs. Carstairs," Mrs. Hendricks said. This time the sniff was audible.

Elizabeth had endured far worse than the disapproval of a housekeeper during the past two years. If nothing else, she thought, such experiences gave one the strength to know that there was really nothing that could not be endured. And those experiences had also given her the ability to evaluate a situation she found herself in without hysteria or magnification. That might come later, of course, but so far…

"Thank you, Mrs. Hendricks," she said simply, and with real gratitude.

The room she was taken to was nothing like she had expected. She supposed she had been anticipating she would be hidden away among the narrow little attic rooms the chambermaids shared. The chamber she had been taken to was a suite instead, large, airy, and charmingly decorated in shades of yellow and dull gold.

Apparently, when the earl had said she was his guest, his housekeeper had taken him at his word. Which spoke well of his control of his household, Elizabeth conceded. And again she found herself surprised at that revelation. She had no doubt that if Mrs. Hendricks believed she could get away with it, Elizabeth *would* have been relegated to the attic, out of sight and out of mind. That she hadn't been was surely because the housekeeper knew the earl would check on her arrangements.

"Is there anything else, Mrs. Carstairs?" the woman asked. "I shall, of course, have your luggage brought up as soon as it arrives."

The housekeeper's face was tight with the force of her disapproval. Elizabeth knew that as soon as Mrs. Hendricks got downstairs, she would verbally vent her frustration at being so misused by the earl. Not to the maids, of course. That would be beneath her dignity.

Perhaps to the cook, if their relationship were of long-standing. Almost certainly to Dare's majordomo.

And his reaction, perhaps more properly his relationship to the earl, would determine how Elizabeth would be treated by the staff during her stay. And so, she thought, feeling for almost the first time the effects of the long stressful night she had just passed through, she might as well take advantage of this period of forced cooperation. *In for a penny, in for a pound,* she decided.

"A bath," she said.

"A...bath?" the housekeeper repeated, as if she had never heard the word before.

Judging by the clean scent of sandalwood soap that had surrounded the earl as he sat beside her in the carriage this morning, that was very far from the truth.

"Before the fire, perhaps," Elizabeth said, ignoring the housekeeper's reluctance. "And please tell them that I like the water very hot."

She turned away, walking over to the windows to pull aside the jonquil silk draperies so she could look down on the garden. What she had just done was a trick she had learned from her mother. Always assume that the servants are going to do exactly what you have told them to do, her mother had said. And then deal with it later if they do not.

"Of course," the housekeeper said faintly.

More grist for the mill in her tale of mistreatment, Elizabeth thought, her smile hidden by her position.

"Thank you, Mrs. Hendricks. That will be all, I think."

She waited until she heard the door close before she turned around, infinitely grateful to be alone at last. Away from the judgmental eyes of the servants. Away from the earl's probing questions and his mocking smile.

Her own smile faded, the momentary amusement at imagining the consternation below stairs disappearing in the reality of her situation. As she had told Dare, the unknown was always more frightening than the known, no matter how awful the known had been. And the unknowns in this situation...

She had no idea what Bonnet was up to. She had believed that she knew what the Earl of Dare wanted from her, but so far nothing had gone as she had expected about that. And, of course, she also had no idea what she should or *could* do about either.

Chapter Three

"And where did you find *her,* my lord," Ned Harper asked, as he helped Dare out of his coat.

It usually took the aid of one of the footmen to get the earl into his perfectly tailored jackets, but taking them off was not quite so much a challenge as to require the presence of a third party in the earl's bedroom. Perhaps, Dare thought, that was not to his advantage. Not if Ned was in the mood to lecture.

"At Bonnet's," the earl said easily. "I won her."

He had given Elizabeth into the more than capable hands of his housekeeper. Although Mrs. Hendricks hadn't spoken a word of protest, the earl had certainly been made aware of her disapproval of her "guest." Her nostrils had flared in distaste, and she had never looked at Mrs. Carstairs as he had given his instructions.

"She was at the Frenchman's?"

"Directing the servants and announcing the scores between hands."

"At least you know she can count," the valet said dismissively. "Perhaps you can get her a position in one of the shops when you've finished with her."

"I don't think she's equipped for working in a shop, Ned," the earl said mildly.

"I suppose that after yesterday I should have known something like this would happen...."

The words, their tone clearly chiding, faded as the valet crossed the room. Smiling, Dare didn't ask for an explanation of what Harper had meant. Nor did he reprimand his valet for what had sounded very much like insolence.

Their relationship had long ago slipped from the rigid bonds that normally governed the roles of master and servant and matured into a deep, abiding friendship. Ned Harper was one of the few people who always told the Earl of Dare exactly what he thought. Which was, of course, one of the reasons Dare valued him.

Only Ned and Ian did that, he acknowledged, stepping in front of the dressing table's mirror to remove his stickpin. Actually, the earl thought with a smile, neither of them hesitated in expressing the most brutally honest opinion about his actions. At least the youngest Sinclair still held him in some awe. Of course, the gap between their ages alone was enough to ensure that Sebastian probably always would look up to him. Thank God someone would, he thought in amusement.

"Then what *are* you planning to do with her?" Ned asked when he returned from his errand, as if the break in the conversation had not occurred.

He had handed the coat to a footman waiting outside the bedroom door. From there it would be carried to the kitchens to be brushed and aired. Now Harper began to unwind the earl's cravat.

"*Do* with her?" Dare repeated.

"You have a mistress. Unless you're thinking of taking on another one. And since you seldom have leisure to visit the first…"

"My nights have been…otherwise occupied," the earl said, smiling at his valet in the glass.

Harper's dark eyes met the blue ones reflected in the mirror. "Exactly. So what would you be needing with the Frenchman's whore."

"What makes you so sure she's a whore, Ned?"

The valet's snort was expressive.

"Seriously," the earl said softly.

Again, Harper's eyes lifted to meet his master's. They were no longer derisive. They held on the earl's a long moment before his lips pursed.

"Well, let me see," he said. "One, she was working for Bonnet. Two, you won her on a hand of cards. Three, she's painted like a Maypole. And four, there isn't enough fabric in the bodice of her gown to make a good codpiece. Will you be needing some more reasons?" Ned asked sarcastically.

"Do you know, Ned, I believe I will."

"You don't have time for this," Harper warned.

"I know," Dare acknowledged.

"Shall I find a house for her?" Ned asked, removing the silver-striped waistcoat.

The earl slipped the lawn shirt over his head before he answered. He turned, wearing nothing from the waist up, and held the shirt, still warm from its contact with his body, out to his valet. "It seemed to me that there might be enough room here for one more person," he said.

"Not if you want to keep your staff."

"Are my servants so sensitive that a woman's pres-

ence might drive them away? If so, I'm not paying
them enough.''

"Not *a* woman," Ned said, taking the shirt and
folding it over his arm. "*That* woman. Mrs. Hendricks, for one, will never put up with it, my lord. No
decent woman would."

"Then I suppose Watson will be forced to find another housekeeper," the earl said, meeting Ned's eyes.

Then he walked across to the bed and sat down,
holding out one leg, still neatly attired in knee britches
and silk stockings, which delineated the well-
developed muscles of his calf. Harper watched him a
long moment, and then, lips tight with disapproval, he
threw the earl's clothing over a nearby chair and
stalked over to the bed. He stooped and put his hand
on the heel of the earl's evening slipper. He pulled it
off, and held it in both hands, still squatting on the
floor before Dare.

"If you are willing to let Mrs. Hendricks walk out,
as long as she's been here, then you've got a bee in
your bonnet for sure," Ned said bitterly. "I knew as
soon as I saw that woman she was trouble."

"She's *in* trouble, Ned. Would you have had me
leave her to Bonnet's tender mercies?"

"Yes," Harper said shortly, grasping the other shoe
by the heel and pulling it off roughly.

The valet carried the shoes over to the door and
handed them to the waiting bootblack. When he had
closed the door, he returned to look down on his master, who was stretched out comfortably on the bed,
ankles crossed and hands locked together behind his
head. The broad, dark chest was bare, and the skintight
britches stretched over a flat stomach, narrow hips and
muscular thighs.

The earl's eyes were closed, the dark lashes lying against his cheeks like miniature fans. A lack of sleep during the past few days had left the fragile skin under them discolored like old bruises. Fatigue and grief had deepened the normally unnoticeable lines around his mouth.

Grief, Ned thought. He had known what this was all about from the beginning. The earl hadn't been in time to rescue his friend, so he had rescued Mrs. Carstairs instead.

And here I am, Ned thought, *nattering on at him like a schoolmaster because he's brought some woman home. What does it matter if he wants to bring every strumpet in Gravesend home with him?* Harper thought, unfolding a blanket he took from the foot of the bed and spreading it carefully over the earl. *He's more than earned the right to do that, even if they don't want to be rescued.*

Smiling at the thought, the valet walked across the room and pulled the heavy draperies across the windows. The room darkened as if it were twilight instead of midmorning. Ned waited for his eyes to adjust, and finally, unable to resist the impulse, he walked back to the high bed, almost tiptoeing so as not to chance waking the sleeper.

Even as a child, this was the Sinclair who could be counted on to bring home the strays. Any sick or mistreated animal Val had ever encountered had found its way back to the warmth of the Sinclair stables. Everyone believed that Mr. Ian was the best of the lot, and in a way, Ned supposed they were right.

But I wouldn't be trading this one, Harper thought, adjusting the cover he had laid over the broad chest, which rose and fell with a regularity that told him the earl was already deeply asleep.

I hope to God you don't disappoint him, he thought, remembering the flawless beauty of the woman who had waltzed in through the front door of the town house this morning as if she owned it. *Whatever your story is, lass, I hope it, and you, are worthy of his interest.*

He watched a moment more, at least until the tense muscles in the handsome face had relaxed, giving way to exhaustion, and then Ned Harper turned and, picking up the clothing he had laid over the chair, tiptoed out of the room.

"More sole?" the Earl of Dare asked.

Elizabeth looked up from the contemplation of her plate, where her original portion of fish resided untouched. The delicate sauce with which it had been dressed was congealed unappetizingly around it.

"Or perhaps not," Dare said softly, his eyes rising from the dish to meet hers. He signaled the butler with the lift of one dark eyebrow, and a footman obediently slipped her plate away. "I'm sorry if you found the fish unappealing. Perhaps there might be something else that—"

"Thank you, my lord, but no," she said. "I find...I'm afraid I'm really not very hungry."

"Indisposed, Mrs. Carstairs?" the earl asked, his deep voice touched with amusement.

Again the dark, highly expressive eyebrow arched. Its meaning was as clear to her as it had been to his majordomo before. He was mocking her. Mocking what he believed to be her false claim of being ill.

They both knew why she might attempt to invent

an illness tonight, but that wasn't the kind of woman she was. Whatever else she might have become during the past two years, she wasn't a coward. Of course, the earl had no way of knowing that.

"I am *not* indisposed," she said. "I am rarely *indisposed,* I assure you, Lord Dare. I am simply…not hungry."

"May I tempt you with a sweet? Or a nice cheese, perhaps?"

"No, my lord, you may not," she said, and then hearing the sharpness of her tone, she added more politely, at least on the surface, "Thank you, but no."

"Cook will be devastated," the earl said, lifting his wine to his lips. He watched her over the rim of the glass a second or two before he drank.

"You, yourself, have made an excellent dinner. My compliments on your appetite. And your servants are very well-trained for a bachelor household. My compliments on the service tonight, as well."

"Why, thank you, Mrs. Carstairs," he said, smiling, seeming not the slightest bit annoyed by her comments. "Your approval of my staff is very kind. And I hope their…service was also satisfactory in preparing your bath this morning?"

The question was highly improper, and he certainly knew it. It was intended to convey two messages, and she had understood the import of both. The first was a reminder, she believed, of her own recent "service" at Bonnet's. The second was clearly meant to warn her that nothing went on in the Earl of Dare's household about which he was not informed.

"The arrangements for my bath were very satisfactory, I assure you," she said. "I was told by one of

the footmen who brought up the water that you yourself bathe. Quite frequently, I understand.''

That was a lie, of course. Under Mrs. Hendricks'
watchful eyes, the footman hadn't said a word, but
unless Dare stooped to question his servants, he
couldn't verify that. Perhaps it would give him pause
to believe that information passed both ways.

His lips tilted in response. ''My staff seems much
inclined to gossip about simple household…affairs,''
he said.

He appeared unannoyed by her comment. Which
was not, of course, what she had intended.

''Another warning, my lord?'' she asked innocently.

''Simply a realization. Apparently my servants are
not so well-trained as you have led me to believe.''

''Or perhaps they are simply bored,'' she suggested.

He inclined his head, as if he were thinking about
the possibility, but he let the silence build between
them as the footmen removed the rest of the dishes.

''More wine?'' he asked when that had been done.
Again he signaled and the servant approached to refill
their glasses. Hers was still untouched, a fact he was
almost certainly aware of.

''Thank you, no,'' she said, and the footman who
had been approaching stepped back to his place
against the wall.

''I thought you might feel in need of some Dutch
courage.''

''Really?'' she said, her voice conveying what she
hoped was a note of surprise. ''I wonder why?''

He laughed, the sound again as pleasant as she had
found it to be this morning. And when his laughter
faded away, he was still looking at her, his blue eyes
serious for almost the first time since she had met him.

"Because you're a woman alone with a man about whom you know nothing. A man who won you in a game of cards. I've been trying to imagine all day what you must be feeling."

"And what did you…imagine my feelings to be, my lord?"

"A degree of curiosity, I suppose. Even anxiety perhaps. Or am I wrong?"

She hesitated, but what he had said was only what anyone in her position might confess to feeling.

"No," she admitted. "You aren't wrong."

He lifted his glass again, moving it in a small salute in her direction, before he brought it to his lips.

"Were you planning to satisfy my curiosity?" she asked.

"You may ask me anything," Dare said graciously.

"Why did you bring me here?"

"My mistress is jealous of her position."

It was the closest he had come to admitting what she had supposed all along to be his purpose. He was interested in her sexually. Bonnet had offered her "services," and that had titillated the earl's interest.

This, then, was why he had forced the Frenchman to stake her instead of his house. Dare had now openly confessed his intent, and the fear and dread she had fought all day tightened her chest, making it hard to breathe.

"I thought," the earl continued, "she might not be pleased if I took you there. And I own only the two houses in London, you see."

It took a second or two for the meaning of that to penetrate her anxiety. He had confused her again. Deliberately confused her. He was playing with her, as a cat will play with an exhausted and dying mouse, trying to make it jump and run again.

Cat and mouse was, however, a game she had played successfully for over two years. And it was one at which she thought she was perhaps the better gamester.

"So you brought me to *this* house instead," she said.

"There *is* a great deal of room," Dare agreed, again lifting his glass.

And then his hand hesitated, the journey never completed, as his eyes examined her. His scrutiny began with the arrangement of her hair. She had dressed it very simply, adorning it with a sprig of jasmine, which she had taken from one of the huge vases of flowers in her room.

His slow and careful appraisal surprised her. And unnerved her. For reasons she had not attempted to analyze, she had taken great pains over her appearance tonight. And yet, until now, Dare had hardly looked at her.

True to his word, he had had her things sent over from Bonnet's. As she had unpacked the *portmanteau* this afternoon, she realized there was really very little to choose from, *if* one were not planning to entertain strange gentlemen in a gambling hell. None of the gowns the bag contained had seemed appropriate for a quiet dinner at home.

She had finally chosen the least revealing, one she had brought to the Frenchman's house in the very beginning. It was more properly a day gown than half dress, although the fabric was a very fine blue silk. It was clearly several years out of style, something a man of fashion like Dare would be well aware of. At least it was modest, however, covering far more of her bosom than the one she had worn last night.

"My compliments, Mrs. Carstairs," he said finally, after he had studied her for several long seconds. Not long enough to be insulting, perhaps, but very close. "I find I much prefer the lily *ungilded*," he added softly.

He meant without the cosmetics Bonnet insisted she wear. They had been included with her things. She had not used them tonight, of course. Surveying her reflection in the looking glass in her room, however, she had been surprised to find she had grown so accustomed to wearing them that her cheeks and eyes appeared almost colorless without the paint.

"Thank you, my lord," she said simply.

His prolonged examination was as improper as his question about her bath, but she didn't want to antagonize him. And indeed, he had offered her no real insult. Not openly. At least, not yet.

"I wonder if you would consent to join me briefly in my study. There are some things we should discuss before I leave," Dare said.

She had been trying to read the tone of the first sentence, and so it took a second or two for the sense of the second to penetrate. "Before you leave?" she repeated in surprise.

"I'm afraid business calls me away for a few days. My apologies for leaving you alone," he said, still watching her.

She tried to keep her relief from showing. He had not said when he was leaving, but that had sounded as if…

"Of course," she said faintly.

"Harper, my valet, will see to your needs in my

absence. He will assign one of the maids to serve you tomorrow. I'm sorry I failed to think of that this morning.''

It had been over two years since Elizabeth had had an abigail. She wasn't sure she remembered what it was like to be waited upon. The thought that he had been remiss in not providing her with a maid hadn't even crossed her mind. After all, in spite of what the earl had told his housekeeper, she was well aware that she wasn't here as his *guest*.

''If all goes well, I should be back within the week,'' the earl continued. ''I've asked Harper to meet us in my study. He's probably waiting there now.''

She examined the information, looking for hidden pitfalls; however, this seemed to be a reprieve, if anything. Dare was to be away on business, and she would be left alone. He had implied it would be for a few days. Perhaps long enough for her to find a way to get a message to Bonnet?

She didn't know what game the Frenchman was playing, but she knew he would never have allowed her out of his clutches if it had not been to his advantage. So she was certain there had been more to the game of cards in which he had staked her than appeared on the surface.

''If you would be so kind as to come with me....'' Dare said, bringing her attention back to the present.

He was already standing, and there was a footman behind her chair, ready to pull it back so that she, too, might rise and join the earl in his study. Where she would be introduced to his valet. It all seemed harmless enough. Already her mind was working on the possible implications of the earl's absence. *And* on its possible advantages.

''Of course,'' she said.

* * *

She wasn't sure what she had been expecting in the Earl of Dare's valet, but it was certainly not the man who was waiting in the room to which Dare led her. Small and undistinguished, it seemed Harper might be more at home in the stables of a country estate than in this vast and elegant town house.

"Mrs. Carstairs, this is Harper, my valet," the earl said.

There was something in Dare's voice. A note of amusement, perhaps? And Elizabeth thought she knew why when she confronted the open dislike in Harper's eyes.

This was the same assessment, the same judgment, she amended, Mrs. Hendricks had made this morning. And one which had been absent from the earl's eyes, she realized. Whatever his servants thought her to be, apparently Dare had not yet made up his mind. Or perhaps he had decided it didn't matter what she was.

"*Mrs.* Carstairs," Ned Harper said. There was a subtle, but obvious emphasis on the title.

"*Mr.* Harper," she said, echoing it.

The small barb struck home. His brown eyes widened, and he glanced at Dare before they came back to her face. At least the contempt that had been in them before was gone, replaced by wariness. Elizabeth found she infinitely preferred the latter to the former.

"Ned will see to your needs while I'm gone," the earl explained again, this time for his valet's benefit. "You have only to ask him for anything you need."

Except Harper can't arrange what I need, she thought bitterly. And neither could the Earl of Dare, no matter how rich he might be.

"Thank you, my lord," she said.

"That will be all, Ned," Dare said softly. It was clearly a dismissal, but the valet didn't move, his eyes tracing over her boldly now. Far too boldly for a servant.

"You're making a mistake," he said finally, his tone flat and hard.

Since he hadn't used the earl's title, Elizabeth wasn't perfectly sure which of them he was addressing, but Dare seemed to be in no doubt.

"And that *is* my privilege, of course," he said.

There was no anger in his voice. Again, she thought she sensed amusement there instead, and she wondered about the relationship between master and man. It was beyond her realm of experience. Her father's valet had been a toadying, simpering idiot, whom no one held in respect, not even the other servants, despite his superior position in the household.

It was obvious that Ned Harper, however, was accustomed to speaking his mind, no matter the subject—even one so personal as the earl's relationship to a woman. And he seemed to expect that Dare would attend to his opinion.

Harper's mouth had tightened, and his eyes, if possible, had grown colder as they rested on her face. Elizabeth controlled her features, unwilling to give him the satisfaction of knowing she had noticed his dislike.

"That will be all, Ned," Dare said again, even more softly.

The valet's eyes held another second on her face, and then he turned and almost stalked from the room.

"I apologize for Ned's rudeness," Dare said after a moment, his voice untroubled. "It wasn't directed at you, I assure you. He's angry that I'm not taking him with me."

He moved to stand beside the fire. He put both hands on the mantel, looking down into the flames. The fine, wine-colored cloth of his jacket stretched across a broad back and well-defined shoulders.

Elizabeth was well aware that gentlemen often created the appearance of muscle by the artful use of buckram padding. It was obvious, however, just as it had been this morning when she had watched him climb the stairs, that the Earl of Dare had never been called upon to resort to such stratagems.

She pulled her eyes away, turning her head a little, so that she wouldn't be tempted to look at him any more. Ned Harper was standing in the doorway to the study, watching them. He held her eyes a long time, and then he shut the door, taking pains that its closing didn't make any sound. She looked quickly back at the earl, but he hadn't moved, unaware that his valet had been spying on them.

"Why aren't you?" she asked.

"Taking Ned?" Dare said, as he turned to face her. His hair was blue-black in the firelight. "A quick business trip. I won't have need of his services."

She wasn't sure this time if the use of the word had been deliberate, but it brought them back to the crux of the matter. Back to what she thought he wanted from her.

"And I'm to stay here in your absence?"

"Of course," Dare said. "I assume you don't wish to return to Bonnet's."

She said nothing, wondering if he would let her go if she said yes. And, more importantly, wondering what Bonnet would do to her if she showed up at his door tomorrow.

Because she wasn't here by accident, of course. Or by a turn of fate. Henri Bonnet, despite his unquestioned skill at gaming, left nothing to chance.

"Or do you, Mrs. Carstairs?"

"No, my lord," she said softly.

"Then I shall see you when I return."

The question she wanted to ask him trembled on her tongue. She watched as he walked across the room until he was standing before her. He held out his hand.

"Sleep well, Mrs. Carstairs," he said. "Tonight and every night until I return. I promise Ned will take very good care of you while I'm gone."

Reluctantly, she placed her fingers in his, and he raised them slowly to his lips. She could feel the warmth of his breath as he brushed his mouth across them, the lightest possible touch.

He did not release her hand, but he raised his head and his eyes held on her face. Finally, at whatever he saw there, he smiled at her.

Something moved within her chest, an unexpected jolt of reaction, almost painful in its intensity. Her heart began to beat so heavily she was afraid the movement might be visible externally. That he might be aware of the effect he was having.

It had been a very long time since a man had kissed her hand. It was a gesture both romantic and chivalric. And it had been far too long, it seemed, since she had stirred either emotion in a masculine breast.

She had become accustomed to leers. To suggestive comments. To hot, roving eyes that focused on the line of her throat or on her exposed breasts.

It had been too long since a man had treated her not

like a wanton, but like a lady. Her reaction had been simple gratitude, a natural response to Dare's gallantry. Or so she told herself.

Although he seemed to be playing the perfect gentleman tonight, the earl had won her on the turn of a card. And he had not offered her freedom, which a *real* gentleman, one who truly considered her a lady, would certainly have done. So whatever his behavior seemed to indicate...

She pulled her fingers from his and almost fled toward the door Ned Harper had closed only moments before. And despite whatever she had felt as the Earl of Dare had pressed his lips against the tips of her fingers, she did not look back.

Chapter Four

*O*ne more, the Earl of Dare told himself, the now-familiar words repeated like a litany, as he pressed his body more closely into the shadows. He was in the back garden of a small house on the outskirts of Paris. It was well after midnight, but there were still lights on inside. Apparently, and disappointingly, the occupant of the dwelling was either awake or, more likely, reluctant these days to sleep in the dark.

And despite the risks occasioned by his present location and by the task he had undertaken tonight, Dare found himself smiling at that thought. Relishing it.

He had known, of course, that this one would be the most dangerous. And he had added to that danger by saving this particular man for the last. That decision, however, had been both considered and deliberate, and even now, faced with the daunting prospect of the light, he had no regrets.

This was the man who had issued the orders. The one most responsible for what had been done to his friend, Andre. And considering his position in the government, this man, Paul Lefebvre was probably the most intelligent of the five whom the earl had set out from London a week ago to hunt down. And that meant, Dare had decided, that Lefebvre was probably also the one with the greatest capacity to imagine his fate.

At least I hope you've been imagining it, you bastard, Dare thought, the smile on his lips without amusement. *I hope you've been living in a state of absolute terror, dreaming about my hands fastened around your throat or about the coldness of my blade sliding into the vileness of your black heart.*

For six days the Earl of Dare had stalked the streets of Paris like ancient Nemesis. And in those six days, he had relentlessly found, and killed, four men. Although what had been in his heart when he had begun this quest had been nothing less than cold-blooded murder, he had given all of them the opportunity to fight him. Far more chance than they had given Andre.

Dare put his head against the rough bark of the tree he was leaning against and closed his eyes. The pleasant reality of the garden in which he was standing faded as he allowed himself to picture what had been done to Andre. He had engaged in this painful exercise four times, fueling his rage, so that when he had approached the men whose heated irons and knotted ropes had tortured his friend to his death, his resolve would be strong enough to do what must be done.

These five deaths would not be, however, simply an exercise in revenge, although that was perhaps the strongest emotion at the core of his determination. They were also intended to serve as a warning. And for that warning to have its fullest effect, for it to reverberate within the terror Fouché and his secret police carried out in France, this last man, the one closest to the center of that official corruption, must also die.

Dare hadn't yet been able to determine how Lefebvre had discovered Andre's connection to his network of spies. That information was something which *must* be discovered, something his agents were working on as if their own lives depended it. Of course, their lives *did*. Just as did Dare's.

He had always known that once the secrets his agents knew began to unravel, the broken thread could run through the warp of his organization very quickly. That was why, by design, they knew so little about one another. And why they knew as little as possible about himself as well.

Most of them had probably guessed he was English, Dare acknowledged, as he edged closer to the glass doors that looked out on the garden. Andre had certainly known. It was even possible that he had revealed the earl's nationality, no matter what other knowledge he had, in his agony, managed to deny them.

Who could know what else Dare might have unwittingly exposed to Andre or another agent through the years? And who could know what Andre might have gasped into the ears of his questioners to stop the torment? Whatever it was, Dare could never blame him.

He had almost reached the glass doors, clinging to the shadows the garden's lush foliage provided. The light from the house poured out through the myriad panes and onto the lawn, but it didn't penetrate very far.

Not far enough to protect you, Dare promised, slipping noiselessly into position against the bricks beside the doors. Moving with infinite care, he leaned forward enough to see into the room that lay exposed behind the glass.

There was only one occupant—a man, asleep in a chair. The light from the lamp on the table beside him not only spilled out into the darkness where Dare was hiding, but it also clearly illuminated the sleeper's face.

The muscles were slack, the porcine features empty of expression or humanity. His mouth was open, a thread of saliva trailing from one corner, his hands crossed over his ample belly. And beside him on the table lay a pistol.

Despite the threat the weapon represented, Dare smiled at its placement. At least now he knew that his victim had been imagining this moment. *How many nights have you sat here,* Dare wondered, *waiting for me to come for you?*

Had Lefebvre known when he had heard the news of the first death that Nemesis would also be seeking him? Six nights, then, he had probably gone without sleep, and tonight, too exhausted to stay awake, too tired to watch for his enemy on this most important of all nights…

The earl's humorless smile widened. *I hope you've been thinking about what will happen tonight,* Dare thought, his hand easing toward the handle of the door. It would be locked, of course, but the earl was talented at gaining entrance to places where he hadn't been invited and was not wanted. Surprisingly talented for an English nobleman.

He tried the handle and was shocked that it turned under his gloved fingers. *A trap?* Even if it were, he decided after a brief hesitation, he had no choice but to spring it. He had an unbreakable appointment at a

ball that would be held at Carlton House tomorrow
night. A rendezvous that would, by royal decree, have
to take precedence over his mission in France.

Tonight, then. Or not until he could again arrange
to leave London for a few days, Dare thought, his eyes
holding on the sleeping man. And he wanted this over.

Tonight, he decided, his gaze moving again to the
pistol on the table beside the chair. He took a firmer
grip on his sword, opening his fingers and closing
them, one by one, around the hilt to make sure his
hold was secure. Then he pushed down the handle of
the door and allowed it to swing inward.

He waited a moment, still hidden within the shadows. Nothing stirred, not within the room or in the
garden. It was as silent as a tomb. As still as death.

He eased through the door, taking care that his
sword touched nothing. On booted feet, he tiptoed
across the room until he was standing before the sleeping man. He could hear the soft, snoring breaths he
took, their sounds corresponding to the gentle rise and
fall of the rounded stomach.

Dare placed the tip of his blade against the sleeper's
chin. He held it there a moment, waiting for reaction.
There was none, nothing but the soft, regular in-and-
out sighs of his breathing. Very slowly, the earl applied pressure, pushing the point of the sword against
the man's chin, causing the gaping mouth to begin to
close.

As it did, the man's eyes opened, sleep-dazed and
unfocused. One beefy hand lifted, as if he intended to
brush away whatever annoyance was pushing painfully against his chin. Instead, the hand hesitated in
midair, and his eyes stretched wider and wider around
the mud-colored irises.

"Close your mouth, Monsieur Lefebvre," Dare said softly in unaccented French, "or you will surely catch flies. Your garden door is open, my friend."

The man's eyes, clearly expressing terror, held on Dare's face, but obediently the Frenchman's mouth began to close, the thin trickle of saliva still visible in the lamplight.

"What do you want?" he said.

"Retribution," the earl said. "You ordered the torture of a friend of mine."

It didn't seem possible, but the eyes rounded even more. The Frenchman's tongue appeared, licking lips that had gone dry.

"No," he whispered.

"Yes," Dare said softly, smiling at him. "I have it on the best authority—that of the soldiers who carried out the torture. They all assured me that yours was the name on the warrant."

"What are you going to do?" Lefebvre asked, his voice breaking with fear.

"Ultimately, I am going to kill you, Monsieur Lefebvre, but first I'm going to give you a chance to fight for your life. Something you *didn't* give my friend. Do you have a sword?"

The Frenchman's eyes held on Dare's a long time, reading the cold certainty in their blue depths. Finally he nodded, his chin moving against the tip of the sword. A drop of blood welled around the point.

"Is it in this room?" Dare asked.

Again the Frenchman nodded. Without turning his head, he rolled his eyes toward a display of weapons on the wall. Dare's gaze followed, finding there what he sought.

Still holding Lefebvre a prisoner in his chair by the

tip of his sword, the earl reached to his left and by feel alone located the pistol on the table with the lamp. He lifted it, and in the same motion, stepped back, away from the chair, his sword still pointed toward the Frenchman.

Lefebvre remained in the same position for three or four seconds, exactly as if the sword were still holding him prisoner. Then, very slowly, he lowered his chin, his eyes never leaving Dare's. The earl tilted his head in the direction of the swords which hung on the wall.

"I'm not a swordsman," the Frenchman said.

"What a pity," Dare said, smiling at him.

"In my youth…" Again the thick pink tongue touched against his lips. "You said you would give me a chance," he reminded, his voice almost whining.

The earl's dark eyebrow arched in question.

"Do you know how the Gypsies fight?" Lefebvre asked.

A finger of ice touched Dare's spine. He did know, of course. He had even seen such a fight once in Italy. He looked again at the wall and saw the pair of crossed knives. They were long, their blades broad and very deadly, their hilts guarded like swords.

If he agreed to what the Frenchman had just suggested, he would be a fool, Dare thought. The man's reach was at least two inches longer than his. In a fight such as the one he had proposed, even Lefebvre's bulk would not be a disadvantage. Perhaps, given the rules—or the lack of them, Dare amended—it might even be an advantage.

Dare was not, however, a murderer. If he were, he would have driven his sword, safely and cleanly, through the Frenchman's heart as he slept. The others he had killed had been soldiers, trained in arms. They had therefore had a chance in the duels he had forced on them. Actually, one of them had been frighteningly skilled. If Lefebvre were not, he told himself, that was simply the Frenchman's bad luck.

For some reason, the word echoed. *Luck.* Dare had always been blessed with more than his share. And with more courage than sense, Ian frequently complained. The sudden, unexpected thought of his brother was both comforting and highly uncomfortable. Because he knew Ian would never have approved of what he was doing.

This was not the way his brother did things. Ian would have trussed them all up like birds for the spit and attempted to bring them back to England to stand trial, Dare thought. He was almost amused by the picture of his honorable brother faced with this decision. But it was not, of course, Ian's decision. It was his. And the Earl of Dare was the Sinclair who was known to be guilty of almost every vice except common sense.

The Frenchman was waiting, his face gleaming with rivulets of perspiration in the lamplight. Dare took another step back, away from the chair, and raised his rapier to his chin in the classic swordman's salute. And then, before he could change his mind, he backed across the room and laid the sword and the Frenchman's pistol on the desk below the weapons displayed on the wall.

When he took the crossed knives down, he was surprised by their weight. Holding one in each hand, he walked back across the room and stopped near the chair where the Frenchman was sitting. Never taking his eyes off Lefebvre, he laid one of the knives on the floor and then, stepping off the distance, he laid the other parallel to it, the blades about four long paces apart.

"Get up," Dare ordered, as he straightened.

The words were clearly a command, despite their softness, and the Frenchman obeyed.

"Your cravat," the earl said.

With trembling fingers, Lefebvre untied the ends of his necktie and then unwound the material from around his neck. When he had finished, he held a narrow strip of cloth.

The earl positioned himself between the two knives, his left arm, bent at the elbow, held up in the air. Reluctantly it seemed, despite the fact that this had been his suggestion, the Frenchman joined him. Beside the right foot of each of them lay one of the knives Dare had taken off the wall.

"Your arm," the earl said.

They were close enough now that he could smell the Frenchman, a miasma of unwashed body compounded by the unmistakable stink of fear. The odor was so strong it was almost palpable. Slowly, Lefebvre held up his left hand, his arm bent like Dare's.

"And the cloth," Dare said.

When the other man had handed over the cravat, the earl looped its length around their wrists, once and once again. Then, using his teeth and the fingers of his right hand, he knotted the material around their joined arms, pulling it tight, so that their wrists were now tied together.

"When I count to three," Dare said.

Fool, his heart whispered, and unbidden, the image of Elizabeth Carstairs' face was suddenly in his mind's eye. Surprised to find it there, knowing instinctively that the thought of her would only weaken him, coldly and deliberately, he destroyed it, replacing the cool perfection of her features with the battered, suffering face of Andre.

"One," the earl said.

To his own ears, his voice sounded strangely harsh. He was close enough to his opponent that he could feel the tensing muscles in Lefebvre's upper body.

"Two," Dare counted.

Almost before the syllable had left his lips, the Frenchman sprang, pulling him forward and down as he dove toward the knife at his feet. At the same time, of course, he pulled Dare away from the weapon that was to have been his.

Warned by a subtle tensing when he had begun the count, Dare had been expecting something like this. He jerked his left arm, the one by which he was bound to the Frenchman, unbalancing his opponent enough that he was forced to stumble backward, toward Dare. His fingers barely missed their contact with the knife he had been reaching for.

Although the earl hadn't yet managed to get his hands on his own weapon, he concentrated on preventing Lefebvre from getting into position to grasp the other knife. For seemingly endless seconds, they engaged in an obscene and ungainly duet. They staggered backward and forward, carried by momentum generated by the other's jerks and pulls on their joined arms, moving like flotsam on the tide, never more than a few feet from the knives.

Finally, having gained a momentary advantage by throwing his opponent off balance just as he had bent to grab at one of the blades, Dare lifted his foot and attempted to kick the knife away. The Frenchman reacted to that maneuver more quickly than he would have believed possible for a man of his bulk. He threw his full weight against the earl, at the same time sweeping his foot forward to catch the earl behind the knees.

Dare staggered, almost going down. He put out his right hand to get his balance, and as soon as he had, he turned to see what his opponent was doing. The Frenchman's fingers were closing around the hilt of one of the weapons.

Dare rolled onto his right shoulder, using the weight of his body to pull his opponent backward. This time, however, the Frenchman's hand had already closed over the knife. When Lefebvre fell, he brought the blade around with him, stabbing wildly at the earl.

Tied to his opponent, there was no way for Dare to get completely out of range of the lethal blade, which was, of course, the terrible danger to this kind of fighting. The earl rolled again, in the opposite direction this time, and felt the point of the knife bite into the loose material of the sleeve of the shirt he wore. At the same time, he brought his knees up, catching the Frenchman under the belly and levering him off to the other side.

Frantically, Dare reached out for the remaining knife, which was lying now just beyond his fingers. He strained, his right arm stretched to its full extent, the weight of the wheezing body behind him pulling him back. Desperately the earl lunged forward, dragging Lefebvre a few inches across the floor with him. The tips of his fingers spread over the blade of the knife.

At that exact moment, the Frenchman jerked his arm, pulling the earl back. Frantic to hold on to the knife, Dare closed his hand, drawing the blade within it, but the keen edge sliced into his fingers as he gripped it. He didn't let go, despite the sting of the cut.

He felt a blow on the back of his left shoulder, but by that time, he was already manipulating the knife he had grasped. He slipped his fingers down to the hilt, feeling the slickness of his own blood on the handle.

Then he managed to get his hand into the guard, gripping the hilt, and brought the knife around in time to meet the downward thrust of his opponent's blade. Sparks flew, clearly visible in the dimness of the room. The force of that contact tingled down Dare's arm, setting nerves on fire.

The blades themselves, locked together by their guards, froze in midair, unmoving, as each man tried to drive the other's blade downward by brute strength. That was a battle he probably would lose, Dare recognized. Sheer size would eventually prevail. And before it did…

Dare dropped his right arm, unlocking the blades. The Frenchman's followed. He managed to turn the knife as he did, driving the point downward. Dare's body was no longer there. He rolled away, and then, in the same movement, rolled back toward his opponent. He slashed upward, awkwardly, but somehow, possibly nothing more than Dare's famous luck, the blade caught Lefebvre in the side of the neck.

The Frenchman screamed, a high-pitched, almost womanly sound. He dropped his knife, both hands reaching for his throat, as if he could somehow prevent the gush of blood. Of course, he drew the earl's left hand up with his. Lefebvre's panic was so great that he continued to scream, a high, keening sound.

The noise must have lasted only a few seconds, but to Dare, on his knees beside the dying man, it seemed to go on an eternity. Finally, as the Frenchman's hands slipped off his neck and his body slumped to the floor, the earl inserted the edge of his knife between their joined arms, forcing it upward and through the blood-soaked material that bound them together.

When he was free, Dare crawled to his feet, using the chair Lefebvre had been sitting in for support. For some reason he felt disoriented. He stood, swaying, his hand on the top of the chair. He knew there was something he needed to do before he could leave, but for a moment he couldn't remember what it was.

He looked around the room, but things were slightly distorted, as if he were dreaming. Everything seemed much darker than when he had first entered the house, coming into the light from that night-shrouded garden beyond the doors.

The garden, he thought. He had to get to the garden. But there was something... Again, he forced his eyes to survey the room. He saw the sword and the pistol lying on the table. His brain told him to move, but his body resisted. Perhaps reluctant to leave the support of the chair? He looked down at it and realized that there was blood on the pale upholstery.

The Frenchman's blood was all over him, of course. He removed his hand, wiping it unthinkingly on his trousers, and took a staggering step toward the table. And then another.

By the time he reached it, he was light-headed, as if he had gone without food or water for a long time. He reached out for his sword and saw the trickle of blood spill off his outstretched fingers. Amazed, he watched as it dripped down onto the table, each drop gleaming like a cabochon ruby. His blood, he finally realized.

There was a dull ache in the back of his shoulder. Exactly where he thought Lefebvre had hit him. He laughed, the sound short. The blow he had felt had been from the Frenchman's knife, driven deep into the muscles of his back.

He lifted his hand, and tried to reach the wound on the back of the opposite shoulder. The shard of agony when he did that was severe enough to solicit a gasp.

He put his hands, palms down, on the top of the table, leaning against it. He closed his eyes, riding out the crest of the pain as well as the nausea it produced. When it had faded to a dull, hot glow, he picked up his sword, and retraced his path across the room and to the glass doors.

He had been here too long. There had been too much noise. On some level he knew all those things, but he couldn't seem to assign them their proper importance. The agony in his shoulder and his dizziness overshadowed everything else.

He had reached the doors and had even managed to open one of them when he heard the noise behind him. He wasn't sure what it was, but it was loud enough that he turned in response.

A woman was standing in the shadows across the room. She had both hands to her mouth, so perhaps what he had heard was whatever muffled outcry she had made. Her eyes, widened and staring, were fastened on the body of the man he had fought.

And then they came up to his. She was small, as stout as Lefebvre, and she was wearing a nightgown. Dark hair, streaked with gray, escaped from her nightcap, which was slightly askew.

The Frenchman's housekeeper? Or his wife?

"Murderer," she said in French. She had moved her

fingertips away from her lips so that the word was quite clear.

So clear, so condemning that Dare found he wanted to explain. The word buzzed unpleasantly in his brain like the sound of summer bees. That was what this stupid duel had been about. This was not murder, the earl thought, trying to convey to her what he understood so clearly, despite the encroaching darkness. This had been about honor. His honor.

The Frenchman had shown he had none by diving for the knife before the count was finished. He wanted to explain all that to her. And to tell her about Andre. To justify, perhaps, the stiffening corpse on the blood-stained carpet.

He said nothing, the words forming only in his brain. Nor did he step through the door he had opened. It was hard to think. Hard to make a decision. The light-headedness he had felt before made his head swim.

She reached out to the table beside her. He watched her hand, which moved with infinite slowness, or so it seemed to Dare, toward Lefebvre's pistol. Realizing that there was at least a remote possibility that she could get the thing to fire, the earl took a step backward, out into the darkness of the garden. He pulled the door closed behind him, feeling a sense of relief at that small accomplishment.

He took one last look at the woman. She raised the pistol, holding it with both hands. Her eyes held his as she pointed it toward him. When she fired, smoke billowed from the gun. The ball struck the door, shattering one of the panes of glass.

And finally, stumbling a little in his haste, the Earl of Dare turned away from the house where he had tonight killed the last of the men responsible for Andre Du Cange's torture and death. As he ran, he pressed his hand against the deep burn in his side. He couldn't afford to lose any more blood.

Fool, he thought again, looking at the wall he had scaled so easily on his way into the garden. It loomed impossibly high. On the other side lay his only chance to escape.

He could hear noises coming from the direction of the house. The shot had almost certainly awakened everyone. Soon the servants would come with torches to light the shadows where he was hiding. And if he were still here...

He grasped the lower limb of the tree he had climbed down, and pulled himself painfully up onto the first branch. He waited a moment, willing the roar in his head to subside. Willing the agony in his side and shoulder into a dark corner of his mind, trying to close it in and lock it out of his consciousness.

He put his foot up on the top of the wall, gasping aloud at the tearing agony in his side. He sat atop the stones for a moment, fighting to stay conscious.

Finally, hearing more noise from the house, he pulled himself upright, balancing carefully on the narrow ledge. He threw his sword onto the ground on the other side. And then, ignoring what his mind told him about the impossibility of what he was about to do, given the condition of his body, the Earl of Dare followed it.

Chapter Five

Seven days, Elizabeth thought, prowling restlessly around the suite as the sun began to set again over London. Despite its size and beauty, in those long days this chamber had become little more than a prison.

She had heard nothing from Bonnet, and her anxiety had built until her nerves were stretched to the breaking point. So much for believing that the past two years had taught her to face everything with equanimity, she acknowledged bitterly.

The earl had not returned. She wasn't sure that shouldn't be cause for rejoicing, but for some reason she had found herself listening to every household noise during the last two days, anticipating that if she listened hard enough, she might hear his voice.

She knew that Ned Harper shared her anticipation. And her anxiety. She could not have said exactly how she had been made aware of that, but she had recognized his worry just the same.

Harper had been surprisingly courteous to her during his master's absence. Perhaps Dare had been telling the truth when he said his valet was angry with him rather than with her that first night. In any case,

Harper had checked on her every day. Her meals, which she had requested be brought to her room, had arrived under silver covers, the food still hot and appetizing, despite having traveled from the distant kitchen.

The first night after the earl's departure she had eaten dinner alone in the huge, formal dining room, every bite taken under the watchful eyes of Dare's majordomo and two footmen. She had not eaten there since.

She imagined because of that she had been roundly cursed below stairs, especially by whichever maid was required to carry up her tray. She had asked them for nothing else, however, except bathwater, and she was, after all, she remembered, her lips tilting in amusement, the earl's valued guest.

The abigail Harper had sent her was newly up from the country and little more than a child. Elizabeth supposed he had hoped that would displease her, but it hadn't, of course. The girl chatted endlessly about her experiences in this great house. Unwittingly, she had given Elizabeth far more information about the household and the people in it than she could possibly have acquired by exploring on her own.

She had listened to Maggie's endless narratives and had watched the outside world from the windows of her room. She now knew by sight most of the tradesmen who made deliveries here. And she had already decided on which she would approach about taking a message for her to Bonnet.

A redheaded, freckle-faced boy brought two buckets of beer for the servants' dining room every night, carrying them carefully by the handles as the foaming liquid sloshed over his scuffed and broken brogans. Of all those who came through the back garden to the kitchens, he seemed to Elizabeth the most likely candidate for her errand.

As young as he was, he would probably be eager to earn something extra and yet not on such terms with the earl's older servants as to gossip about the opportunity. He might even see her request as an adventure, something that would appeal to a boy of that age. At the very least, or so she fervently hoped, he wouldn't have nerve enough to report her to Watson, Dare's intimidating butler.

So she had begun a draft of her message to the Frenchman this morning, and now the final version was ready. She had only to decide if she would try to talk to the boy tonight or tomorrow night.

She couldn't imagine why Bonnet hadn't contacted her. Of course, it might simply be part of the cat-and-mouse game he loved. By now, he could be certain she would be willing to do anything he demanded. And she would be, she admitted bitterly, letting the silk draperies fall back against the darkening glass.

Tonight, she decided. And if she were caught, she would say she was in the garden because she had needed a breath of fresh air. Since she hadn't been out of the house since Dare's departure, that desire would be hard to dispute. Hard even for Ned Harper to question, although his dark eyes saw far too much.

He didn't trust her. She knew that, and she almost admired him for it. Because she couldn't be trusted. Not to do anything except what Bonnet ordered her to do. There was too much at stake to chance doing anything else. And honor was something Elizabeth Carstairs had given up a long time ago. Along with her freedom. Her will. And her soul.

Tonight, she told herself again, pushing those painful admissions from her mind. *Approach the boy tonight, and have done with it.*

Leaving the house had been easier than she'd imagined it could be. She had sneaked down the servants' stairs and had been out into the back garden in a matter of seconds, without encountering anyone. No questions to answer, she thought gratefully. Not yet, at any rate.

She had even found a dark linsey-woolsey cloak, hanging on a peg by the kitchen door. Not only would it conceal the light color of the gown she wore, it would ward off the chill that had arrived with the twilight.

As she waited for the boy, she could hear the voices of the servants, drifting out of the house and into the gloom. Their laughter. Even the occasional word, distinguishable only because the speaker had raised his voice in jest or in admonition.

She peered into the shadows which obscured the other end of the path that led from the alley to the kitchen door. It seemed that the redheaded boy was later than usual. Because it was Saturday, she wondered?

As she considered the possibility, someone appeared at the end of the path. Someone or…something, she amended, watching its halting progress through the darkness. The shape seemed too large to be a person. Certainly too large for the boy.

She ran back toward the house, positioning herself against the kitchen wall, where she would be hidden by shadow. Ivy covered the stones behind her, she realized belatedly, and she shivered at the brush of leaves against her neck, wondering about their eight-legged inhabitants. Her eyes, however, never left the shape that was slowly coming toward her down the walkway.

Two men, she realized. One supporting the other. As they came closer, despite the fading light, she recognized that one of them was the Earl of Dare. And the other...

Was no one she had ever seen before, she decided. Her eyes came back to Dare's face. It was contorted, and despite his companion's help, his feet were dragging.

"Just Harper," she heard the earl say as they approached.

The other man nodded and then helped Dare to the tree beside which she had been standing only minutes before. Without his companion's support, the earl slumped against its trunk, his head hanging as if he were too exhausted to hold it upright.

The other man continued up the path, past Elizabeth's hiding place, and pounded on the kitchen door. She couldn't see who answered his knock, but the man quickly disappeared inside, leaving the earl alone in the darkness.

She was near enough that she heard the breath he drew. It was ragged, the end of it almost vocal. Almost a groan. Inarticulate. Suffering. Like a wounded animal.

Elizabeth's first impulse was to go to him. After all, Dare had come to her rescue. Or was she giving him more credit than he deserved? Perhaps she was even creating a melodrama out of whatever was happening here. This was probably something very prosaic. Perhaps Dare was drunk. Perhaps—

The door opened, interrupting her search for an explanation that wouldn't demand she become involved. The man who had brought Dare into the garden came out of the house, followed by Ned Harper. Again, Elizabeth tried to push closer against the ivy-covered wall behind her, knowing instinctively that Harper wouldn't want her to see whatever was going on here. The resultant rustling of the leaves seemed very loud. She froze, eyes locked on the men starting down the path.

Neither of them seemed aware of the noise. Or of anything else. Their attentions were totally directed toward the man slumped against the tree.

"You bloody fool," Ned said softly, his voice without anger or censure, but rich with concern, despite the chiding words. "I told you you'd need me."

Dare laughed. The sound was low, but it was also now familiar. She had heard him laugh before, and on those occasions she had enjoyed hearing his laughter. Neither had been like this. She could almost feel the pain that cut the sound short, stealing his breath.

"Pay Captain Stark, Ned," the earl said after he'd recovered. "And make it double. He's more than earned his money this time."

"I'll take care of him," Harper assured soothingly, slipping his shoulder under Dare's arm. "He knows that right enough. The captain's not worried about his money. Let's get you inside first so we can see what damage you've done."

"Whatever it is…" Dare began, but the words ended in a gasp as Harper lifted him away from the support of the tree.

Behind them, coming from the alley that ran at the back of the gardens of this row of elegant town houses,

the same alley from which the earl and his companion
had appeared only moments before, came the sound
of whistling.

The boy, Elizabeth realized, raising her eyes to the
end of the path. Harper had made that identification at
the same time. Fumbling in his pocket, he pulled out
a sack of coins, judging from the sound they made as
he tossed it to the other man.

"That's the boy with the beer," he said. "Get rid
of him."

The man Dare had called captain had been trying
to get on the other side of the earl, so that between
them they could help him into the house and then up
the back stairs. It was apparent to Elizabeth that they
didn't want anyone to see what they were doing. Not
even, it seemed, the boy who brought the beer.

Stark had caught the sack with one hand, and then
turning, he hurried down the path and disappeared into
the darkness. His eyes lingering a moment on the
shadows there, Harper finally brought his attention
back to the task at hand.

"All right, lad, up we go now," he encouraged
softly, shifting the earl's arm more securely over his
shoulder and eliciting another smothered groan in the
process.

If there had ever been anyone less likely to be referred to as "lad," Elizabeth thought, it was the Earl
of Dare. Just as the thought formed, the earl's knees
bent, and his body sagged. Unprepared, Harper staggered under the suddenly dead weight, almost dropping his master onto the path.

Against all her self-protective instincts, Elizabeth
stepped out of the shadows and ran to slip under the
earl's other arm. As she did, she looked up into his

face. It was ashen, covered with a film of perspiration. She could feel the heat emanating from his body even through his clothing. His eyes were closed.

"He's fainted," she said, straightening her back so that she was now supporting some of his weight. She was surprised at how heavy he was. Of course, since he was unconscious...

The blue eyes opened, thick, black lashes moving upward slowly. He blinked once, like a sleepy owl, and then his eyes focused on her face. He didn't appear surprised to find her helping to hold him up.

"You have to help us now, my lord," Harper said. "You have to try to walk."

Dare turned his head, regarding his valet with the same steady appraisal he had just afforded Elizabeth. Then, obediently, he took a step and, belatedly, she and Harper moved forward as well. For some reason, Elizabeth couldn't take her eyes off his face. Maybe because she was really expecting him to faint again at any moment. Because, of course, by now she knew he wasn't drunk.

There was no smell of spirits. Nor any fragrance of the sandalwood soap that she had noticed in the carriage. The shirt the earl was wearing was made of rough homespun and smelled of brine and tar. It was open at the throat, and she could see the strong, brown column of his neck and the top of his chest, the skin there dark and roughened with hair.

She pulled her eyes away, confused by the emotions this man's body created in hers. Those were something she could not afford to feel, she told herself fiercely. They were not allowed. Not in her world.

They had reached the three low steps that led up to the kitchen door. At least he hasn't fainted again, she thought, but she couldn't think how they would manage the inside stairs.

"Eau d'…onions" Dare said. The words were breathless, a little thready and enunciated with difficulty as they helped him to negotiate the first of the three low steps.

He was referring to the odor coming from the cloak she was wearing, Elizabeth realized. Caught off guard, she laughed at the absurdity of his mentioning its smell at a time like this. She had, of course, been aware of the scent emanating from the garment as she swung it around her shoulders. She hadn't minded, more interested in its potential for concealment and warmth than in its aroma.

"I must confess, Mrs. Carstairs, I prefer the other," Dare said.

His lips lifted, the attempted smile more like a grimace as they almost dragged him up the second step. If possible, his face was more colorless than it had been before.

The scent she had worn that night at Bonnet's, of course. Although it had been included with the other cosmetics sent from the Frenchman's, she hadn't applied it to her wrists or her throat since she had been here. That was something Bonnet had made her wear. Like the cosmetics. And therefore she had chosen *not* to wear it here. A small and meaningless rebellion, she knew, but somehow it had made her feel better.

"All right now, my lord," Harper said softly. "That's enough talking. We don't want anyone to hear us."

He meant the servants, who should all be in the dining hall by now, waiting for the boy to bring the beer. And probably wondering why he was late.

"I'm here," the captain announced behind them. He had the boy's buckets, one in each hand.

"Get on his other side," Ned ordered.

"He needs to take *your* place," Elizabeth said.

Harper's eyes fastened on hers. It was obvious he was surprised by her suggestion. And not particularly pleased that she'd made it.

"*You're* the only one of us who can take that beer in without causing comment," Elizabeth explained. "And if you don't do it soon," she warned, "someone will come out here to see what's keeping those buckets."

Their eyes held, wills warring for supremacy. After a few seconds, however, Harper gave in. Because she was right, of course. The captain, whoever he was, couldn't appear in the servants' dining room without eliciting questions. And neither could the earl's "guest." Ned Harper, however…

"Here," he said, gesturing Stark forward with his free hand.

The man set the beer down and traded places with the valet. During the exchange, Elizabeth was forced to bear more of the earl's weight than before. He sagged against her, and when she looked up, his eyes were again on her face.

He didn't bother to verbally apologize for a situation he could do nothing about, but his apology was in his eyes. At least there was regret there. And that was the only reason she could imagine for its presence.

"Wait for me," Harper said.

"On the first landing," Elizabeth whispered.

She knew he had intended them to wait here at the back door. Once more she had contradicted his orders. The valet longed to protest. She could see that quite clearly in his face, but again, she was so obviously right that he didn't say a word, lips tightly set against whatever he wanted to say.

Not the way to win Harper over, she thought, turning her face away from the valet and, with the captain on the other side, helping Dare up to the top step.

She had time to wonder why she would want to win Harper over, before the captain opened the door. Together they managed to get the earl through the entrance and closer to the greater challenge—the narrow servants' staircase that rose frighteningly before them.

"Thank you, Mrs. Carstairs," Ned Harper said grudgingly, throwing the words over his shoulder as he bent to tend to his master. Ned and the captain had helped Dare onto the high bed, and then Harper had paid the man and had sent him away. Only the three of them were in the earl's bedroom now as the valet felt the earl's forehead.

He's probably wishing me to the devil, Elizabeth thought.

She didn't move, however, her gaze on the waxen features of the man on the bed. Dare's eyes were closed, and in the light of the lamp Harper had just lit, his pallor was far more frightening than it had been downstairs.

Of course, then he had still been able to tease her about the smell of the cloak she'd pilfered. And able to laugh at Harper's admonition that he had known the earl should have taken him with him. That had all been before they had made that nightmare journey up the stairs. None of them had felt inclined to laughter after that. Especially, she supposed, not the man who had done his best to stifle the sounds of his suffering as they had maneuvered his injured body up those narrow steps.

"He needs a physician," she said.

It was obvious to her that Dare did. And it was just as obvious that Ned Harper wasn't planning to send for one.

"No," the earl said.

The strength of his denial was a little surprising. He still hadn't opened his eyes, and now his mouth was again clenched against the pain.

"He'll be fine," Harper said.

And you are either a fool or a liar, she thought. "I know something about caring for injuries," she offered aloud.

Her grandmother had taught her a great deal about herbal medicines. And she had grown up in a house with four brothers. Someone always had a bruise or a broken head. However, considering the condition of the man on the bed, she believed that whatever was wrong with him was much more serious than either of those.

Harper turned to look at her, his hands hovering over the rough shirt Dare wore. The valet met her eyes, probably trying to read the truth of what she had just claimed.

"No," Dare said again.

After a long hesitation, Harper said, "Thank you, Mrs. Carstairs. We'll be fine."

He did not look back at the earl when he spoke this time, his eyes holding on hers. Harper's were cold and determined.

"Whatever's going on here—" she began, only to be interrupted.

"Thank you. And good night," the valet added.

He waited, his eyes pinning her, his hands not moving to succor his master. And he wouldn't, she realized, until she was out of the room. A subtle form of blackmail, perhaps, but surprisingly effective, given that she had just noticed the spreading bloodstain on the homespun shirt.

The stain was low on Dare's right side, just above where the borrowed garment was tucked into the earl's own dark trousers. The spot was bright red, and therefore fresh, probably brought on by their inept efforts in dragging him up the stairs.

"Feel free to wake me at any time if you need advice, Mr. Harper," she said, her voice too sharp, fighting a fear she shouldn't feel.

After all, it was nothing to her if the Earl of Dare bled to death. If Ned Harper was too stubborn or too stupid to see to it that his master was properly cared for, then it was nothing at all to her, she told herself, as she turned and left the room, almost slamming the door closed behind her.

She stood outside a moment, listening to the silence of the great house. The servants were at dinner. Her own meal, which had been brought up before she had gone to the garden, awaited her in her chamber. The perfect time for someone to enter or leave the house unseen. And, of course, the earl would certainly have known that.

She could make a mystery of this if she wished, she supposed. Wondering how the Earl of Dare had been injured on a business trip and why his valet intended to prevent him from getting proper medical attention after sneaking him into the house while the servants were at their dinner. She could worry about it all night, allowing her mind to work out possible answers to those questions. And she could fret anxiously over what was going on in the room she had just left.

Or she could acknowledge that she had quite enough problems of her own to take care of. *What the Earl of Dare does behind the closed doors of his own home is nothing to me,* she told herself firmly.

All tonight had really meant to her was that she had missed an opportunity to give the beer boy her message. Tomorrow night, she determined, trying to put the events of this evening out of her mind. After all, it was obvious that none of the principals had welcomed her interference. And maybe they would have so much to think about now that they would forget for a while that she was even here.

Nothing, she told herself, *will please me more.*

"Brandy," the earl suggested when the door had closed behind Elizabeth Carstairs.

"I should think drink is the last thing you need," Harper responded, cutting the shirt away to reveal the long strips of cloth that had been wrapped around the earl's waist.

Dare knew they would be stained. He was well aware that the wound had broken open as they had helped him up the stairs. There wasn't much he could do about that, of course. Not with time so limited. Nothing but let Harper bind the hole even more tightly than the captain had.

"The Regent's ball is tonight," Dare said.

Harper looked at him then, eyes lifting from the stained bandages to his face. "And what has that to do with *this?*" Harper asked. "Or with brandy?"

Dare closed his eyes again, not to shut out Ned's grim features, but because the room was spinning drunkenly around his head. "I have to put in an appearance," he said.

"With coffin or without?" Ned asked.

Dare laughed, and was again reminded of why that was a bad idea. He pressed his hand against the bandage, just above where the ball lay. Doing that didn't help appreciably with the pain, but it might keep his guts from spilling out of the hole.

At least that was the sensation he had every time he forgot and laughed. Despite the fact that he knew intellectually that wasn't possible, given the size of the wound in his side, it was a particularly unpleasant feeling.

"Don't do that," Dare said, the words breathless and without force.

"Don't tell you the truth?"

"Don't make me laugh."

"It seems to me you've got little enough cause for amusement," Ned said.

Harper was now using the scissors to cut through the layers of the bandage. The metal blade was cold against the heat of Dare's skin. He had felt the fever building all day, and he had fought its effects. Because he had known, of course, what he had to do tonight.

"You are a constant source of amusement, Ned," the earl said. "That's one thing I value about you."

He was discovering that if he didn't move and took only the most shallow of breaths, the pain was bearable. Of course, he had not yet figured out a way to attend the Regent's ball without doing those two things.

Whatever the cost, however, Dare didn't have a choice about putting in an appearance at Carlton House tonight. Once there, he could plead illness or an accident and leave early. He would only have to manage to stay upright for an hour or so, but whatever his condition, the Earl of Dare *had* to attend the Regent's entertainment tonight.

He couldn't take the chance, as remote as it might be, that anyone might put together with his indisposition what had happened in France during the past week. And he certainly couldn't afford to alienate the Regent. Dare didn't want to lose his place in the prince's inner circle, and Prinny was well-known for taking offense at the slightest provocation.

"Brandy won't get you on your feet," Ned warned.

"No, you'll do that, of course," Dare said. "The brandy will, hopefully, help me to stay on them. At least long enough to make my bow to the Regent."

The very thought made his side ache. No choice, he told himself again. Then he could come back here and finally give in to the pain and the fever. Ned would take care of everything. Dare knew that.

Ned couldn't, however, take care of tonight's performance. There was no one else who could do what he had to do tonight. And the sooner he did get it over, the better.

"You've been shot," Ned said.

He sounded shocked, and Dare fought the urge to laugh again.

"What did you think had happened?" he asked, gratified by how normal the question sounded. As long as he didn't move. As long as he was flat on his back, unmoving, there was breath for everything. And when he remembered not to laugh, there was also a blessed, if brief, freedom from the grinding agony in his side.

"I thought you'd let your guard down. Maybe one

of them had managed to prick you with his sword and—''

"Shoulder," Dare said. "And it was a knife."

Again, Ned's eyes came up to his face. "You really are a bloody fool," he said again. "How bad is that one?"

"Your tender ministrations on the stairs didn't manage to break it open, if that's what you're asking."

"You're lucky I didn't leave you clinging to that tree out in the garden," Ned said savagely. "I wish I had."

Dare almost laughed, stopping the reflexive response just in time. "Mrs. Carstairs would have rescued me," he said.

"What are you going to do about that?" Ned asked.

"About…Mrs. Carstairs?"

"About the fact that she saw you."

"I shall lie through my teeth, Ned. Just as I always do."

There was a small silence.

"That ball will have to come out," Harper said.

"A prospect I shall look forward to," the earl said. Despite the determined lightness of his tone, it was probably obvious to his valet that he wasn't. "But *not* until after I've made my bow to my beloved prince. I think the puce, Ned. It should show the accidental spot of blood less than the blue, don't you think?"

"*I* think you're a bloody fool," Harper said again, the words more caustic this time.

"Tiresome, Ned. Find a new phrase, if you please. You have quite worn that one out."

"Save that tone for them fops you'll party with tonight, *milord,*" Ned said. "And for that fat bastard who occupies the throne. And not one of them worth your dying for,'' he added bitterly, the words almost thrown away as he turned from the bed.

"But I'm not doing this for them, Ned," the earl said softly. Reluctantly it seemed, the valet looked back, meeting his eyes. "I do what I do for Ian. For Sebastian. For all those other soldiers who are someone else's brother. Or someone's son. Someone's husband…"

There was not a trace of mockery or amusement in the quiet voice, which was usually, deliberately, full of both. And again silence built in the room, until Dare broke it.

"Prinny and his sycophants have nothing to do with this." The long fingers touched lightly against the bluing hole the Frenchwoman had blown in his side. "Despite the fact that I am most certainly one of them," the earl added, smiling at his valet.

For a long moment, Ned held his master's eyes. Finally, he shook his head, but he made no more arguments. And, just as Dare had known he would all along, despite his reservations, it was Harper who made it possible for him to do what they both knew had to be done.

Chapter Six

Dare had finally resorted to resting after each step. And considering the necessity of that, it might well be morning before he reached the safety of his room, he imagined. At least no one was up at this hour. No one around to see this pitiful excuse for—

A door opened somewhere on the second floor, drawing his attention upward. A wavering light moved down the hallway, coming toward the head of the stairs. The earl closed his eyes in relief, his hand still gripping the railing for support. Harper had finally realized he was home.

"She *must* be jealous."

Dare opened his eyes and tried to focus them on the figure standing at the top of the stairs. At first, the lamp seemed too bright to look into. The burn behind his eyes, dried by the rising fever, almost matched that in his side. But he knew the voice, of course.

"She?" he asked.

"Your mistress," Elizabeth Carstairs said. "I would assume that is the only reason you would be out at this hour."

"You're up very late as well, Mrs. Carstairs," he

said pleasantly. The tone was no more difficult to achieve than the one he had used all evening. Easier perhaps, because she did make a pleasant picture standing at the top of his staircase, lamp in hand. Almost as if she were welcoming him home. *Almost.*

"Or up very early, perhaps," she said. "I suppose that would depend on your point of view."

"Or on your occupation," Dare suggested, leaning against the wall. He wasn't certain he was up to a prolonged matching of wits with Elizabeth Carstairs, no matter how appealing the picture she presented.

She was wearing a leaf-green velvet wrapper. The rich fabric clung to her body, molding every curve and indentation, shimmering subtly in the lamplight. The garment was so revealing that he wondered, the thought probably fever-induced, if it were possible she was wearing nothing under it.

"And *your* occupation, of course, requires that you go out socially. Even…tonight?" she asked.

The brief hesitation before the last word was telling. Had she had almost said "in your condition?" Dare supposed she was afraid saying something like that might be dangerous. It would remind him that she had a too intimate knowledge of his affairs.

He wondered if he were expected to forget she had helped him from the garden into the house. Or that she had been in his room this evening when Ned and Stark had levered him up onto his bed. Or that she had been the one who had insisted Ned call a doctor.

Now, however, she was parsing her words, trying, it seemed, to avoid any open reference to things they both knew she had witnessed. The result of some hard-learned lessons about minding her own business? Learned from Bonnet, perhaps?

"As a matter of fact, my…occupation did require it," he said. The silence lasted a few seconds before she broke it.

"I take it, then, you *haven't* been with your mistress."

"I have been attending my prince. Should I have given him your regards, Mrs. Carstairs?"

"I have not had the pleasure of making the Prince Regent's acquaintance, my lord."

He couldn't decide if that was intended to be a very suggestive double entendre or a simple denial. And he was far too tired to try to puzzle her meaning out.

"No introduction at court?" he asked instead. "Would you like me to arrange one?"

"I think not." And then, her eyes on his face and her lips almost smiling, she asked, as if she were really interested in his answer. "Could you?"

"I'm one of Prinny's dearest friends," he said, mockingly. "I have had the Regent's private assurance of his undying favor."

"You were at Carlton House." This was not a question.

He inclined his body slightly in agreement and then wished he hadn't. The fury in his side had subsided as soon as he'd stopped climbing the stairs. And while engaged in repartee with his guest, he had almost managed to forget the pain. At least he had for the last two or three minutes, which was far more forgetfulness than he had managed most of the night.

"Did you dance?" Mrs. Carstairs asked, smiling openly now.

"*Not* with grace," he said truthfully.

"I'm sure Grace was vastly disappointed," she said, her voice amused. "The puce is lovely."

He laughed and tried to stifle the gasp that ended it.

"Are you going to stand on the stairs all night?" she asked after the sound of that aborted laughter had died away.

"No," he said softly.

With a small frisson of surprise, he realized that was the absolute truth. His knees bent, suddenly without the strength to hold him up. Luckily, he was still gripping the railing. It was the only thing that prevented him from falling down the steps he had mastered with such painful difficulty.

Not falling was an academic consideration merely, and one in which he had found he was not particularly interested at the moment. The light Mrs. Carstairs held had dimmed, and when it finally brightened again, swimming slowly back into focus, she was kneeling beside him.

"Harper's right," she said. "You *are* a bloody fool."

"Harper and Ian are always right," he whispered.

He hadn't intended for his agreement to be a whisper. It seemed that even his voice was out of strength. Determination. Need. Whatever had gotten him through the seemingly endless hours of this seemingly endless evening.

"Who is Ian?" she asked.

She had set the lamp on a table at the top of the stairs, and it shone down on them both, illuminating her features very clearly. She was so near he could smell her. It was the same scent she had worn at Bonnet's, probably caught and held in the rich folds of the velvet robe. Her hair, loose and very long, slightly curling, brushed his cheek as she knelt beside him.

''My brother,'' he said. ''Next in line for the title. He'll never forgive me if he's forced to inherit it.''

She laughed, as he had intended. At the sound, despite his exhaustion, he managed to lift his head enough to look at her again. She was so beautiful she took away the rest of the little breath he had gathered to tell her about Ian.

In the low light, she seemed ethereal. Almost angelic. Her skin translucent and glowing.

As he examined her features, she didn't turn away in pretended confusion as she should have done. As the women he had talked to at the ball tonight would most certainly have done had he looked at them as searchingly as he was looking at her. She was unwilling, it seemed, to play the games that were so much a part of what was happening between them.

And something was happening, he acknowledged. Something significant, Dare thought. And he bloody well wished he could think clearly enough to know what it was. Like everything else, however, that thought seemed too difficult to hold on to.

''Do you have brothers, Mrs. Carstairs?'' he asked instead, thinking about how angry Ian would be if he died. And *not* because of the title, of course.

''Four of them,'' she said brusquely. ''And they taught me to recognize when a gentleman has had quite enough Dutch courage. If I help you, do you think you can stand?''

''Brandy,'' he explained, without answering her question. He hated to admit openly that he really didn't believe he could stand. ''Where's Harper?''

''Asleep?'' she guessed. ''Perhaps he tired of waiting up to put you to bed.''

"He's done it often enough," Dare admitted. "Waited up."

"As he has waited for you all week," Mrs. Carstairs said.

She had put her shoulder under his arm again. Using it and the support of the railing, Dare was able to get himself off his knees. That seemed to be as far as it was possible to move right now. "A moment," he breathed, closing his eyes against the vertigo.

"As many as you like," she said. "I've been immeasurably bored in your house, my lord. You can't imagine how entertaining I'm finding your current adventures."

"Because I keep falling on my knees whenever I see you?"

She laughed, and he felt the warmth of her breath against his cheek. It was sweet and clean. The dark, musky scent she wore seemed to have clouded his brain. All he could think of was that if he turned his head, his mouth would be very close to hers. Close enough that—

"Up we go," she urged. "A mere handful of steps, my lord, and you'll be at the top."

Obediently he lifted his right foot, and the agony lanced through his side. He fought to stay conscious. Fought not to fall, taking her down the long flight of steps with him. Fought not to make a bigger fool of himself in front of her than he already had.

Dare was quite accustomed to playing the fool. Playing the fop, as Ned had so accurately characterized the men who danced attendance on the Regent. The earl had never cared before what anyone thought about him. Or about the role he had perfected through the years. For some reason, however, he found that he cared quite a lot what Elizabeth Carstairs thought. He actually cared whether she believed he was a coward or a drunkard.

"I'm not really drunk, you know," he said, when he again had breath enough to speak.

"I know," she said soothingly.

"A little brandy," he whispered, taking the next step.

He stepped up with his left foot this time. An easier process, he found. And, he discovered, an infinitely more interesting one. It put his leg in close alignment with hers, as they moved simultaneously up the step. Hip to hip. Almost as if their bodies were joined. That image wasn't one he could afford to think about right now, Dare decided, taking the next step. He already had quite enough on his plate.

"Almost there," she said encouragingly.

He looked up and realized they were. Only two more steps and he would be finished with this, and perhaps she would let him rest while she went to wake Harper. He wondered idly why he hadn't suggested that before.

Then, as they made the next step, her body moving against his, he remembered the reason. Having Ned help him up the stairs wouldn't be nearly so interesting as having Mrs. Carstairs at his side, he admitted.

"Why are you smiling?" she asked.

"Because we are almost at the top?" he suggested innocently.

"An unquestionable excuse," she complimented. "But not, I think, the truth behind *that* smile."

"You are far too astute, Mrs. Carstairs," he said, gasping a little as the pain again took his breath.

"Elizabeth," she said.

He glanced at her as they made the next step. She wasn't looking at him, deliberately not meeting his eyes. And that surprised him. She had not turned away when he had rudely examined her features, but now, having offered him permission to use her given name, she did.

"Elizabeth," he repeated, finding that he liked the feel of the word on his tongue. The name fit her. It was classic and elegant, a little regal, just as she was. Except, of course...

And then suddenly, in the middle of that unwelcome thought, they were at the top. She allowed him to lean against the wall, and as he rested from the ordeal, he examined the length of the hallway that led to his rooms. That distance seemed almost more daunting than the stairs.

"I think you'd better awaken Harper," he said.

She hesitated, her eyes searching his face. "Will you be all right if I leave you here?"

He smiled at her. Not the one he had employed tonight at Carlton House. This was the one he saved for Ned. For Ian, when he was able to get away from London to visit his brother. The one he would give Sebastian, if he ever saw him again.

"Will I fall again at your feet in abject worship, do you mean?"

"Is *that* what you've been doing?" she said. "Had I realized that was your intent, my lord, I should never have attempted to stop you." And then she returned his smile.

Despite his exhaustion, he recognized that hers was different, as well. Not the same as the ones he had had from her before. This one didn't taunt. Or mock. Nor was it bitter. Or professional.

And with that, something moved in his chest. Hard and cold and almost as painful as the wound in his side. *Professional,* he thought again, hating the word.

"My lord?" she questioned softly, her smile fading. "Are you faint?"

"No," he said.

He wasn't, of course. He was sick instead, an unexpected agony gnawing at his gut that had nothing to do with the ball that was still there. "I'm not faint. Just…get Harper," he ordered harshly.

She held his eyes a long heartbeat. He couldn't imagine what she was reading in them, but whatever she saw, he couldn't do anything about it. His feelings, at least at this moment, were beyond his control. That sudden agony of emotion beyond his ability to hide.

"Of course," she said finally, and turning away, she left him leaning tiredly against the wall at the top of the stairs.

"It's no good," Ned said.

And then the valet added an obscenity Dare had never heard him use before. One he echoed in his own mind, however, as he tried desperately to rebuild his failing courage. Because, of course, Ned was going to have to dig for the ball again. They both knew that. What Dare didn't know was how much more of this he could bear.

"I'm sending for a surgeon," the valet said, throwing the forceps into the bowl he had placed on the table beside the earl's bed. "It's too deep."

"It's not lodged in anything vital," Dare said. "If it were, I'd be dead by now."

"Maybe you are, and just too stubborn to stop talking."

Dare remembered this time not to laugh. Truth be told, the inclination to find any of this amusing had faded after the first probing. And for someone who laughed more often at himself than at anything else, that was disheartening in the extreme.

"Pay the surgeon enough and you won't have to worry about him keeping quiet," Ned said.

"I always have to worry."

"Taking the chance that the surgeon might talk is no more dangerous than letting this go septic," Ned warned.

"Then get the ball out. Do whatever you have to do," Dare ordered, closing his eyes. "And, Ned, short of calling a surgeon, I don't really care what that is," he added softly.

He must have dozed off. Maybe he was still sleeping. Dreaming, perhaps. Because he would have sworn the scent of that damnable perfume was all around him. *Her* perfume.

He could feel Ned's fingers moving over his stomach. They were cool against the heat of his skin. Reluctantly, he opened his eyes. He had had a few minutes' respite from the pain, and he found he had almost been unwilling to come back to this. Back to the brutal, but necessary probing.

"And did your jealous mistress have another, perhaps equally jealous lover, my lord?" Mrs. Carstairs inquired.

She didn't look up, her eyes still watching her fingers touch against the hot, swollen skin. He didn't know how she had known he was awake. Maybe a change in the tone of his muscles, responding reflexively to the knowledge that *she* was touching him, that it was her hands which were moving over his body.

Of course, there was nothing sexual about what she was doing. Actually, he couldn't think of anything *less* sexual.

"Here," she said softly, pressing down.

The pain was enough to provoke a groan he couldn't have suppressed had his life depended on it.

Her eyes came up at that, focusing on his face. "Exactly," she said. She sounded as if she were pleased.

"Can you reach it?" Ned asked.

"Of course," she said.

Her voice sounded calm. And supremely confident. Unlike the edge of panic he could still hear in Ned's.

"Perhaps more brandy, my lord?" she suggested.

His head was swimming with blood loss and what Ned had already given him. And the liquor hadn't helped with the pain. Not enough that he could notice.

"Just do it," he said.

To his own ears, the order sounded harsh. The same edge of panic he had heard in Ned's voice, but he truly didn't know how much more he could take. *Bloody fool,* echoed in his head.

He felt her hands again on his stomach, and he tried to brace himself, at least mentally, against the onslaught of the pain, but when it came, he was helpless against it, overwhelmed and defeated. It seemed to go on and on. As endless as the night he had just spent at the Regent's elegant London palace.

And the worst of it was, he wasn't even sure before he passed out whether or not she had been successful.

The muttering had been growing in volume, and the earl's head thrashed back and forth against the pillow.

It was almost as if he were in some unimaginable torment, Elizabeth thought worriedly, leaving her chair and coming again to stand over the bed, as she had done countless times already tonight.

She put her fingers against his forehead, hoping to find that the fever had broken. His skin was still on fire, hot and dry beneath her touch. She squeezed out the cloth she had left in the bowl of water on the table beside the bed, laying it across his brow.

Then, hoping to lower the fever, she dipped the cloth in the water again and again, reapplying it to his brow. Where the touch of her fingers on his face seemed to soothe his agitation, however, the feel of the cloth appeared to increase it.

The nearly inaudible words he had muttered gradually grew louder. Occasionally there was a phrase that was intelligible. And those reinforced her impression that Dare was suffering from some terrible nightmare, which was the product of his delirium.

He seemed to be begging someone to stop. She couldn't decipher enough of what he was saying to be perfectly certain of the action he was protesting, perhaps her own probing two nights ago for that elusive bullet. But somehow…

"No more," the earl said clearly. "Please, God, no more."

"Shh," she whispered, leaning nearer.

She brushed the black curls off his brow, in preparation for laying the cooling cloth against it again. And then her hand hesitated, its motion arrested.

For a long moment, she studied his face in the low light of the lamp. For the first time since she had met him, it was fully exposed, vulnerable to her inspection, and without the benefit of the habitual mockery, which she now knew he wore like a mask.

His features were far stronger than she had realized before. More masculine, despite their undeniable beauty. And in spite of the parched lips and the grayish tone illness had given his skin, they were infinitely appealing.

She forced herself to look away, her gaze falling on the glass water jug Harper had brought up earlier. Her grandmother had taught her that fever burns up the body's natural moisture. That was the real danger of a fever that wouldn't break, of course. It would burn up the body before it burned itself out.

She put the cloth back in the bowl and poured some of the water from the jug into a tumbler. Holding the glass in her left hand, she slipped her right gently under the earl's head. She eased down on her knees beside the bed, raising his head carefully and tilting the rim of the tumbler against his lips.

They were slightly open, and she hoped that with the cooling touch of water, they would open even more. And if she was very lucky, she could get some of the moisture into his mouth and from there down to bathe the parched dryness of his throat.

"My Lord Dare," she said softly.

There was no answer, of course. The grip of the fever was too strong for him to break its hold, but at least the delirium seemed to have abated with her nearness. A response to the comfort of human contact in the midst of whatever horror he had railed against, she told herself. A response that had nothing to do with her personally.

She allowed the water to trickle out of the glass and into his mouth. His lips moved, just as she had hoped.

His tongue appeared, tasting the wetness. Encouraged, she tilted the tumbler again. He swallowed, and only a small stream of liquid escaped from the lax corner of his mouth.

She wiped it with her thumb, smiling at her success. And when she looked up, Dare's eyes were open, watching her. Or so it seemed. After the initial shock, she realized that they saw nothing, at least nothing in the present. He was still lost in the throes of whatever horror he had fought these long hours as she had kept watch.

"Kill me and be done," he said, his eyes locked on hers.

"No one is trying to kill you, my lord," Elizabeth said. Of course, considering that she had recently dug a ball out of his side, it was very possible, she supposed, that he was right and she was wrong. However, that realization would not be inducive to letting the earl rest. And he needed to do that if his body were to heal. "You've been dreaming," she comforted.

There seemed to be some acknowledgment of what she had said in the fever-bright eyes. Some cognizance. But then that belief was shattered when he spoke again.

"They are killing him," the earl whispered urgently.

"I promise you, my lord," she said softly, "no one is being killed." She set the glass down and dabbed his forehead with the dampened cloth, but he turned his head away, obviously irritated.

"Torturing him," Dare muttered, his eyes again imploring her to do something. "Have to get him out."

"Shh," she said automatically, but her heart

stopped at the desperate words, which seemed to echo her own long nightmare.

Whether it was her unthinking command or his own weakness, the fevered eyes closed, Dare's eyelids falling downward suddenly as if he were too exhausted to hold them open any more. And with their closing, the frantic words ceased.

Slowly, Elizabeth sat back on her heels, watching his face. It was relaxed in a sleep that appeared more natural. Perhaps now that he had voiced his fear, he could rest. Perhaps he believed she would do something for whoever was being hurt.

Torturing him. She repeated the words mentally, trying to imagine what else Dare might have said that she could have mistaken for them. That was her nightmare, of course, and not his. Apparently she had imposed her own fears on his senseless, incoherent delirium. *Torturing him. Have to get him out.*

The phrases echoed again and again in her head, as she tried to think what the Earl of Dare might really have said. Or, if she had heard them correctly, why he might have muttered those phrases. Finally, unable to resolve the question, she put her hand on the table for support and rose. She laid the cloth she held back in the bowl and looked down on the sleeping man.

In the long, silent minutes she stood there, the nightmare didn't return. There were no more whispers. No more appeals for help. Whatever had troubled Dare had been forgotten, it seemed, lost in the healing peace of sleep.

If only her own nightmare could be as easily destroyed, Elizabeth thought. If only there were someone *she* might appeal to for help. Finally, she shook her head over the strangeness of the coincidence and re-

turned to the chair where she kept vigil over the Earl
of Dare.

Every time Dare opened his eyes, the shadows in
the room were different. But they always seemed to
be ominously creeping their way across the floor toward his bed. And every time, someone was in the
room with him, sitting in the chair beside the windows.
Watching the shadows? he wondered. Protecting him?

Dare's eyes lifted to the chair again, seeking the
familiar figure of his valet. This time there was light
from the windows behind the chair, so he knew it was
morning. And he discovered that the person sitting
there now wasn't Harper.

Her hair had been put up again, and the soft curls
that clustered on top of her head, the color of new
butter in the sunlight, were threaded with a thin blue
ribbon. She was wearing a white muslin gown,
sprigged with flowers of exactly that same shade. To
Dare's discerning eyes, it was obvious the dress was
several seasons out of date.

He would have to do something about her clothes,
he thought. And then he realized he had no right to
buy her clothing. And no responsibility to do it, either.
After all, Elizabeth Carstairs was neither his wife nor
his mistress.

As he watched her face, her eyes lifted from the
book she had been reading. They met his and held on
them assessingly a long moment. Then she closed the
book and laid it down in her lap, marking her place
with her thumb.

"You're awake," she said. It sounded like a pro-
nouncement.

"And, more surprisingly, I'm alive," he ventured. At least he thought he was.

She laughed. He wasn't sure whether she was laughing at the uncertainty of his tone or at his surprise.

"You had doubts about my course of treatment, my lord?" she asked. "Shame on you." She stood up, putting the book she was holding down on the chair. "I hope you don't mind. I have made free with your library."

"Of course," he said, closing his eyes. He didn't think he had ever had a stranger conversation in his life. Especially not with a woman.

"It's actually quite excellent," she said. "It needs to be properly catalogued, of course."

"I'm delighted you approve. I shall hire someone to catalogue it immediately. Unless you think I might be safe to wait until perhaps tomorrow."

"Do you read them?" she asked, her fingers against his cheek.

She was feeling for fever, but to Dare it felt almost like a caress. He could feel the movement of his whiskers, surely longer than a morning-after beard, under her fingertips.

"How long...?" he asked.

"Three days. More than I had hoped, but the fever finally broke last night. I *do* believe you will live, my lord, at least long enough to see to the cataloguing. I must confess, however, that in all honesty there were occasions when even I doubted."

"And you don't now?"

There was a long pause, and he opened his eyes again. He hadn't even been aware they had closed. It was just that he was so tired. She was smiling at him, he realized. The sunlight from the windows behind her made a halo around her figure, like those Renaissance portraits of the saints.

"I don't now," she agreed softly.

"Thank you," he said.

Using a strength he didn't know he possessed, he lifted his hand a few inches from where it lay to touch her fingers. He caught them in his, wanting to tell her in some small way how grateful he was. And to tell her without the customary mockery he hid behind. He owed Elizabeth Carstairs his life, and he was well aware of that.

Her smile faded, and she pulled her fingers free, the movement quick and decisive. Almost as if she were afraid his touch might contaminate them.

"I'll get Harper," she said. She turned, leaving the book she had been reading open in the chair. Obviously forgotten in her haste to leave the room.

For a long time he watched the shadows, trying to see if they moved. Waiting for Harper. And hoping she would return.

Not allowed, Elizabeth told herself fiercely. She turned, retracing the path she had just taken across her room. She had been walking back and forth since she had summoned Harper and sent him to his master's bedroom.

Her own departure had been little more than a retreat. It had been a *rout,* she admitted bitterly. She had been driven out by the touch of a man's fingers against her own. Weak, trembling fingers that almost lacked the strength to grip her hand.

And his weakness should argue against what she had felt. A heated stirring in her blood, which was unfamiliar, but which she had immediately recognized.

She and Ned Harper had shared the nursing duties during the long days of Dare's illness. The valet had given out the news to the household staff that his master was indisposed. Supposedly the earl had suffered an inflammation of the lungs after getting chilled on the way home from the Regent's ball.

According to Harper's story, the master had gotten caught in an unexpected rainfall while getting into his coach. The dampness of his clothing and the night's dropping temperature, despite the fact that it was almost June, proved to be too much for his delicate constitution.

In reality, Maggie had confided, the earl had been rather the worse for his excesses at the Regent's party. *If you know what I mean,* the girl said with a smirk, repeating the words exactly as she must have been told by someone on the staff. Elizabeth doubted Maggie knew what she was implying, but she herself certainly did.

Just as she knew, of course, that the tale was far from the truth. She had kept her own counsel, not responding to Maggie's wide-eyed confidences, her lack of interest carefully suggesting that what the Earl of Dare did was of no concern to her.

Nor was it, she told herself. Other than the actions which affected her own life, of course. She turned and walked back to the window. She spent a moment looking down into the garden, trying to think what she should do. Because finally she had heard from Bonnet.

The note had been under her cup of tea, brought up with her breakfast tray on the very morning after she had removed the bullet from Dare's side. When she had lifted the cup away from the saucer, the scrap of paper had been revealed. She had known at once what it was, and seeing it, her heart had hesitated. She had had to force her fingers to unfold it.

Its message had been brief and to the point. She was to watch the Earl of Dare and to report anything she saw that was unusual about his activities or about his household, using this same method of communication. And in the difficult days that had just passed, she had had two anxieties, one almost as troubling as the other.

She had done what Harper had asked. She had removed the ball from the earl's side, closing her mind to the pain she was inflicting. She told herself as she worked that this agony was necessary to save his life. Ironically, it was the same thing she had told herself about her actions for the last two years.

Then had come her natural concern over whether the Earl of Dare would live or die as a result of what she had done. And for at least one night, as she had confessed to him, she had really not been sure. Now, however, it seemed the danger that he might die from his wound had passed.

She dropped the curtain and paced across the room again. Twelve steps. Then twelve steps back to the window again. And in the course of that short, restless journey, nothing about the trap she found herself in had changed.

It would never change, she acknowledged bitterly. Not until... She took a breath, denying the thought. That was her only chance of freedom, of course, but it would come at a cost that would be even more difficult to bear than this.

So she would endure this betrayal because she could not endure the other. After all, she told herself again, it had been only the touch of his fingers. The touch of the hand of a man about whom she knew nothing.

Other than the fact that he could laugh in the face of pain and illness. And more important, that he could laugh at himself, a rare and unusual gift. Or the fact that his courage was far greater than her own. Greater courage than she had previously been able to imagine, which gave her, ironically, a glimmer of hope in her own long nightmare. And the fact that he was playing a role. What that role might be...

Not allowed, she told herself again, the litany determined. Single-minded.

Speculating about the man who had won her in a hand of cards was something she couldn't afford to do. And trying to determine whatever dangerous game the Earl of Dare was playing was *not* the task Bonnet had given her. All he had demanded was that she watch and report. Watch the Earl of Dare and report anything she felt was unusual about his behavior.

Her sudden smile was bitter. She supposed the fact that she had removed a bullet from one of the members of the Regent's toadying and simpering inner circle might be exactly the kind of ''unusual'' event the French gambler was interested in. And now that she was certain Dare would survive, she could no longer find any reason to delay her report.

No reason beyond the touch of trembling fingers against her own. No possible reason beyond the way that they had made her feel. *Not allowed,* she repeated, dropping the draperies and pacing across the expanse of the rich oriental rug that covered the oaken floor of her room. *Those feelings were not allowed. They would never again be allowed for the woman Elizabeth Carstairs had now become.*

Chapter Seven

The early-morning knock on Elizabeth's bedroom door several days later was unexpected. Her breakfast tray had already been brought up from the kitchens, and thankfully it hadn't included any more correspondence from Bonnet.

By now, Maggie knew that she liked to enjoy her morning tea in bed—undisturbed by chatter. Therefore, the abigail *shouldn't* be upstairs for at least another half hour or so.

Knowing Maggie as she did, however, Elizabeth supposed she shouldn't be surprised by the break in the routine she had tried to establish. The child probably had some bit of gossip from below stairs that she was bursting to share, sure that Elizabeth would be as excited over the prospect of hearing it as she was over having an opportunity to tell it. And given her situation, Elizabeth decided it might be prudent to listen.

"Come in," she called, settling back more comfortably against the pillows behind her. She hid her anticipating smile as she lifted her cup and watched the door, expecting the girl to emerge, wide-eyed with excitement. When it opened, however, it wasn't Maggie who stepped through it and into her bedroom.

For the past few days Elizabeth had tried *not* to think about the Earl of Dare. She had been determined not to remember his trembling fingers lifting to touch hers. She had denied his hold on her emotions by reminding herself of other emotions. And of other loyalties.

Denying the impact of a man who hovered very near death, however, was quite a different proposition from denying the impact of the man who was standing in her bedroom. Until now, she had seen the earl only in formal attire. Although his taste in evening clothes was impeccable, the style and color of those garments hadn't become him nearly so well as did the coat of navy superfine he was wearing this morning.

His waistcoat was a sedate blue-and-white stripe, his cravat tied in so simple a manner that it would allow him to turn his head freely. And the coat and waistcoat were complimented by skintight fawn pantaloons, which disappeared into a pair of gleaming tasseled Hessians.

"I do beg your pardon, Mrs. Carstairs," Dare said, his eyes alight with amusement. "I could have sworn I heard you give me permission to enter. I didn't realize you were still in a state of *dishabille*, or I promise you, I should never have intruded."

"I thought you were the maid," she said, managing to say the words almost without embarrassment.

After all, he was the one who had come calling at such an ungodly hour. How had he expected to find her? Deliberately, she completed the arrested motion of her cup, sipping her tea, and at the same time watching him over its rim.

His eyes examined the room before they came back to hers. They were far bluer than she had remembered them, perhaps because they were reflecting the dark hue of his jacket. Or perhaps, she admitted, they seemed more vibrant because she had spent the last three days trying to make them fade into insignificance.

"I trust they have made you comfortable," he said politely.

Behind her cup, her lips tilted, but she answered in the same vein. "Very comfortable, thank you, my lord."

"Good," he said.

His gaze was now on her face. She was aware, however, that after his eyes had circled the room, they had touched briefly on the low neckline of her *negligé* before they lifted to meet hers.

The silence after his comment stretched awkwardly for a few seconds. She felt no compunction to ease the strained atmosphere by making conversation. *He* was the one who had come calling at an hour almost guaranteed to find her in some state of undress.

And with that thought, the possibility that Dare had come to her chamber for something other than conversation was suddenly in her head. She had expected this from the very first night he had brought her to his home. Then he had disappeared on his "business" trip, leaving her in Harper's care. And when the earl had finally reappeared, almost a week later, he had been in no condition to make any physical demands.

She wondered that he could make them now. It had been only three days ago that he had awakened from the fever, so weak he could barely hold his eyes open. So weak that his fingers had trembled...

Again, she denied the memory of their touch. And the memory of what had been in his eyes.

In reality, this very early visit could be about something very different from what she was thinking, she acknowledged. Dare *was* dressed for traveling, it seemed.

"Would you like to sit down, my lord?" she asked, her inquiry as polite as his earlier one had been.

His lips quirked minutely at one corner and were then controlled. Almost unconsciously, his fingers touched the spot on his side from which she had recently, and reluctantly, dug out a bullet. "I believe I prefer to stand, Mrs. Carstairs," he said. "If you'll forgive me."

"Then…?" she hesitated, her question obvious.

"You're probably wondering why I've invaded your privacy."

He waited, but she said nothing in response. It was almost an unanswerable comment, especially since she didn't wish to put notions into his head. She *was* wondering why he was here, of course, but this was his house. And she was his "guest." She had never been more aware of her status than at this moment.

"I've come to thank you," he said, his voice holding a depth of emotion she had not heard there before. "Ned assures me that he should never have been able to remove that ball."

"My Lord Dare…" she began, and his voice calmly overrode her protest.

"My life may be worthless," he said, without any trace of mockery or amusement. "Indeed, people would assure you that is the case. But since it *is* my life, and the only one I shall ever have, I suppose, you have my undying gratitude for saving it."

Again, the silence in the room was profound. Elizabeth could think of nothing to say to that seemingly heartfelt expression of his gratitude. Finally, she put her cup down on her saucer.

"Shall we say simply that the score is now even, my lord?" she said, her voice as soft as his, as free of mockery.

He tilted his head, one dark eyebrow lifting in inquiry. It was a gesture she had noticed before. An attractive one, she admitted.

"Even?" he repeated.

"You rescued me from Bonnet. I rescued you from...an inconveniently located bullet," she finished.

"And you are, of course, wondering how that ball came to be there," he suggested.

"Am I?" she asked.

"I should think most people would be."

"I am *not* most people, my lord."

"Indeed you are not, Mrs. Carstairs," he said softly.

She looked down at the tea in her cup, wondering what he thought of her. Some part of her wanted to explain. To recount for him all the reasons for what she had done. To pour out the painful chronicle of the events that had brought her to where he had discovered her.

She didn't, of course. Because none of her reasons, valid though she felt them to be, could alter the outcome of her choices. And for an English nobleman like Dare, the outcome would be all that was important. All that would ever be important as far as his opinion of her was concerned.

"Whatever I did for you, my lord," she said, choosing her words carefully, "I should have done for anyone in that condition. I'm very glad it has turned out so well."

"No questions asked," he said.

"No, my lord," she said. "No questions asked. Providing," she added, "you will agree to abide by that stricture as well."

The dark eyebrow lifted again.

"That you will ask *me* no questions," she responded to that unspoken inquiry.

"I don't believe I have done so yet, Mrs. Carstairs."

"No, my lord, you haven't. However, human nature being what it is…"

"You anticipate that one day I shall," he said. "You may be right, Mrs. Carstairs. I'm afraid, however, that it won't be any time soon. I regret to inform you that I have been called away for a few days. Whatever secrets you wish to keep should be safe from me. At least for the time being."

"Then you don't intend to abide by our agreement."

"I don't believe *we* agreed to anything. *You* very graciously volunteered a willingness not to ask about the events leading up to…my recent injury. You then suggested I should do the same. You will notice, I hope, that I didn't agree to those terms." He held her eyes a moment, almost daring her, it seemed, to protest. When she didn't, he added, "If you need anything—anything at all—while I'm gone, you have only to tell Harper."

"Leaving Ned behind again," she said mockingly. "Hasn't he yet convinced you that is apt to be dangerous?"

He laughed, and then winced, the long fingers once more touching the place on his side. "I believe you offered to ask no questions, Mrs. Carstairs,'' he reminded her.

"So I did. May I wish you a good trip, my lord?"

"I shall certainly hope for a better journey than the last,'' he said. He held her eyes, and then he inclined his head before turning toward the door.

"God keep you safe, my lord,'' she whispered.

Elizabeth could not explain the impulse that had prompted that wish, but she didn't bother to deny, not even to herself, that she truly hoped He would.

The earl turned to face her again, obviously surprised. "*If* He undertakes to do that,'' he said, ''I am sure it will be due entirely to your intervention on my behalf. You are bound to be more in favor with the Divinity than I.''

"No, my lord, I am not,'' Elizabeth said, her voice devoid of the quiet amusement his held. That denial was only the truth, and for some reason she felt compelled to make it to him.

Because that was something else she had given up two years ago. Any claim to the Almighty's favor or consideration. And any hope for His forgiveness.

"Then we shall be sinners together, Mrs. Carstairs,'' Dare said softly. And when he smiled at her, exactly as he had on the stairs that night, her heart turned over.

She didn't return his smile, but she found that she was incapable of releasing his eyes, and after a moment, he spoke again, that endearing tilt appearing at the corner of his lips.

"Did they call you Lizzie?"

"I beg your pardon, my lord?" she asked, bewildered by the out-of-context question.

"Your brothers. Did they call you Lizzie?"

"Only when they wished to annoy me," she said truthfully. And was rewarded by his laughter. "God speed, my lord," she said softly before the sound of it had died away.

He opened the door and stepped out, pulling it closed behind him. In the room he had just left, Elizabeth Carstairs' eyes fell to her cup. After a moment, however, her lips tightened, and she raised the tea to her lips, determined not to dwell on that conversation or on the man with whom she had just had it.

When her breakfast tray went back to the kitchens an hour later, however, the note she had prepared last night to go between the cup and its saucer lay in tatters, and another had been hastily substituted in its place.

"It's obvious she's been sent here to spy on you," Ned said.

"And equally obvious that she isn't giving Bonnet any real information," Dare said, holding the note Ned had just shown him. "In spite of what she knows. And that's what I find really interesting, Ned. Is it possible she's on to Maggie?"

"I don't know how she could be. The chit's smart. I'll give her that, even if she is my own blood."

"Then the pertinent question seems to be why Mrs. Carstairs is *not* telling Bonnet I'd been shot?"

"The pertinent thing to *me,* my lord, is that she could. She's spying for the Frenchman. And she already knows far more about your affairs than is safe. You wouldn't take a chance on calling in a surgeon when your life hung in the balance, but you allow a woman you *know* is a spy to run free in your household."

"What would you have me do with her, Ned?" Dare asked.

"Shag her," Ned said coarsely. "Get it out of your system. And then send her back to the gambler."

Dare said nothing for a few seconds, and then he again lifted the note that had been sent down to the kitchens with Elizabeth's tray. "With all that she knows, this is what she writes Bonnet," he said. "Spy she may be, but she isn't giving him anything that might be useful to him. Or to anyone else."

"She will," Ned said.

"You are probably right," Dare acknowledged. "It must be obvious, even to you, Ned, that Bonnet has some hold over her. There has to be a very good reason for a woman like that to end up in an establishment like his. And I confess I'm curious as to what that reason might be."

"I can suggest a few," Ned said bitterly.

"I'm sure you can. I could as well. Mrs. Carstairs herself has provided me with her version of how she came to be working in the Frenchman's hell. However, none of those seem feasible to me. There's something else going on here, and I want to get to the bottom of it."

"Before or after she betrays you?"

Dare laughed. "Preferably before, of course. Watch her while I'm gone. And Ned..." The earl hesitated, thinking about the poor timing of this necessary journey, just as he had been since Harper had told him about the notes. "Whatever you do, don't let her leave."

"And why not, my lord? I can't think of anything that makes more sense than her leaving," the valet said. "Good riddance."

"Actually, I believe that's the same sentiment Bonnet expressed," the earl said. "But…I don't want her under his influence again. Especially since she's lying to him. I'm not sure what might happen if he discovers that."

"Carstairs," the earl's brother said, shaking his head slightly, a small, familiar crease forming between the earnest hazel eyes. "I don't remember any Carstairs."

"Four sons," Dare said. He tipped the last of his father's excellent pre-embargo brandy into his mouth before he added nonchalantly. "And at least one daughter, whose name is Elizabeth. I'm not sure about any other daughters."

He had waited until the last afternoon of his three-day visit to broach the subject of Elizabeth to his brother. He wasn't completely sure of the reasons for his reluctance, perhaps because he suspected that Ian would react much as Ned had. And he really didn't want to listen to those same arguments again.

"Younger? Or older?" Ian Sinclair asked.

Dare's lips pursed slightly as he thought about the question. "They annoyed her by calling her Lizzie. So she's probably younger, I should say."

Ian laughed. "You annoy me, Val, but I'm not sure one should speculate that my annoyance with you has anything to do with the fact that you're older than I."

"My apologies."

"For annoying me?" Ian asked in obvious amusement.

"Of course. That has never been my intent, I assure you."

"Rubbish," Ian said cheerfully, and then he

downed the dregs of his own brandy, "What have you been up to other than searching for an elusive family named Carstairs?" he asked.

"Very little," Dare said, reaching for the decanter which stood on the table beside him.

The small intake of breath that unthinking movement evoked was audible. Too betrayingly audible, Dare feared, for someone as astute as his brother. Ian's eyes lifted quickly and held on his face as he carefully straightened, brandy forgotten.

"The *little* you've been up to appears to cause you pain," Ian said.

"I thought health was a forbidden topic. Shall I inquire about yours?"

"You shall *not*," Ian said softly.

The middle Sinclair brother had been invalided out of the army almost a year ago. A very long year, during which his recovery from the terrible wounds he had suffered in Iberia had been frustratingly prolonged. And Ian Sinclair was not a man who enjoyed ill health.

Despite his strength of will, however, he couldn't force his body to heal more quickly or to recover its strength and vitality, it seemed. Ian could and did, however, forbid anyone who loved him to take note of his painfully slow convalescence. And "anyone who loved him" certainly included his older brother.

"Would you care for more brandy?" Ian asked.

"Not enough to require you to get up and get it," Dare said.

Ian laughed. "I'm quite capable of serving my guests," he said, proving the point by doing exactly that.

Dare watched as his brother limped across the room.

Ian held out his hand for Dare's glass, smiling at him, and when he had refilled it from the decanter, he returned to place it in his brother's hand.

"Bravo," Dare said.

"Thank you," Ian said.

His smile seemed a mixture of embarrassment at having shown off his progress mixed with pleasure at having such definite improvement to demonstrate. And he had known, of course, that his audience would be appreciative of that improvement.

"The name may even not be Carstairs," Dare said, knowing from experience that any further comment about his brother's condition would be unwelcome. "But surely there can't be that many families with four sons, who also have a daughter named Elizabeth. I've gone through my acquaintances within the ton, at least all those I can remember. You, however, traveled in different circles from mine. I have been hoping that you might be willing to examine yours as well."

"I'm beginning to believe your inquiry is more than idle curiosity. Or am I wrong?"

"I won her in a game of cards," Dare said bluntly.

"Won *her* in a game of cards? Good God, Val, do you mean the sister?" Ian demanded, his voice climbing with each inquiry.

"I told you, her name is Elizabeth," Dare said, his eyes holding on his brother's.

"Even for you, that seems…a bit extreme. And in that case, what in the world makes you believe her family would be one within the ton? Or did you win her from one of those four brothers?"

The suggestion was obviously mocking. Ian would be unable to conceive of a brother wagering his sister on the fall of a card. Dare had seen stranger things, but, as he had reminded his brother, they traveled in very different circles. At least since he had begun his operations against the French several years ago.

To divorce himself from any association with his brothers had been a conscious decision on Dare's part, undertaken to protect his family if his role were ever discovered by the enemy. That was why he had put about the story of their supposed estrangement and why he made his monthly visits to Ian in secret.

"I won her from Bonnet. I believe the Frenchman was mistreating her."

"And so *you,* of course, felt compelled to rescue her," Ian said. "I might have known it was something like that."

He had returned gratefully to his chair by the fire, his normally serious eyes now reflecting amusement over his brother's lifelong propensity for chivalric actions. His weakness for playing knight errant was directly counter to the image the rest of the world held of the Earl of Dare. An image Dare had worked very diligently to create.

"And then I discovered that she's been clandestinely communicating with the Frenchman," Dare said. "Harper assigned his niece to be Elizabeth's abigail. She's the one who found Bonnet's notes. And Elizabeth's to him."

"Harper's niece is spying on the woman you won in a hand of cards, who is spying on you?" Ian said. It was obvious he was highly entertained by the tale, at least until he realized the significance of what Dare had just said. "Do you mean to say she is living in your home? A woman from Bonnet's gaming hell?"

"She isn't what you think," Dare said.

"I know that compared to you I've led a relatively

sheltered life, Val," Ian said, "but even *I* am aware of the kind of woman who works for someone like Bonnet."

"That's one of the things that puzzles me. She is nothing at all like what one would expect such a woman to be. She's refined. Educated. She was reading Virgil as she watched..." Dare broke the sentence, reluctant to reveal to his brother how seriously he had been injured on his last mission. "And she was reading it in the original Latin," he carefully amended his original thought. "I swear I could take her to Carlton House, Ian, and she wouldn't put a foot wrong."

"I'm sure Prinny would be delighted to welcome her. Of course, he has an eye for beauty, and, they say, a not too discriminating taste for—"

"Don't," Dare ordered.

Again Ian's gaze lifted to his face. "Good God, Val," he said, his voice as quiet as his brother's, and touched with wonder. Or sympathy perhaps. "This isn't... I mean you can't possibly be *interested* in this woman."

"She isn't what you think," Dare said again.

Ian said nothing for a moment, but his eyes had widened. "I'm not sure it's important what *I* think. But you must admit the possibility exists that she is...less than pure," he finished carefully. "Even if you *are* attracted to her, you must be aware the fact she is working for Bonnet suggests that."

"He offered her to me," Dare said. "Sexually offered her," he added softly.

The earl would probably have shared that information with no one else, but he trusted Ian implicitly, both to keep his counsel and more importantly to provide the kind of logical assessment of the situation that he wasn't sure he was himself any longer capable of making. As he waited for his brother's response to that revelation, the silence in the room was complete, broken only by the occasional low sound of the fire.

"Then she has probably been offered to others," Ian said softly. Despite the cruel truth of that statement, his eyes were compassionate.

"I know. I'm not even sure that offer was exclusive to me the night Bonnet made it."

"There were others present?"

Dare inclined his head.

"Then…?" Ian said, his eyes still on his face.

"You are about to propose what Ned has already suggested," Dare said. "That I take her, and get her out of my system."

"You've always valued Ned's opinion," Ian said delicately.

"I value it now, but I find I'm not ready to send her away. Nor am I ready to set her up in her own establishment."

"You can't have her living in your home. Your people won't stand for it. Never mind what the rest of society will say."

"Ah, but I am the Earl of Dare, who is noted for his idiosyncrasies. *I* can damn well do anything I please," Dare said, his lips tilting in a mocking smile, "and no one will think it strange."

"The sooner you put this…attraction into perspective, the better," Ian warned, ignoring his brother's bitter comment.

"The better for whom?" Dare asked. "I think she's in trouble. I think that bastard has some hold on her, and she's being forced to do what she's doing."

"Forced to spy on you?"

"Exactly," Dare said.

"Or is that simply what you'd prefer to believe?" Ian suggested quietly.

"Perhaps. But until I know for a fact…" Dare began and then hesitated, reluctant to put into words what he knew both Ian and Ned believed about Elizabeth Carstairs.

"Until you know for a fact that she *is* Bonnet's willing accomplice, you don't intend to turn her out."

"Would you?"

"I'm the Sinclair who never gets involved with such difficulties. Without your periodic visits, my life would be far duller than it is at present. I have to confess, I've missed you," Ian said with a laugh.

"My apologies for that as well. I was…unavoidably detained. I promise it won't be so long the next time."

"I wasn't chiding you. There's no reason for you to make that trip from London so frequently. I'm well aware you only come to see for yourself that I've managed to survive another month without pointing my toes upward in the family crypt."

"That might have been true in the beginning. Now I come because…" The words faded, and the laughter deserted the blue eyes. "Because I miss you," Dare finished softly.

Ian laughed, deliberately destroying the emotional solemnity of that confession. It was a singularly pleasant laugh, Dare thought. And another thing he missed when he was forced, as he had been lately, to forgo his customary visit to the family's country estate, where his brother had taken up residence on his return from the Peninsula.

"Flattery you learned at Prinny's knee, no doubt," Ian said easily.

He would know that Dare was telling the truth, of course. Despite the three years that separated them, they had always been close. They knew one another far too well for the subterfuge of mockery and indifference that served the earl so well with others to work here.

"I have an ulterior motive," Dare said, pushing carefully up off the too comfortable sofa. "Rack your brain for a family that fits my description. I intend to get to the bottom of the mystery of Elizabeth Carstairs."

"And you intend to protect her from Bonnet until you do?"

"Of course. Would you have me do anything less?" Dare asked, smiling.

He had crossed the room to stand before Ian's chair. He noticed, but didn't mention, that his brother made no effort to stand again in order to see him out. In the light from the tall windows Dare could clearly see the lines of suffering that the past year had etched into the handsome face before him. Suffering which might never be openly acknowledged, but which had certainly taken its toll.

"What I *would*," Ian said softly, looking up at him, "is to have you take care of yourself. What's wrong with your side?"

"You are far too observant."

"And you haven't answered my question."

"Mrs. Carstairs recently dug a ball out of it. One Ned couldn't manage to remove. I find myself…grateful."

The smile had faded from his brother's lips. "Then I find myself grateful to Mrs. Carstairs as well," Ian said.

"If you think of any possibility as to who she might be, send me word," Dare said.

"You could bring her here," Ian suggested.

"I don't dare risk the competition," Dare said, smiling, "as much as I appreciate the offer."

With that, he turned and crossed the room to the door. He sketched his brother a salute before he disappeared through it.

Behind him, Ian Sinclair looked down into the fire that blazed cheerfully beside him. His lips twisted, and his closed fist lifted and fell to the arm of the chair. He had been aware intellectually of the danger his brother faced, but to find that Val had been shot somehow made the hidden battle Dare was fighting all the more real. And, of course, all the more frightening as well.

Chapter Eight

"There's a very good edition of Ovid on the lower shelf," the Earl of Dare said.

He watched Elizabeth Carstairs' hand hesitate over the volume she had been reaching for. She turned, looking down on him from the top of the library stair on which she was rather precariously balanced.

"I didn't know you were back, my lord," she said. "I hope you have had a pleasant journey."

Dare contrasted the polite disinterest in her tone to what he had heard there the morning he left. Of course, she had had several days to come to the realization that she had revealed too much that day.

"A very pleasant journey, thank you. And you, Mrs. Carstairs? How have you managed to fill the long, empty hours since I've been away?" he asked.

There was a sudden rush of color underlying the fair skin, and Dare regretted that unthinking remark. He had only intended to be amusing. He realized now, however, that she thought he was making fun of what she had said to him that morning. And nothing could be further from the truth.

Whatever had prompted her seemingly heartfelt

concern for his well-being, he treasured it. It had comforted him through the trip to the country, almost overcoming his unease over the notes that he now knew were going back and forth between Elizabeth and the French gambler.

"I've been reading my way through your library, my lord. And I thank you for your suggestion, of course. I'm afraid, however, Ovid is not to my taste."

"Too florid?" Dare asked, propping his hip casually on his desk. From where he stood, he had a very enticing view of two neatly turned ankles, covered by thin white silk stockings.

"Too...romantic," she said.

She met his eyes, hastily raised from their contemplation of her hemline. In hers was no trace of embarrassment over what portion of her undergarments might be revealed by their relative positions. Dare wasn't sure his had achieved that same nonchalance.

"And you disapprove of romance?" the earl asked.

"I don't *disapprove* of it. I'm simply not personally disposed toward the emotion."

Dare laughed. "Not a romantic, Mrs. Carstairs?" he mocked. "You are surely a discredit to your gender."

"Are all the women you know inclined to romance, my lord?"

As she asked the question, she put her fingers on the edge of the nearest shelf and began to step down. Dare immediately straightened and walked across the room to offer his hand. After a few seconds, she put hers into it and allowed him to help her down the stair.

"They or their mamas," the earl said, looking into her eyes and smiling.

"And yet you have escaped the so-called matrimonial trap?"

"Perhaps I haven't met the right woman," Dare suggested.

"Oh, I believe your bride, when you find one, could hardly be considered a *woman,* my lord. Even at your age, you should be expected to choose from the girls enjoying their first or second Season. Someone very young. Healthy enough to fill your nursery to overflowing. At least until constant childbearing breaks her health or results in her untimely death from puerperal fever."

"I'm feeling guilty already, Mrs. Carstairs, and I'm not even betrothed," he said, his smile widening.

"How many men have you known in your circle who have buried more than one wife, my lord?" she demanded.

"All I can say in my defense is that I, personally, have buried none. And have, as yet, wed none either," he added.

"And I wonder that you haven't," she said, sounding as if she were really interested. "Perpetuating the family line is usually considered a responsibility that goes with a title."

"Despite the fact that you apparently feel me to be of a ripe age to marry," he said ruefully, "I *do* have two younger brothers. Perhaps that makes me less concerned that the Sinclair line might die out."

"Ah, yes. The brother who will never forgive you if he is forced to inherit. I had forgotten."

Dare wished he hadn't told her about Ian. Possibly the effects of fever or blood loss had loosened his tongue.

"My brothers and I are estranged," he said. Whatever mistake he might be making in allowing Elizabeth Carstairs in his home, he didn't intend Ian or Sebastian to suffer for it. "They don't approve of the way I live."

"Then we have something in common," she said.

Other than her comment about her own brothers, this was almost the first personal reference she had let slip. Dare thought there had been an edge of bitterness to her voice when she made it.

And if he were correct in his supposition that she had once been a member of the relatively small circle which composed the English ton, then he could imagine the feelings of her family in regard to the situation he had found her in at Bonnet's. What he couldn't imagine was why they hadn't done something about it.

"Disapproving brothers?" he asked.

There was a small silence.

"I simply meant we share a way of living that evokes disapproval," she said.

"Does that disturb you, Mrs. Carstairs?"

"I suppose we should all like to believe our choices are acceptable to society."

"And if they are not, we have the option of changing our behavior."

"Of course, my lord," she said calmly.

"Then why don't you?"

"Change my behavior?"

"If you are worried about society's disapproval," Dare said reasonably.

"Why don't *you,* my lord? At least my choices seem less likely than yours to result in serious injury."

He laughed and watched her eyes respond, almost unwillingly it seemed. "I'm glad to know that what you have chosen isn't dangerous. Somehow that night at Bonnet's, I had a very different impression.''

"The impression that what I did was dangerous, Lord Dare?" she asked, her voice puzzled. "In what way?"

With his thumb he touched the corner of her mouth, exactly where the drop of blood had clung the night a furious Bonnet had dragged her from the salon where they were playing cards. Elizabeth didn't move, her eyes on his. Then he drew his thumb upward, tracing lightly over the fair skin that had already begun to discolor by the time he had brought her to his home.

"Danger from Bonnet," he suggested, his voice very soft.

"I was in no danger, my lord," she said after a moment. "Henri's temper sometimes escapes his control, but his anger is short-lived and seldom has serious consequences."

He nodded, his thumb still moving over her cheek, no longer illustrating his point, but now simply caressing the smoothness of her skin. He expected her to turn her head. To step away from him. To do something. However, her eyes were steadfast, the tinge of color in her cheeks the only sign of any possible discomfiture.

"I'm glad you never felt yourself to be in danger," Dare said. "I had meant to offer you my protection, Mrs. Carstairs."

"I have no need of your protection, my lord."

"So I now understand. However, if you find that you *ever* do need someone to fight your battles, may I offer my services?"

She smiled a little, mockingly he thought. Mocking

his offer? Perhaps even mocking him, he acknowledged, but her eyes were unamused.

"I'm flattered, Lord Dare," she said, "but somehow…"

"But somehow, you don't believe I could protect you?" he finished for her.

She said nothing.

"Sometimes people are not what they seem, Elizabeth," Dare said. "For example, you are not, I believe, exactly what you have portrayed yourself to be during our short acquaintance. It shouldn't surprise you to find that others are not as they portray themselves, as well."

"I'm afraid I don't understand, my lord," she said. "Are you suggesting that *you* are in some way… playing a role?"

The question hung in the air between them. And then Dare smiled at her again. "We all play roles. Part of the excitement of any new relationship is in discovering the secrets that the other person is guarding. And when we have done so, keeping those secrets is part of the trust inherent in any friendship. Or in any other type of relationship, I suppose."

"And you believe that we have a friendship, my lord?"

"I believe we are both guarding secrets, Elizabeth. I'm simply suggesting that if you ever need a friend, someone you can trust, someone to help you with a problem that may seem insurmountable when you are facing it alone, I'm very willing to play that role."

She held his eyes a long time, searching them. And then her lips tightened as if she had reached some decision. Apparently, however, it was not the one he had hope for.

"Thank you, my Lord Dare. I am singularly aware, I assure you, of the honor you do me."

"*But* you have nothing you wish to confide," he said, accurately reading her tone.

"I have no problems that require your intervention. And I'm sure I don't know from whom you believe I might need protection."

He nodded. "Fair enough. I pray you will not forget the offer, however. *If* that need should ever arise."

"Of course not, my lord. I promise you I shall not forget. Should that need ever arise," she added softly. "And now, if you'll excuse me…"

He was reluctant to let it go. And even more reluctant to let her go. He had made his offer, hoping for her trust, and it had been rejected. Other than physically forcing her to tell him the truth, there seemed nothing else he could do. If he resorted to force, a method he knew Ned for one would approve of, then he would be little better than Henri Bonnet.

"Will you join me for dinner, Mrs. Carstairs?" he asked.

"Are you dining in, my lord?"

"I have been looking forward to it," Dare said truthfully. "I've been hoping you might advise me on what to do with my sadly neglected library."

She held his eyes again, and they dared her to deny his invitation. After a moment, she looked back at the cluttered bookshelves that surrounded them, filled with leather-bound volumes stretching upward to the high ceiling.

"Perhaps…" she began, and then she hesitated. "Since I am living under your roof, my lord," she said finally, "I suppose I could make a start on putting them in order."

"You are my guest, Mrs. Carstairs. I did not mean to imply that you yourself should undertake the task. It's simply that I know so little about the process. The neglect is of long-standing, I'm afraid. My father was not bookish. Nor am I, of course."

"It would give me something to do to occupy my day," she said. "And a way to repay your...hospitality."

Her eyes came back to his. They seemed as steadfast as they had always been, but he believed he could detect a hint of anxiety in them as she waited.

"My hospitality, like my offer of friendship, has no conditions, Elizabeth. I hardly expect you to sing for your supper."

The corners of her lips lifted, the smile almost mocking again. At least her eyes were no longer anxious, he thought.

"I believe you would be disappointed if I tried. My voice was described by my governess as merely adequate, my lord. My brothers were less kind."

He laughed. "Brothers tend to be brutally honest about our failings."

"Are yours?"

"Frequently," he admitted. "But then I told you, I believe, that we are estranged."

"And the estrangement is of long-standing?"

"I'm afraid so," he said regretfully.

"How bizarre. I'm sure Maggie told me that's where you had gone. To visit your brother, who is ill. I had hoped for a healing of the breach in your relationship."

"You are all kindness, Mrs. Carstairs."

"I was Elizabeth only a moment ago."

"That was *before* you began rattling family skeletons."

"I beg your pardon, my lord. If the subject is painful to you…"

"Perhaps we can discuss our assorted brothers over dinner," Dare suggested softly and watched her smile fade. "Or is it only *my* family skeletons you are willing to rattle? We dine at nine. I am so looking forward to having you join me."

He bowed slightly and walked back to the desk where he had laid his gloves when he had come into the room. He picked them up, running the supple calves' skin through his fingers a moment before he turned around. For some reason he was inordinately encouraged to find she was watching him.

"By the way, a package arrived for you today," he said. "I've instructed Watson to have it sent up to your rooms."

"A package, my lord?" she asked, her brow furrowing. "I'm expecting no package."

The anxiety was back, and that was not what he had intended. He had been hoping to give her pleasure, and instead he'd worried her. Surely another indication that, despite what she had told him, she was afraid. Of Bonnet? Or of something else?

"This is a gift," the earl explained. "I hope you will receive it in the same spirit in which it is given."

"A gift, my lord?" There was a hint of chill in her tone.

"Forgive me, Mrs. Carstairs, but I find that Bonnet's rather questionable taste in fashion offends my sensibilities. He obviously had no idea how to dress you. And although you clearly know what becomes you, the garments you brought with you to the Frenchman's are several years out of date. I hope you'll indulge my desire to see you dressed as you should be."

"Am I to understand that you have taken the liberty of purchasing some items of clothing for me, my lord?" she asked, her voice now openly full of ice. And anger.

"You allowed Bonnet to dress you," Dare reminded her gently. "And *he* has no taste. Mine, on the other hand, is reputed to be excellent. Indulge me," he said again.

The color had risen very strongly in her cheeks, and Dare realized that he was holding his breath, waiting for her fury to overcome her careful control, wishing for some break in the barriers she had erected against every emotion.

"Do I have a choice?" she asked bitterly.

"Of course. We all have choices. I believe that was the focus of our earlier discussion."

"I believed the focus of our earlier discussion concerned friendship. And trust."

"As well as an offer of protection," he reminded her.

"I had not thought you meant *that* kind."

"That kind?" he repeated, puzzled by the emphasis.

"The kind of protection one offers to one's mistress," she said. "I have always thought that a strange euphemism. Now I know how right I was."

"I have given you no insult," Dare said.

"A gentleman does not buy clothing for a..." She stopped before she uttered the word, but they both understood what she had been about to say. *For a lady.* Which Elizabeth Carstairs had, at least at one time, obviously considered herself to be.

"For a friend?" Dare finished when she broke off

the sentence. "I have never had a woman as a friend. Forgive me if I have overstepped the bounds of such a friendship. That was not my intent, I promise you."

Again she refused to answer, and her eyes were still cold. And hurt, Dare realized in regret. He had truly intended no insult. And he had certainly not intended to cause her pain. But he didn't know what else to say to repair the damage.

"Until tonight, Mrs. Carstairs," he said instead of attempting another fruitless apology. He bowed slightly, and then he walked across to the library door and through it, closing it behind him.

In the silence he had left behind him, Elizabeth took a deep breath and put the tips of the fingers of both hands over her mouth. Her lips trembled, her eyes burned, on the verge of tears. Ruthlessly she suppressed the emotions that had caused both reactions.

For two long years, she had understood exactly who and, more important, what she was. And she had dealt with the knowledge. Why did it now seem so hard, so impossible to accept the cost of what she had done? A cost she thought she clearly understood.

We always have choices, the Earl of Dare had said. He was wrong, of course. She had no choice. And no matter what she believed she saw in the Earl of Dare's eyes, she knew she still had none. She was as trapped as she had ever been, and not even Dare, with all his wealth and position, could protect her.

"Nothing since you've been gone," Ned Harper said, easing the earl's coat off his broad shoulders. "Not unless they've discovered some other method of passing their messages. And we sent the last one on to Bonnet after you saw it, so they've no reason to suspect that they should change the procedure.''

"Maggie told her I was visiting Ian," Dare said.

They were sequestered in the earl's bedroom. Harper had insisted on examining the wound in his side, which, judging by the relative ease of movement he had enjoyed during the last twenty-four hours, Dare believed was healing nicely.

"I don't believe it," Ned said, shocked into stillness, the earl's coat hanging from his hands.

"Then how else could she know where I have been?"

Ned shook his head, his mouth compressed as he tried to think. "I'll speak to the girl. Of course, it's always possible the Carstairs woman has some other source of information."

"Bonnet, do you mean? In that case…"

"In that case?" Ned repeated as Dare let the sentence trail.

Harper had removed the earl's waistcoat and was helping to pull the lawn shirt over Dare's head, exposing the strips of linen Ned himself had wrapped around the earl's waist three days ago. They were still clean and white, not marked by any seepage or discoloration from the wound.

"In that case," Dare said again, "I think I should pay a call on Monsieur Bonnet."

"On Bonnet? Are you sure that's wise?" Ned asked, untying the ends of the cloth bandage.

"If he knows enough about me to put a spy in my own household and to pay another to report on my comings and goings, then I'm not sure what I have to lose by letting him know I'm aware of his interest."

"You believe Andre talked?" Ned suggested.

"We've always known it was possible something was revealed during the questioning. Torture does strange things to a man's mind. Perhaps Andre really believed he had told them nothing. Or perhaps whoever betrayed Andre knows more about my affairs than we would wish."

Ned was touching the place on his side, running his fingers over the hole the ball had made. Despite the fact that the wound was obviously healing, and the area around it far less swollen and bruised than it had been three days ago, there was a small sound, a subtle intake of the earl's breath, when Harper touched it.

The valet's eyes came up at the sound. "Did you tell your brother about this?"

"Only under duress," Dare said with a laugh. "It's hard to hide things from Ian. He has always seen through me."

"Did you tell him about the woman?"

"I asked him to help me discover who she is," Dare said. "That's the kind of intellectual puzzle at which Ian excels. And the search will give him something useful to do."

"I can tell you who she is," Ned said. "She's Bonnet's whore, and the sooner you come to terms with that, the better."

"You and Mrs. Carstairs apparently have a lot in common," Dare said. Again Ned's eyes lifted from their examination of the wound. "She, too, professes to have an unromantic nature."

"There's nothing romantic, my lord, about being—"

"That's enough," Dare ordered, his voice overriding his valet's. Ned's eyes remained locked on his. They were bitter.

"I swear, she'll lead you to your death if you trust her," Harper warned. "Whatever you think she feels for you is *your* romance. And in the game you're playing, you can't afford a mistake of that kind."

"Indulge me, Ned," Dare said softly. The tone was almost the same as he had used downstairs to Mrs. Carstairs. As were the words. "Whatever mistakes I make will be on my own head."

"There's a purpose to the chances you usually take. A good and noble cause. But to put yourself at risk for…" Ned hesitated, and then he substituted another word for the one he clearly longed to use. "…For a woman," he said, "is worse than foolish."

"She's in trouble."

"Did she tell you that?" Ned sneered.

"If she had, I might not have believed her. Since she hasn't…" Dare tilted his head, eyebrows raised.

"You'll do what you like, of course. You always do."

"Of course," Dare agreed. "I think the black tonight. I feel a need to change my image. Mrs. Carstairs doesn't believe I can protect her. Perhaps a more somber attire will make me appear more…reliable."

"You've offered her your protection?"

"A gentleman can do no less for a lady in distress."

The smiling blue eyes dared Ned to disagreed. The valet's lips twisted, but he held his tongue. Dare put his arm around Harper's shoulder and squeezed the smaller man close to his side. Whatever silent communication passed between them with that gesture, they didn't speak of Mrs. Carstairs again. And when the earl went down to dinner, he was dressed in black, the most sober of the many suits of evening attire he possessed.

Chapter Nine

"More wine?" Dare asked.

Elizabeth lifted her gaze from its unseeing contemplation of her plate to meet his eyes. They were sapphire in the candlelight. Jewellike, surrounded by their frame of long black lashes. Incredibly beautiful.

And, she decided in disgust, she had already had quite enough wine. Too *much* wine. It was totally out of character for her to notice the color of a man's eyes, much less to describe them in such hyperbolic terms, even to herself.

"No, thank you, my lord," she said, her voice colored by that discovery.

"I had thought you were enjoying the wine, Elizabeth. We agreed it is an excellent vintage."

"I *was* enjoying it, my lord," she said, amending her tone. After all, she hadn't intended to be rude. Dare had done everything possible to make this evening pleasurable. And surprisingly, despite her misgivings this afternoon when he had invited her to dine with him and her trepidation as the dinner hour approached, the experience *had* been enjoyable. "The claret is excellent, as you well know. If I drink any more, however, I fear it will go to my head.''

His eyes assessed, and then his lips tilted slightly at the corners. Despite her refusal, he turned to his major-domo and signaled with a raised eyebrow.

Without further protest, Elizabeth watched as one of the footmen stepped forward to refill her glass. Just because it was full didn't mean she had to drink it, she told herself, watching the liquid sparkle in the candlelight as it flowed into her glass. At the beginning of the meal, she had felt a need for the courage the wine would give her. Now, however...

She was aware of the subtle effects of what she had already drunk. A slight relaxation in her customary wariness. A willingness to engage in the flirtation he had begun this afternoon in the library.

Of course, it was possible those feelings could not be attributed entirely to the wine. It had been so long since a man had treated her to anything but insult, she had found herself unconsciously, almost against her will, responding to the earl's attentions. And other than the gift of the dress, Dare had not put a foot wrong.

She had not worn the gown, of course, although watching Maggie unpack the modiste's box had caused an unaccustomed, and unexpected, surge of anticipation. Fully revealed, the dress had proven that the earl's claim was not without merit. His taste *was* excellent, and apparently he *had* known as well as she what would become her. There was no doubt the gown would have.

Her coloring was delicate, and it had been over-whelmed by the garish hues Bonnet forced her to wear. Dare's gown was fashioned of a subtle dusk-rose silk, with a cunningly designed overtunic of cobweb fine lace, the color of old ivory. She had spent far too much time in her room this evening fingering the material and dreaming of how she would look in it.

She had not dared to try it on, because she had known it would be perfect. And she had also known that once she put the gown on, she would not have been able to resist wearing it for him. For *him*. She couldn't believe she had thought that. However, it was nothing less than the truth. She had desperately wanted Dare to see her in that gown.

Thankfully for her pride, she had won that particular battle of will. She was wearing the same blue silk she had worn the first night she had dined here. He had made no comment about her appearance, which was perfectly proper, of course, but she had been unaccountably disappointed that he hadn't complimented her. Perhaps her refusal to wear his gift had angered him.

"I think I should like to see that," the earl said softly.

"You would like to see me…inebriated, my lord?" she asked after a moment, almost having lost the thread of the conversation in thinking about the dress.

"I should like to see you less anxious," he said. "And less controlled."

"Less *controlled?*" she questioned the strangeness of his wording. "For a woman in my position, my lord, that would be a luxury, and one I'm afraid I can't afford."

"And I find myself wondering why not?"

She realized with surprise that somehow her wineglass was back in her hand. So he would like to see her less controlled? she thought a little bitterly, raising it to her lips. Her intent for the past two years had been to achieve *more* control, over both her emotions and her destiny.

"For a woman alone," she said, "forced to live by her wits, every word must be guarded. And every action."

"Every emotion?" Dare suggested softly.

"Of course," she agreed. "Our emotions embroil us in situations we would do better to stay out of. And we might avoid them, if we allowed our intellects to guide us."

"How dull life should be."

"And how safe," she said.

The earl laughed, putting his wineglass down on the table. It was empty again, although it seemed to Elizabeth that the footman had filled it only a moment before. At the same time he had filled hers, she thought, her eyes examining her own goblet. Which, she realized with a start, was as empty as the earl's. Almost guiltily, she put it on the table, lifting her eyes in time to catch Dare's nearly indiscernible signal to his butler.

"No more wine, I beg you, my lord," she said quickly.

"I'm sorry. I had thought you were enjoying yourself."

She had been. Far too much. The evening had been an exercise in nostalgia. Very good food, served by a perfectly trained and unobtrusive staff. An excellent vintage chosen to compliment the meal. And a man whose attentions were both courteous and flattering, and in no way improper or insulting.

As the evening progressed, she had let down her

guard. For her, that was a gift as rare as the gown that was still lying across the bed in her room upstairs. And tonight, too, had been his gift. Unlike the gown, she had not found the will to refuse.

"I am enjoying myself," she admitted, raising her eyes to his.

"I could not be more pleased," Dare said. The quiet words sounded sincere.

"Not even if I had worn the gown?" she asked, smiling.

She was teasing him again. Flirting with Dare as if he were a suitor. Something she had not done since her Season. That had been so many years ago the excitement of those events had almost faded from her memory.

During the short weeks of the London Season, however, there had been this same sense of anticipation. A sense that the next man she was introduced to on some crowded dance floor might be the man of her dreams. The man she would fall in love with and would one day marry.

Those dreams were dead, and so she wasn't sure what she was anticipating tonight. All she was sure of was that this was that same sweet expectation. And Dare had given that back to her. Whatever happened, she would always remember this night. And she would be grateful.

"I should very much like to see you in that gown, Elizabeth," he said, his voice soft, its tone almost seductive.

She said nothing, because she would very much have liked for him to see her in it as well. She had acknowledged that weakness to herself, but she couldn't, of course, admit it to him.

"Did you even try it on?" he asked.

"I couldn't afford to," she said, holding his eyes.

He knew exactly what she meant. That was clear from the sudden quirk at the corner of his mouth. A very enticing quirk, she thought. A very enticing mouth. Which, she realized belatedly, she seemed to be staring at. She raised her eyes again, and found his on her face. He wasn't smiling anymore.

"I want to dance with you," he said softly. "I want to waltz with you while you are wearing that gown."

"Waltz with me, instead of poor neglected Grace?" she asked, her smile spontaneous at the memory, maybe even a little giddy with wine and pleasure.

She wondered if he would remember. Was she the only one who seemed to have inscribed every word of their exchanges on her heart? Men, of course—

"I might even manage to do so with grace this time. Thanks to you."

"No more gratitude, my lord," she ordered, laughing. "I'm afraid you are giving me more credit than I am due. I believe that luck played an equal role in my success *and* in your recovery. You owe me nothing. If all this is because you believe I saved your life…"

"All this?" Dare echoed her words.

"The gown. The dinner. Your offer."

The last word, which had definite connotations of marriage, in their circle at least, lingered in the air a moment as his gaze held hers. And when he spoke, there was no amusement in the quiet words.

"I gave you the gown because I thought it would become your beauty instead of warring with it. I invited you to dinner because, I confess, I enjoy being in your company. More than I have enjoyed the company of any other woman I've ever know," he added softly.

Listening to him, Elizabeth realized she had forgotten to breathe. She was surprised to find that her heart was still capable of beating, as full of emotion as it was. Her throat had tightened, and again she fought the unaccustomed burn of tears.

"And I made my offer," Dare said, his voice even softer than it had been before, "because I believe you are in a great deal of trouble. And because I would really like to help you, Elizabeth. If you'll let me."

The silence grew, stretching too fine, like the sudden thinning of the air around her head. Elizabeth thought she had never wanted anything in her life more than she wanted to tell him. To make him understand, even if he couldn't help.

Because he couldn't, of course. There was nothing anyone could do to free her from the trap she was in. A trap baited with the most powerful lure of all. More powerful even than the one Dare was using.

If it had not been for the wine, perhaps she would have been able to formulate some witty or provocative answer to distract him. To deny convincingly that she needed his help. To deny that she had been moved by what she had heard in his voice.

She did none of those things. Instead, without warning, she stood, pushing back the heavy chair. And then she fled, leaving the Earl of Dare sitting alone at his table.

He wasn't sure it was the moonlight, as bright as day, pouring into his bedroom that awakened him. Perhaps it had been the intensity of the dream itself that pulled him from sleep. Almost certainly wine-induced, it had at least taken the place of the nightmares that had haunted him since Andre's death.

He pushed the tangled sheet off his legs and rose, his body aching with the hard, physical need created by the images his brain had contrived to torment him. Contrived, because he had not known Elizabeth as she would have been then. As she had been in his dream. Young, innocent and untouched.

Those pictures were fantasies, fabricated by what he knew about the lives of other women in his circle. Pictures of Elizabeth during her Season, a girl rather than the woman she was now. Dancing with a dozen beaux in some London ballroom. Riding or driving on Rotten Row. Being courted and feted, as beautiful as she was now, but without the control that dictated her every action. And without the terrible sadness that haunted her eyes.

Dare walked across to the tall windows, knowing that he wouldn't be able to go back to sleep. Not until he had put those images from his mind, along with the sense of regret over not having known her as she would have been then.

Thinking about Elizabeth, he knew he had never before loved a woman. He had been infatuated. When he was young. *And foolish,* he completed the familiar phrase in his mind, smiling at the truth behind it.

A pretty face and a winsome figure would attract his eye. And then, as the acquaintance deepened, the shallowness of the mind behind the smile would begin to pall. The trivial conversation, devoid of anything but social pleasantries, would begin to bore him. And whatever charms he had thought he saw in her features would eventually fade. And she would be forgotten.

Until now. Until *this* woman, he acknowledged.

This woman, who lectured him about the inequities of marriage in his class. Who did sums in her head and read Virgil in the original Latin and found Ovid too romantic for her tastes. As he pushed back the draperies to look out on the garden, he realized he was smiling at the memories.

He looked down on the familiar vista of manicured garden that stretched beneath his windows. His heart hesitated, missing at least a few of its normally measured beats, and then, as he watched, it began to hammer in his chest.

Elizabeth Carstairs was moving across the smooth lawn below in an endearingly childlike parody of a waltz. Her right hand held the fingers of an imaginary partner as her steps glided over the close-mown grass. With her left hand, she was holding up the skirt of the gown he had had made for her. His gift, which she had refused to wear.

As she dipped and swayed and circled, dancing alone in the silvered moonlight, he could almost hear the music she so obviously felt. He had told her at dinner that he wanted to dance with her while she was wearing this gown. And now she was waltzing across his garden as if she were waiting... *As if she were waiting...*

In a matter of seconds, Dare had found the doeskin pantaloons he had worn home from Ian's, hopping on one foot and then the other as he struggled to pull them on over his bare buttocks. He threw a shirt on over his head, not bothering to tuck it in. Harper had sent his evening shoes down to be cleaned, but the Hessians stood gleaming by the hearth, already returned by the bootblack.

They were not, however, designed for dancing. And

the gliding figure on the lawn was far too graceful to
be hampered by a clumsy partner. Laughing a little at
the absurdity of what he was doing, Dare ignored the
boots and opened the door of his chamber. Like a boy
stealing sweets, he looked both ways, up and down
the hall, searching for any witness to his act of mad-
ness before he hurried, broad feet bare, down the
stairs.

He knew every inch of the house, of course, and in
a matter of seconds he was standing before a set of
glass doors that would lead directly to the garden. He
was relieved to find that Elizabeth hadn't disappeared.
She was still dancing, her slippered feet skimming
over the grass as lightly as if it were the fine parquet
that covered the floor of the ballroom.

He thought about leading her there, but somehow
he knew instinctively that would destroy the magic.
She belonged to the moonlight. To the night. And to
the drifting shadows that played over the rose and
cream of her gown, turning it silver and old gold as
she twirled.

Magic, he thought again. He slipped the lock on the
door and, moving as silently as she was, stepped outside.

She was humming. The sound drifted to him
through the stillness. As she circled, he saw that her
eyes were closed, her head tilted slightly back, completely lost in her fantasy. Smiling again, the earl
moved nearer, making no sound on the damp lawn.
He waited until she had circled within three or four
feet of him before he spoke.

''May I have the honor of the *next* dance?''

With the sound of the first word, her eyes flew open.
The hand that had been holding her skirt dropped it

and lifted to press against the pulse in her throat instead. Lips parted, eyes widened, her breathing rapid, from shock or from the exertions of the waltz, she stood perfectly still, just staring at him.

"I didn't mean to frighten you," he said truthfully.

He had thought, as he looked down on her from his window upstairs, that she was dancing for him. That she had intended him to see her and then join her. He knew now that she had never expected anyone to witness this. Not him. Not the servants. That's why she had come here, so that no one would ever know she had worn his gown. Worn it to dance in the moonlight.

"I'm perfectly harmless, I promise you," he said, smiling at her. He held out his arm, wrist up, exactly as he would have had they been in a ballroom.

After a moment, she closed her mouth, catching her bottom lip in her teeth before she spoke. "I thought you were…"

"A ghost?" he suggested. "I don't believe we have one. At least I've never seen any."

"I thought you were the product of my imagination."

He cocked his head, considering the statement, wondering if that could mean what it sounded as if it meant. And wondering, if so, why she had told him.

"Were you imagining *me?*" he asked. For a moment she said nothing. He could see the indecision in her eyes.

"You *said* you wanted to dance with me," she said finally, neither a confirmation nor a denial.

"I do," Dare affirmed softly. "More than you can possibly imagine."

"I think…I believe I *can* imagine, my lord," she whispered. "I think I know exactly how much."

Again Dare wondered if that could be as encouraging as it had sounded. But even if it were not, he had come here with the sole intent of dancing with her, so why was he hesitating, he wondered, trying to read every nuance of her response?

"Then...shall we dance?" he invited.

She laid her fingers over the top of his wrist, and together they walked to the end of the lawn, moving slowly, just as if they were preparing to open a ball by leading out the first dance. Her chin was held high, the curls clustered atop her head gilded by the moonlight. She looked like a queen, he thought. Or an angel. He knew that he had thought the same thing before, but he couldn't remember when. Or where.

When they reached the edge of the garden, he turned in a half circle and, hand still on his wrist, she gracefully followed his lead until they were facing the doors from which he had exited the house. Then he turned toward her, bowing slightly. When he straightened, he realized she was looking down at his feet. She raised her head, and her eyes, filled with laughter, met his.

"Barefoot, my lord?" she said, that laughter caught in the husky timbre of her voice as well.

This was the way her voice should sound, full of life and joy. And it *would* always sound this way, he decided, if he were allowed anything to say about it.

"My choices were rather limited," he said. "Forgive my disreputable state of undress, my lady, but if I trod on your toes, you shall surely feel it less painfully this way."

"Are you planning to trod on my toes?" she asked, the laughter he had relished in her eyes and her voice hovering now around her lips.

As he had on the stairs that night, he longed to put his mouth over hers. To taste her. To slowly kiss her laughter into passion.

"I shall never trod on your toes," he vowed softly instead.

He put his hand at her waist, and she gathered her gown, lifting it away from her slippers. Then she gave him her other hand. They stood for a long, slow heartbeat, looking into one another's eyes.

Finally, the corners of her mouth began to tilt. "Shall I hum, my lord?" she asked. "Or shall you?"

"My voice is not even 'merely adequate,'" Dare said, returning the smile and watching hers widen. "And my brothers less kind than yours."

"Then I suppose," she said, "as unpleasant as it may be, it's up to me."

The first notes were slightly quavering, but when he didn't laugh, her voice strengthened. He waited until she had found the rhythm, and then he swung her into the familiar steps of the waltz.

It should have been awkward, even ungainly, given his lack of footwear, the uneven surface of their "dance floor" and the quality of the music. It was neither. It was as if they had danced together a thousand times. Their steps blended in perfect harmony, their bodies moved in unthinking, joyful alignment.

They circled and swirled across the grass, the hem of her gown occasionally trailing, unnoticed, in the dew. Their eyes had held a long time, and then finally she had surrendered herself to the pleasure of the moment, just as she had when she had been dancing alone. She closed her eyes, letting her head fall back, trusting him to guide her. Trusting him.

Long minutes slipped away, and neither of them

seemed aware of their passage. After a while, she ceased to hum, and the music they moved to sounded only in their heads. Even then, their steps didn't falter. Gradually, however, after a very long time, they did begin to slow.

By then the distance required by etiquette, precise to the inch, which should have separated their bodies had lessened. Without either of them being exactly sure how it had come to be, her cheek was resting against his chest. They no longer circled. Or twirled. It seemed that they no longer moved, except to sway, weight shifting imperceptibly from one foot to the other.

Faintly, away in the distance, the sound of a farrier's cart moving over the cobblestones of a street drifted into the garden. A sure sign that morning was breaking over the sleeping city.

Slowly, the earl lifted his head from where it had been resting against softly perfumed curls. The sky was definitely lightening, he realized. It was not yet dawn, but it *was* the lesser darkness that precedes it.

Reluctantly, he released her hand, stepping back, increasing the distance between them again to that prescribed by the dictates of society. Elizabeth, too, raised her head, looking into his eyes.

He took her hands in his, and then he stepped back one step—far enough to see her. Slowly, he surveyed her slender figure, up and then down. He had been right, of course. The gown was absolutely perfect. Perfect for her.

"Thank you, my lord," Elizabeth said.

"It's perfect," he said.

"It was perfect," she agreed.

Not the dress. The dance, then? he wondered. The

night? Or the fact that he had held her? That her head had rested on his shoulder, her breasts pressed against his chest?

"And I will never forget," she whispered.

As she spoke, she began to disentangle her fingers from his. Unwilling to have it end, he refused to let her go. She stopped struggling, her eyes looking up into his.

"My lord?" she questioned.

He released her hands then, but only to put his around her upper arms. She made no effort to break away, her gaze still locked on his. He pulled her to him, and then he bent, turning his head to align his mouth over hers.

Unconsciously, her head tilted backward, just as it had when she had been lost in the beauty of the dance. He placed his lips over hers, the kiss gentle, without pressure or demand. Exactly as he would have kissed her had she been the Elizabeth of his dream. Virginal and untouched.

For an eternity her lips were unmoving. Unresponsive. And then, like the bud of a flower responds to light, they opened. Moist and warm and sweet, her mouth lay under his, acquiescent to his invasion. And to his control.

For a woman in my position, my lord, that's a luxury, and one I'm afraid I can't afford, she had told him, and yet she had surrendered that careful control to him.

His tongue invaded, exploring. And was met, its every movement answered. Just as their bodies swirled in unthinking harmony in the dance, so their tongues touched. And then retreated. And then entangled again. Simply another form of waltz, this one as old as time, mirroring an even older and more primitive series of movements.

After a moment, he put his arm around her waist, easing her body nearer his, again savoring the feel of her breasts flattened against his chest. Her right hand lifted to caress the back of his head, slender fingers threading through the curling thickness of his hair.

Her other hand found his cheek, trailing, as it had once before, over the abrasiveness of his morning beard. He had been ill then, and that caress had been prompted by concern. This was something very different, and he understood everything it represented. For her. And for him.

He deepened the kiss, bending her upper body slightly back and pressing his hips into hers. His erection was incredibly powerful and painfully constricted by the pantaloons. The thin, supple doeskin would be almost as revealing of the contours of his arousal as would his total nudity.

He felt her reaction. Surprise? Or fear? He eased his aching body back in response to her recoil, lessening the contact between them, an act of will he couldn't believe he had been able to accomplish. He had been, only because he didn't want to frighten her. He never wanted to see fear in her eyes when she looked at him.

In spite of that self-imposed restriction, he wanted her. He wanted to make love to her more than he had ever wanted to make love to any other woman. More than he had ever wanted anything in his life.

He wanted to strip the gown he had designed from the body he had been envisioning as he sketched it in the shop of London's premier dressmaker. He wanted to see the beauty that lay beneath the silk completely exposed. The smoothness of her skin, milk-white, blue-veined. The shapeliness of legs and slender ankles he had only glimpsed. The firmness of small breasts, that he had felt harden with desire as they moved against his chest.

And when he had examined every inch of her body—with his eyes, with fingers that he knew would tremble with need, and with lips and tongue that even now longed to caress each hidden, secret place—then he would lay her on the dew-touched grass that surrounded them and push into the sweet, wet heat he had created.

His fantasy. His need. As real to him as the dance had been for her. And all he needed to make it a reality was her permission. Some sign that she wanted him, too.

Instead, she turned her head as she tried to step back, breaking the kiss and the contact between their bodies. He could have held her, of course. He could have used his strength to control…

Control. The word reverberated in his head. She had willingly given herself into his control, and unless he intended to abuse her as, furious, he had watched Bonnet do, then he had to respect her choice. Her decision.

No matter what she had been or done in the past, what she did with him was under her control. That had been implicit in everything he had said to her. Reluctantly, he released her, stepping away. Removing himself from a temptation which was stronger than any he had faced in his life.

It was light enough now that he could see her face. She was looking up at him, eyes wide and dark. The moonlight had been kinder than the dawn. In its harsher light, her eyes were again haunted. Not with sadness perhaps. There was, however, clearly some painful emotion there he was unable to read. Or interpret.

He heard the breath she took, almost a sob. And then, as she had done before from the dinner table, she turned and ran across the lawn, entering the house through the French doors.

Behind her in the morning stillness, Dare raised his head, looking upward into the brightening sky. After a moment, he closed his eyes, moving his head back and forth in a slow denial.

What was she? That was the question he should have answered first. By the time he had known how important its answer would eventually be, however, it had been too late to ask the question.

Bonnet's whore. That's what Ned had called her. And even Ian, who seldom judged the actions of others, had warned against the involvement. And even if she *were* Bonnet's whore...

He took a breath, as deep as the one Elizabeth had drawn. And even if she were, he acknowledged, the words as bitter as gall as they formed in his heart, she was still, and always would be, the woman he loved.

Chapter Ten

"**M**y Lord Dare," Henri Bonnet said. "But how charming to see you again."

Dare wasn't sure it was pleasure he heard in the Frenchman's tone, although the gambler's greeting seemed, on the surface, as ingratiating as it had the first night the earl had come to play in these rooms. Whatever emotion had first appeared in Bonnet's black eyes had been quickly hidden, and when they were lifted again after his bow, Dare could find nothing there but welcome.

"*Monsieur Bonnet*," he said, his tone filled with hauteur.

"My house is again honored by your presence, my lord."

The gambler's hand invited him into the main salon, where there were several games of chance under way. Dare's gaze swept over the players, recognizing many gentlemen of his acquaintance among them. The public rooms seemed filled to capacity, the noise fueled by Bonnet's notorious generosity with the wine.

At the faro table, the most popular in the salon, a woman dealer presided. She was wearing a low-cut emerald gown, and the unnatural copper color of her hair, gleaming in the light from the crystal chandeliers, was almost as garish as her dress. Her face was pallid, an overapplication of powder, the earl guessed, an unsuccessful attempt to hide a raddled complexion perhaps.

Dare's lips flattened as he compared this woman to the one he had danced with in the moonlight last night. There had to be an explanation for why someone like Elizabeth Carstairs had ended up at Bonnet's, Dare thought again. And he intended to hear it, if not from Elizabeth herself, then from the French gambler.

"And what is your pleasure, my lord?" Bonnet asked, his smiling eyes on Dare's face. "As you can see, we are able to accommodate almost every taste—faro, ecarte, baccarat, basset, piquet."

The inflection had been questioning, as was the Frenchman's expression. Dare met his eyes and held them for a moment before he said, "Only a little information, *monsieur*. If you please."

There was the briefest hesitation before Bonnet said, his tone almost as congenial as before, "But of course, my lord. I will be delighted to tell you whatever you wish to know."

"I want to know how Mrs. Carstairs came to be working for you." Deliberately, Dare allowed his eyes to focus on the woman dealing cards from the faro bank across the room. "She is not, I'm sure you'll admit, the kind of woman one would expect to find in your establishment."

"Elizabeth?" the gambler repeated, as if the question were the last he had expected. "And how is Elizabeth, my lord? I have wondered so often how your relationship was progressing. I trust she has proven to be as…satisfactory for your purposes as she always was for mine.''

Dare's eyes came back to the Frenchman's face. There was a long silence, and during it the gambler's smile slowly faded.

''And exactly what were your purposes for Mrs. Carstairs, Bonnet?'' Dare asked, his voice very soft.

''To entertain my clientele, of course. Elizabeth can be very entertaining. When she chooses,'' the Frenchman said with a laugh. ''As I'm sure you've discovered for yourself.''

''And yet you've already replaced her,'' Dare said, ignoring the innuendo. His eyes moved back to the faro dealer. ''And with someone who seems very popular with your patrons.''

He was controlling his fury. He didn't know what information he had expected Bonnet to give him. Everyone had told him what Elizabeth Carstairs was. He had hoped the gambler could explain the unexplainable and ease the pain that had been gnawing at him even more strongly after last night.

''Her name is Marie, my lord. If you're interested—''

''I'm *not* interested,'' Dare interrupted, turning back to the gambler. ''I'm not interested in anything other than the information I asked you for. And the comparison between your Marie and Mrs. Carstairs only serves to make me more curious.''

''A personal interest?''

''Curiosity. After all, we both agree that Mrs. Carstairs isn't your usual…employee.''

Bonnet laughed again. This time the sound seemed to express relief. ''She was certainly above average, my lord," he said. "Those qualities were, of course, what caught your eye."

"And exactly how did she come to be working for you?" This time as he asked the question, Dare's voice was much softer, perhaps even menacing.

"Her husband owed me money, my lord. When he died, I offered Mrs. Carstairs a way to pay his debts."

"*Which* she was under no legal obligation to pay," Dare said.

The Frenchman's lips tightened minutely. "A moral obligation, if you will."

Dare laughed, the sound abrupt and ugly. "Are you attempting to convince me that an English gentlewoman would feel an obligation to come to work in a gaming hell because of her husband's gambling debts? Do you take me for a fool, Bonnet?"

There was a sudden gleam in the Frenchman's dark eyes that said exactly that. He *did* take Dare for a fool. And since that was the role the earl had played with such success for so many years, he supposed he shouldn't feel this surge of anger on seeing the contempt in Bonnet's eyes.

"My Lord Dare! No, no! Of course not, my lord," Bonnet said soothingly. "That is the story Elizabeth herself concocted. I have always hated to contradict a lady."

"A lady?" Dare interrupted, pouncing on the word.

Bonnet shrugged, a very Gallic gesture, and leaned closer, as if he were about to make a confidence he feared might be overheard. "And from a very good family," he said, his voice lowered almost to a whisper, despite the noise that swirled around them. "A name you would recognize if I mentioned it. Which, and I'm sure you will forgive me, my lord, I promised Elizabeth I should never let slip past my lips.''

He raised one long, white finger and drew an X over his pursed mouth. And then he smiled at Dare as if they were fellow conspirators.

''And you still haven't explained how a woman of such an illustrious family would come to be in your employ.''

Again the dark eyes considered his face, and Dare waited through their examination. Finally, the Frenchman inclined his head as if bowing to the inevitable.

''Elizabeth ended up here because she suffers from...a very passionate nature, shall we say. Leave it at that, my lord. I would never seek to malign anyone because of past transgressions. We have all suffered from those, I think. I cast no stones.''

''I'm sure you are discretion itself, *monsieur.* However, I find that I am even more curious as to the nature of that...transgression,'' Dare said. ''Since you've already suggested it, I think you can hardly plead the higher moral ground of now closing your lips. Whatever your promise to Elizabeth.''

The bastard was lying, Dare told himself, holding on to his temper. He longed to pound that smirk off the gambler's face. It was the same urge he had had to defend Elizabeth when Ned had called her whore. Logically, he knew his anger was misplaced.

Whatever Elizabeth Carstairs had been in the past, lady or wife or daughter of some noble family, she had been working in this infamous London hell for more than two years before he met her. And Dare himself had been offered her sexual favors almost as casually as Bonnet offered his patrons wine and cigars. That fact alone didn't argue that she still possessed an innocence worthy of defense, no matter the spell she had cast.

"An unfortunate pregnancy, my lord. By the time her family discovered her condition, the cad who was responsible for it had fled. It was too late to lure any unsuspecting suitor to take his place at the altar. They did the only thing they could in the circumstances." Again the Frenchman shrugged. "Not an uncommon situation, I think, even among the English nobility."

"And the family's solution?" Dare asked.

There was a growing sickness in the pit of his stomach. Despite what the Frenchman had suggested, he knew how unusual it was for a gently reared English girl to find herself in that particular kind of trouble. At least without the culprit around to be called to account by her father or her brothers. And Elizabeth had had four of those.

"They sent her to a convent, of course. In a rather remote part of Ireland. It's amusing when Elizabeth tells the story."

"A convent?" Dare repeated unbelievingly. Whatever he had expected the Frenchman to say, it wasn't this. A hasty marriage to someone not of her own class perhaps, which would explain why the name Carstairs had not been familiar to him or to Ian. Or even the pretense of a marriage. But a convent...?

"Of course, Elizabeth found the accommodations not to her liking. A little too much of a good thing, if you take my meaning. Or perhaps I should say that for Elizabeth's nature there was too *little* of a good thing," the Frenchman insinuated with a smile.

Again Dare fought the urge to pound the suggestive smirk away. "So she left," he said.

"As soon as the child was born, I believe. At least as soon as she could travel."

"And the child?" the earl asked, feeling his nausea roil again, almost as strong now as his anger at Bonnet.

The Frenchman shrugged. "I have no idea. I doubt Elizabeth has. A most inconvenient birth for someone of her class, you understand. I would imagine she preferred to forget it as rapidly as she could."

"She left the baby, and came back to England."

"With the help of someone she had met there. An Irish gentleman who was more than willing to bring her back to her native country, in exchange for her...favors."

The knowing smile had returned, and the Frenchman lifted his eyebrows as he said the word. Her *favors*. Sexual favors, of course. Dare found that he wanted to close his eyes, so that he wouldn't have to see Bonnet's face. Just as he wanted to close his mind to the sordid tale the gambler was unfolding.

This is what he had asked for, but he had no way of knowing whether any of it were true. He had known, however, that the question of why Elizabeth had ended up in Bonnet's employ would require an explanation that would be as sordid as this. He found himself wishing that he had never demanded an accounting. It was better *not* to hear this. Better *not* to wonder how much was truth and how much invention—whether Bonnet's or Elizabeth's.

Events such as these would certainly be enough to cause the kind of estrangement between Elizabeth and the brothers she had hinted at. Dare had professed that his brothers disapproved of his life, and she had echoed that. In her case, it seemed that claim must have had some merit. Otherwise, why would her family have allowed her to end here, dealing cards for Bonnet and being offered to his clientele like some prize?

Her favors. The same ones Bonnet had offered him. The favors many in London might already have enjoyed. And this was the woman he had treated like an innocent last night, as bewitched by the moonlight and her seeming virtue as she had probably been bewitched by the man who had deflowered her.

"And how did she then come to work for you?" Dare forced himself to ask.

"Her 'rescuer' owed me money. That part of the story she contrived has some validity. Only he wasn't her husband, and, as far as I am aware, he isn't dead. He left her with me in lieu of his debts. Elizabeth was a bargain I was more than willing to accept. She was almost as popular as Marie." The gambler's eyes moved to consider the faro dealer before they came back to Dare's. "Two very different women, each appealing in her own way. Something about Elizabeth's aloofness attracts. Despite her rather checkered past, she manages to project an innocence still. Almost a gift," Bonnet said. "Especially when one knows the truth," he added softly. "As you and I both do, of course. In bed, all that maidenly fragility fades away rather spectacularly, doesn't it? A remarkable transformation. Don't you agree, my Lord Dare?"

When one knows the truth. As you and I both do…
Bonnet's words echoed over and over in his head as the wheels of the carriage rolled smoothly over the streets of a sleeping London. Dare had stayed at Bonnet's long enough to lose a few hundred guineas at

the faro table and to drink far too much of the gambler's wine.

His decision to stay had been deliberate, a very painful form of masochism. As he watched the red-haired woman interact with Bonnet's customers, he had forced himself to picture Elizabeth in these same rooms. Made himself imagine her engaged in the same provocative and suggestive banter with which the faro dealer entertained those gathered around her table.

For two years, this was the role Elizabeth had played, and he wondered if she had played it half so well as the one she had assumed last night. His lips tightened in disgust. Both Ned and Ian had warned him, but he had refused to acknowledge until tonight the reality of what Elizabeth Carstairs was.

Because he hadn't wanted her to be that. He had wanted her to be the romantic creation of his own mind. Of his own desires.

He knew it was entirely possible that the Frenchman had not told him the truth. It was even possible that Bonnet didn't know Elizabeth's true story. Nothing, however, could change the fact that for two years she had done what he had watched the woman called Marie do tonight. And she must have done it very well, or a man like Bonnet would never have kept her.

The Frenchman would have had no compunction in putting Elizabeth out on the street if she had failed to satisfy his customers. *Satisfy.* All the sexual connotations of that word echoed in his head, and in the darkness of his own carriage, the earl allowed the escape he had not permitted himself before.

He closed his eyes, putting his head back against the leather seat, and for a brief moment, his mind filled with the unwanted images of last night. All of them.

From the time he had pushed aside the curtain and had seen the graceful figure on the lawn beneath his window to the moment when she had fled from the evidence of the effect she had on his body. Running away like a virgin, frightened by her first exposure to the power of a man's animal nature.

The earl's self-castigating laughter was bitter. He opened his eyes, having found memory almost as agonizing as the present. There were aspects that were still puzzling, such as why Elizabeth had not given the Frenchman the information about Dare's wound and its cause. It was possible, he supposed, that she could still be a loyal patriot and at the same time be a woman of the lowest morals. There was many a thief in Whiteside who would willingly die for his King and the Crown.

Dare hadn't gone to Bonnet's to investigate the Frenchman's interest in his activities. Whatever the gambler suspected about Dare's involvement with the war effort could be dealt with, even if Elizabeth had passed on information to him. After all, Bonnet had already suspected something or he wouldn't have required Elizabeth to spy on the earl's household. And since Ned was carefully monitoring her activities, tonight's mission had been strictly personal in nature. Especially after last night.

Dare shook his head, his lips again flattening as he remembered what he had felt then. Bonnet had been right about one thing. Despite what she had done during the past two years, Elizabeth seemed incredibly unmarked. Innocent. Untouched.

The carriage bumped to a stop, startled, Dare looked up to find it had drawn up before his own town house. The footman was already opening the door and letting down the steps. The journey had been too short to resolve the feelings he had needed to deal with. The earl found himself reluctant to enter his home. As long as he was in the coach, he could lick his self-imposed wounds in solitude and not have to make any decision about what to do with Elizabeth. Now, however...

Summoning every ounce of willpower he possessed, Dare stepped down out of the coach and walked into the house, even managing to exchange the customary commonplaces with his butler. His mind, however, was upstairs in the bedroom where Elizabeth was sleeping. A room he had entered only once before, the morning he had left to visit Ian.

He handed over his hat, gloves and cane, and allowed Watson to divest him of his evening cape. Then, rudely leaving his butler in midsentence, he climbed the stairs. His hand on the railing, he moved up them far more slowly than was his custom, remembering the night she had found him on this very staircase. Remembering her body moving in unison with his as she helped him climb them. Remembering.

Despite the pain inherent in those memories, he didn't stop until he had reached the door of her chamber. And then, surprised by his reluctance to force a confrontation he knew was long overdue, he hesitated, his hand raised in midair to knock.

She would be asleep. And there was no reason that what he needed to say couldn't wait until morning. The delay would allow him time to clear the effects of Donnet's wine from his head. And it would give him a few more hours to come to terms with something he had known intellectually from the very beginning of this relationship.

Known and rejected, because he hadn't wanted it to

be true. And because he had been infatuated with her from the first moment he had seen her. Certainly from the time she had challenged his supposed insult to her nationality. From the time Bonnet had gripped her arm and dragged her from the salon. From the time she had reappeared, her eyes wary and the mark of the Frenchman's hand on her cheek.

Of course, Bonnet was well within his right to discipline her, he acknowledged bitterly. After all, she was his. His employee. His whore.

She had been then. And tonight's most bitter realization was that if he put Elizabeth out of his house, she would again become what she had been before. Bonnet's whore. What he and she had shared, their few encounters, which had loomed so important in his own mind, would probably be very swiftly forgotten as she slipped back into the role she had played for two years in the French gambler's hell.

But of course, *this* had been the role. The one she had played with him. The trembling fingers. The haunted eyes. The virginal innocence. With the last thought, the Earl of Dare's hand closed over the knob of the door to Elizabeth Carstairs' room. And despite his anger, or maybe because of it, his fingers were trembling as he turned it.

She came awake too suddenly, the effects of the deep, dreamless sleep too strong to escape so quickly. Her eyes opened to the same moonlight that had called her so strongly last night.

Perhaps that was what had awakened her, she thought. She turned her head away from the windows, preparing to go back to sleep, and saw a figure beside her bed, looming over her in the darkness. She could never be sure what prevented her from crying out. Her heart had leapt and her breathing had faltered, but for some unknown reason, despite her terror, she hadn't screamed.

And by the time she realized that she should, she had recognized him. She didn't understand how she had known it was him, since his face was in the shadows, but there was no doubt in her mind that the Earl of Dare was standing beside her bed, watching her sleep.

The front of his shirt gleamed white as bone in the moonlight, and the diamond stickpin in his cravat shimmered with his breathing like sunlight dancing on the surface of a dark pond. He was in evening dress, she realized, which meant he had been out.

"My lord?" she questioned softly. He said nothing in response, nor did he move.

Her initial panic at awakening to find someone beside her bed had now given way to a very different kind of anxiety. She had hidden in her room all day, making that meaningless journey back and forth across it, pacing the distance off, trying to come to grips with what had happened.

She had told herself a thousand times that it had, after all, been only a kiss. And only a waltz, prolonged though it was far beyond the parameters of any other dance she had ever experienced. She had argued with her heart that what had happened between them had really been nothing beyond those two relatively meaningless events. Meaningless, at least as far as the earl would be concerned.

Dare had probably kissed a hundred women. And he had danced with untold scores. Why should she try to interpret what *she* had felt as meaning anything to him? Anything other than the sexual appetite he had revealed to her at last.

She had been aware all along of why he had brought her to this house. At the beginning there had been no doubt in her mind of either his motives or his intents. *She* was the one who had tried to imagine there was something else involved in his treatment of her. In his treatment up to this point, she amended, her eyes still on the dark, menacing figure.

This was what she had expected from the first night, when he had won her on the turn of a card. And then, when he hadn't touched her, she had allowed herself to fantasize that he had rescued her. But of course, that had never been his intention.

She knew very well there *was* no rescue. Nor could there ever be, not from the very private hell in which she had lived for the past two years. No rescue. No white knight. No reprieve. Especially not from her past.

The time had come, apparently, for Dare to call due his markers. She supposed she should be grateful he had delayed this long. She was instead so bitterly disappointed that, to use a hackneyed and ridiculously clichéd phrase, her heart was breaking. She was surprised to find there was anything left intact enough after these last two years to respond to this pain.

She sat upright in her bed, holding the sheet with one hand against her breasts. "Is something wrong, Lord Dare?"

She willed her voice not to betray her, and with gratitude she heard the calm tenor of the question. There had not been the least revealing quaver in the words.

"Who are you?" he asked, his words as soft as hers.

"You know who I am," she said. "You have known from the beginning who I am."

There was a long silence. As she waited through it, she could sense the very blood flowing through her veins, the slight pulse of it counting off the slow seconds as they drifted by in the darkness. His face was still hidden by the shadows. She wished she could see him. To watch, perhaps, the end of the dream. She needed to watch its death to make it final.

"And what you are," he said.

And what you are. It had not been a question, and she recognized the significance of that. She had known this time would come. They had, both of them, only been delaying the inevitable. Something had happened tonight that had made it impossible for him to do so any longer. And her heart ached for him, as well as for its own grief and loss.

"And what I am," she said. A confirmation of what she had heard in his voice.

"Were you Bonnet's whore?"

She prayed he couldn't see the tears. They had burned her eyes, filling them, and then they had spilled out, trailing hotly over her skin. Running across the same cheek that had rested against his chest last night. She had been sheltered there. Loved and protected. Or so she had imagined.

I thought you were the product of my imagination, she had told him. And he had been, of course. The man she had danced with in the moonlight had not been this cold stranger standing before her, demanding that she confess a truth he already knew. A truth they both had known from the first.

"I was his whore, my lord," she said softly.

One of the tears dropped onto her right hand, which

she realized she was holding within the left, so that they rested together just below her breasts. It was a trick she had learned very early at the gambler's hell. It kept their trembling from being obvious to the men who came there to play. And they were trembling now, she realized, just as they had then.

"I was his well-used whore," she added, and she wondered if Dare would be aware of the bitterness that underlay that confession. Or of the pain.

Sometimes love died. Sometimes it faded into an old and comfortable friendship, still cherished. And sometimes it was killed. Deliberately murdered because it couldn't be allowed to grow and flourish. And it was better that cruel act be done as early as possible. Because otherwise…

Another tear fell onto her fingers. Her throat was too thick to force any other words past its constriction. And of course, there was nothing else for her to say. Finally, she had said it all, as she should have long ago. And she fought not to betray to him that she was crying.

"Tell me why," he said. "Make me understand."

Make me understand. She wanted to. Dear God, how she longed to try. This, too, she had wanted from the first. To pour out for him the whole story. To beg him to understand what she had done and the choices she had made.

But even if he did, of course, it would change nothing that lay at the heart of what had happened. She *had* been Bonnet's whore, and nothing she could ever say to Dare could change the brutal reality of that.

To tell him why might be satisfying, but it would also be pointless. And, far more important, it might be dangerous.

That was the one thing she could not do. She could not make meaningless the terrible sacrifice she had made. She had known for a long time that was the only thing she could not live with.

"No," she said softly.

"There has to be a reason. Something that would be powerful enough—"

"No, my lord," she interrupted what she clearly recognized as a plea: *Tell me something I can believe. Give me some excuse for what you have done.* "There are no reasons. No explanation I can make that would make any difference to what I have done. Or to what I am."

Again the silence stretched between them, so achingly empty in the cold, silver moonlight. So different from last night. Nothing would ever be the same. She understood that. And soon, he would be forced to accept what he could not change. What neither of them could ever change.

And when he had, she thought he would leave. He would run from what she was, just as she had fled from the revelation last night of how much he wanted her. She had left because that physical desire had been out of place in her fantasy. It hadn't fit with the man she had created from the moonlight and the music and her own distant dreams.

She knew that what she had told him tonight wouldn't fit any better with the woman *he* had been imagining. When he realized that, he would leave, and she would never see him again.

"Then why not be my whore as well?" he said softly.

It was unexpected. As was his hand, reaching out of the darkness to grab her wrist. He pulled her off the bed, uncaring that she almost fell. Had it not been for his fingers wrapped so tightly around her arm, she might have. One foot had tangled in the sheet, and as he jerked her up, she had fallen into him, her hand flattening against his chest.

She tried to push him away, but he was too strong. Too angry. Too determined.

He released her wrist, but before she could move, his hands were gripping her shoulders, lifting her upward to meet his descending mouth. The kiss was nothing like the one they had shared last night. Nothing of its gentleness or unspoken concern. It was hard and demanding. He pushed his tongue between her lips, not waiting for permission or response. And then his mouth punished her.

Punished. That was exactly what he was doing, she realized. Punishing her for letting him fall in love with her. For allowing what had happened between them to happen.

And if punishing her would ease his pain, she found she was willing to let him. Perhaps his brutality would even destroy some of what she had felt about him as well. Or ease what she had felt about herself for the past two years. After all, guilt demanded chastisement. Craved it. And who better than the man she loved to chastise her sin.

And so for endless minutes she remained motionless as his mouth devoured her. She hung from his hands like a lifeless doll. Powerless to protest because she knew she deserved whatever he did. She deserved it because of what she was.

And then, as his lips moved hotly over her throat and his hand closed roughly over her breast, kneading it painfully between his strong fingers, she knew with a clarity almost as bright as the moonlight that this was wrong. And that it would destroy them both.

Dare was not this kind of man. Nothing she knew about him had indicated that he would ever take a woman with this brutality. This was his anger and most of all it was his pain, but it was *not* the man she had come to love.

If he did this, everything would be destroyed. All she had believed about him. All she had built up in her mind about the kind of man he was. About what he felt for her. That was fantasy, she knew, but then fantasy was all she had left.

All that was left of the woman she once had been. All that was left of her heart—the foolish hope that someone like Dare might love her enough to forget. Or at least to forgive.

That and the knowledge that because of what she had become, her brother was still alive. And as long as he was alive, there was always hope.

She had had no choice about what she had done with Bonnet. This, however, would be something she would allow to happen, complaisant as one of the prostitutes who sold themselves for food or drink or drugs. They had no place to take the men who paid for their services, so they allowed themselves to be taken standing up. Pushed against the wall of some dark building, skirts raised and legs spread, they were used and then discarded.

If she allowed Dare to do what he intended, then she would truly *be* what he thought she was. No better than those other whores. And the woman she had once been would be completely destroyed. There would not be even the brittle, broken shards she had guarded for so long.

And so she began to struggle, fighting against his strength. And against his anger, which seemed fueled by her refusal.

His fingers dug into the softness of her breast, and his mouth moved to cover it. She could feel the heat and wetness of his tongue through the material of her rail, and the feeling weakened her knees, creating a hot, unbearable pressure between her legs. Longing. Need.

She felt herself slipping into response, almost unwilling to struggle against him when she wanted him to touch her instead. Wanted it and feared it. More than she had ever feared anything in her life because she understood the repercussions of this act for both of them. Both of them, she repeated, fighting now as much for his sanity as for hers.

She twisted and writhed against his hold, finding a strength she didn't know she possessed, and then, suddenly, inexplicably, she was free. She broke away, running toward the door. He was too fast for her, of course. His long arm snaked out and grasped her wrist, pulling her around to face him. With his other hand, he caught the front of her nightgown. It was old, one she had brought to Bonnet's, its fabric now thin and worn. It tore like paper under the power of his fingers.

The sound it made seemed to paralyze them both. Neither moved for endless seconds, locked in a frozen tableau. Then, he released the torn material, and it fell to reveal her breasts. The cold air touched against her nipples, tightening them, and Elizabeth put her hands over her chest, fingers spread, shielding her body.

Slowly, his gaze lifted from her breasts. Their eyes met. As she panted, breathing audible in the stillness, she watched his face change. The revealing moonlight played over his features, as contorted by emotion now as they had once been by the pain of his wound.

His eyes gradually lost the glitter that had frightened her. They fastened on her face, and at what was in them, her tears began again. Unheeded, they traced downward over her cheeks and fell again on her fingers.

"This is not..." he began, and then his voice faded. She waited, watching his face and crying for what she had done to him.

"I'm sorry," he said finally. The words were almost too low for her to hear, even as close as they were standing. "I never meant to hurt you."

"I never meant to hurt *you*," she whispered. She didn't know if he understood, but the agony she had seen in his eyes hadn't lessened. It was raw. Exposed. Totally unguarded.

She had made him vulnerable to this torment, and there was nothing she could do to stop it. Nothing except what she had already done. What he, ultimately, had done.

It was over. He wouldn't touch her again. She knew that. It was in his eyes. Then he turned and crossed the room, disappearing into the shadows. The door opened and then closed.

The sound released her. She fell on her knees and put both hands over her mouth. This time, however, the racking sobs were too violent to stop with her fingers. They echoed through the silence, as the force of them tore through her body.

They didn't cease until two long years of unspoken pain had been released. And when the paroxysm of grief was finally over, Elizabeth Carstairs lay exhausted, unmoving on the gleaming oak floor of her bedroom in the Earl of Dare's town house. All alone in a peaceful spill of silvered moonlight.

Chapter Eleven

Dare didn't sleep, of course. He watched the sun come up over the lawn where they had waltzed, turning the shadows to a tarnished silver and then to bright, lush green. The noises of the awakening city drifted upward, but he was never conscious of them. All he heard were the sobs that had echoed down the hall behind him as he had fled, taking refuge in this room.

He had assaulted a woman. He had torn her clothing with his bare hands, exposing her body. And then he had left her alone, crying in her chamber because he could not trust himself to offer comfort or solace or apology for what he had done, other than the half-strangled one he had managed before he fled.

The knock on his door disturbed him for a moment, requiring more of his attention than he was prepared to give anything other than the problem he had agonized over all night. And so he ignored it, his eyes on the garden below.

His head ached, both from the lack of sleep and from the excess of Bonnet's wine. He wished he could accept his overindulgence as some excuse for what he had done, but he hadn't yet been able to convince himself it could be.

"You've not been to bed," Ned said in surprise, his voice coming from behind him.

Dare hadn't heard the door open. He supposed his valet had been quiet, assuming he was asleep when he had refused to answer.

"I don't need you," Dare said without turning around. His eyes would reveal too much, especially to someone who knew him as well as his valet.

"There's a message from your brother."

He turned at that, trying to read Harper's face. "Sebastian?" he asked, feeling fear crowd his chest.

"It's from Master Ian. And they would send word to *you* if anything had happened to Master Sebastian."

Harper held out an envelope. The earl's gaze lifted from his brother's message to meet Ned's eyes, the coldness in his face forbidding any questions, he hoped, about why he was standing by the window, still wearing the same clothes he had worn to visit Bonnet's hell.

"Put it on the desk," he said, turning back to the window.

"Are you all right?" Ned asked.

He wasn't, of course. He didn't know how to tell Ned about last night, however, without admitting his valet had been right all along. Right about Elizabeth. Right about the damage his involvement with her would do. Perhaps someday he would be able to discuss his feelings, calmly and rationally, but he knew he could not do it now. The pain was too raw; the wound too fresh.

"Thank you, Ned. That will be all," he said instead.

He listened for Harper's footsteps crossing the room

to the door. They didn't, and Dare knew that the escape he had longed for would not be allowed. Ned had, through his loyal service, earned the right to demand answers. Dare wished he wouldn't. He wished that as a friend, Ned would simply go away and leave him alone. Apparently, that was too much to hope for.

"What's happened last night?" Ned asked.

"Nothing you didn't predict," Dare said.

Harper said nothing for a moment. "Read your brother's letter," he suggested. "He may have discovered who she is."

"I know who she is," Dare said. After all, she had told him herself, removing any doubt. And any hope.

"Then maybe you need to know *why* she is," Ned said. "Maybe you still need to know that."

Dare turned, reading in Ned's face what had been in his voice. Concern. And compassion.

"You said she was in trouble," the valet continued. "Nothing's changed about that, no matter what else is different."

Ned was right, of course. Elizabeth Carstairs was still a woman alone and friendless. Dare still believed she was afraid of Bonnet. And he still thought she was in trouble.

The earl walked across and took the letter from Ned's outstretched hand, meeting his eyes briefly as he did. Then he carried it over to the window, breaking the seal, and holding the single sheet out to the light. There were only two lines, scrawled in Ian's unmistakable hand.

"I know who she is. I think I may know why she was there."

Dare read them twice, silently cursing his brother for their careful brevity. Ian had committed no names

to paper, of course. And he had given no details of
what he had found. But apparently his brother had
done what he had asked him to do. He had discovered
Elizabeth's identity, as well as a possible explanation
for how she had ended up at Bonnet's.

Perhaps it would even be a reason that would be
more palatable than the Frenchman's story. Dare
couldn't see, however, how understanding what had
happened could make a difference in how he now felt.
I was Bonnet's well-used whore.

Dare's impulse was to crush the note in his hand
and throw it into the fire. What did unraveling the
secrets Elizabeth was determined to keep matter now?
Knowing the *why* of it all would change nothing.

You said she was in trouble, Ned had reminded him.
Nothing has changed about that. And because he truly
believed she was, Dare found he could no more abandon her than he could have abandoned a starving dog
he had encountered in the street. It wasn't in his nature. Just as last night was not.

He owed Elizabeth more than his apology, of
course. He had offered her protection. And there had
been no caveats in that offer. Nothing that had said
this is offered only if you are pure enough to meet my
standards. Or society's standards. He had offered her
his protection, a pledge and an obligation.

"I need you to pack for me, Ned. For a journey of
at least two days. And inform the stables to have the
coach ready to leave within the hour."

"I'm going with you," Ned said, already moving
to carry out the first of those commands.

"Someone has to watch her," the earl said softly.
If he left her alone, Elizabeth would leave. There was
no doubt in his mind about that. "I think that job will

have to be yours. Out of friendship, if for no other reason. And whatever you do, Ned, don't let her out of the house. Use the footmen, if you have to, to help you keep an eye on her. But whatever happens, don't let her go back to Bonnet.''

''You think she's going somewhere?'' Ned asked. There was a hint of contempt in his voice. Dare wasn't sure whether it was meant for him or for Elizabeth.

''I think she will try if you don't prevent her. And if you don't prevent her, Ned...'' He drew a breath, thinking about the implications of that. And then he added softly, ''I don't believe I should ever be able to forgive you.''

The valet's eyes widened, and finally, reading his master's eyes, he nodded. Reluctantly given, perhaps, but agreement.

''Richardson,'' Ian said. ''I should have remembered the family before, but the Carstairs fooled me. And that *isn't* an assumed name, by the way.''

''She's married?''

For some reason that was painful as well, even given what he already knew. It meant that Elizabeth had once cared about another man well enough to wed him, to commit herself to his care. And apparently like her brothers, her husband, too, had failed to keep her safe.

''She was George Richardson's only daughter, and she was very beautiful. Her father made the best match he could. Not necessarily the best for her, but the best financially. I don't suppose she was consulted about his choice.''

''They sold her to the highest bidder,'' Dare said bluntly, remembering their conversation about the conventions of marriage within their class and about the glaring inequities for women.

"That isn't uncommon," Ian said softly, "as you know. Especially when the family has fallen on hard times. When estates are long mortgaged and unproductive. When there are four sons who must therefore secure some sort of living."

"I don't suppose any of *them* were forced to wed heiresses not of their choosing," Dare suggested. He finished the last of his brandy and set the glass down with too much force.

"Do you need another?" Ian asked.

The earl looked up to find his younger brother watching him. He could have sworn he had caught a flash of pity in Ian's eyes, but if it had been there, it was now hidden.

"I don't think so. Not unless you believe I shall need further fortification to listen to the rest," he said, his tone even more caustic than was his norm.

Ian's lips tightened, but he didn't answer immediately. After a moment he simply went on with his story. "She was seventeen. He was a merchant named Benjamin Carstairs. A green grocer originally, I believe, although he had made a success of his shops." There was a small, telling pause before he added. "Carstairs was old enough to be her grandfather. The marriage lasted more than five years."

"And..." Dare forced himself to ask, fighting the images and trying to reconcile any part of this with Bonnet's story. Trying still to discover the truth about the woman he had left sobbing in her room last night.

"When Elizabeth was widowed, her eldest brother, who was by then head of the family, discovered that Carstairs' holdings had not been so profitable at the time of his death as he had represented them to be when the marriage was arranged. There was enough to secure a more comfortable living for the second brother. He now holds a vicarage at Soames-on-Trent. A captain's commission was purchased for the third. The youngest is still in school, I believe, his fees no doubt paid by the money that came into the family on Carstairs' death.''

''And the heir?'' Dare asked, trying without success to remember any Richardson within the peerage. Trying to remember any man despicable enough to use the money from his widowed sister's death settlements and then abandon her.

''Lives comfortably in the family home in Kent. I don't believe he has seen his sister in several years. At least not in the last two.''

''Your informant was nothing if not thorough,'' Dare said, the bitterness still in his voice.

He considered everything his brother had told him, a wealth of detail it seemed, but still there was nothing in the story that explained Bonnet. Even if her brothers had spent the settlement on themselves, why would they feel ill will toward Elizabeth? According to Ian's account, there had been nothing reprehensible in her behavior. Nothing except the actions of a dutiful daughter, obeying her father's dictates and seeing to her family's needs. Nothing that would give them reason to cast her out and force her into Bonnet's clutches.

He hadn't yet heard any satisfactory explanation for her presence there. Not in either version of what was purported to be Elizabeth Carstairs' story.

''My informant is a former schoolmate,'' Ian said. ''An inveterate gossip, I'm afraid. He always was. He has a mind like a sponge, and he never forgets the slightest detail of people's lives,'' Ian said. ''Sometimes that tendency to prattle about the affairs of others can even be useful.''

''And is that the extent of his knowledge about the Richardson family?'' Dare asked, controlling his voice so that he was pleased to think it revealed no trace of the anxiety he felt as he posed the question.

''Almost,'' Ian said. ''There *is* one more small piece of information. He included it in his letter as an afterthought. It was even written in the form of a postscript. And I wonder if I should have thought to pursue it, if he had not.''

Dare waited through the pause that followed that statement, and finally Ian's eyes came up from their concentration on the pattern made by the last of his brandy as he swirled it gently in the bottom of his glass.

''Captain Jeremy Richardson was taken prisoner by the French a little more than two years ago,'' he said. ''He was one of Wellington's exploring officers, captured behind enemy lines. He was in uniform, of course, so the French couldn't shoot him as a spy. Poor bastard,'' Ian said softly, his eyes hard as he said the word. ''It would have been far better for him if they had, I suppose. They took him to Paris, instead.''

As his brother talked, Dare's mind had been absorbing the information and filtering it through his too intimate knowledge of what the current French intelligence system did to political prisoners. Especially to English officers whom they had reason to believe possessed military knowledge that might prove valuable to Napoleon's Peninsular forces.

''My God, Ian, they have her brother,'' Dare said.

"*That's* the hold Bonnet has on her. He's forcing her—"

"You can't *know* that," Ian interjected, stopping the flow of words. "You can't *necessarily* put the two together. We don't have enough information to draw that kind of conclusion. No matter how tempting it might be to draw it," he added softly.

"*I* have enough," Dare said harshly, the unwanted image of Andre's broken body in his head.

This was the piece that had been missing. The one thing he hadn't known, which made everything else that hadn't made sense about Elizabeth slip into place. The French had planted her in Bonnet's establishment to give her access to the powerful men who frequented his tables. Under the influence of too much wine, those men talked about matters that should never have been discussed in public at all, much less in a gambling hell.

Bonnet had established himself so effectively in London circles as a rabid anti-Bonapartist, however, that few bothered to guard their tongues while in his rooms. And especially not at a private table presided over by a fellow Englishwoman, Dare thought. A woman who was being forced to do whatever the French gambler told her to do because she was trying to protect her brother from unspeakable torment, the effects of which the earl himself had recently seen firsthand.

Forced to do whatever the French gambler told her to do, Dare thought again, *even*... Even what she had admitted to him last night? Even that? As black, hot rage flooded his body, Dare wondered what he would have done faced with such a choice. His eyes lifted again to find Ian's steady hazel eyes on his face.

What would he have been willing to do this past

year, Dare asked himself, to prevent all Ian had been forced to endure? If the French held Sebastian, as they held Jeremy Richardson, what wouldn't he do to prevent his youngest brother from suffering the same fate as poor Andre?

Not treason, of course. Neither Ian nor Sebastian would ever forgive him for that. But as far as he knew, neither had Elizabeth committed treason. Considering her refusal to tell Bonnet anything about Dare's own activities, he suspected she had been playing that same very dangerous double game while in the Frenchman's establishment, feeding him and the French as little of value as she possibly could and still protect her brother.

No treason then, but what of the other things Elizabeth had done to keep her brother from torture? Would Dare give up his reputation to prevent his brothers' deaths or their agonized suffering? And there was no question in his mind that he would.

Would he also give up his honor? Would he do something against every moral precept he had ever been taught? Something that would affect his personal integrity? And he found, holding Ian's eyes, that there was no question about that, either.

And *he* was not Elizabeth Carstairs. He was not a defenseless woman, alone and without the support of her family as she had been forced to make that terrible decision. He wondered if her brothers knew what had been going on. Or had they simply assumed, as he had, that she was at Bonnet's through some fault of her own? Some moral flaw in her character.

The flaw would have been had she *not* chosen to do what the French wanted, Dare thought. She would have condemned her brother to tortures he hoped Elizabeth could only imagine. And there was no shred of honor or morality or virtue in that.

There was no honor in any of this. It was the most despicable of actions, carried out by France's London agent. Bonnet was gathering information for the French from within the heart of the English capital. And Elizabeth had been forced to be his tool, a helpless pawn caught in an unspeakable trap.

And last night...last night...

"I have to go," Dare said, that memory too strong. Too painful. He found he had already risen. Ian's eyes had followed his rise, and the compassion in them this time wasn't disguised.

"What will you do?" he asked.

"Free her," Dare said softly. "And then..."

He stopped, because what he intended after that was something he couldn't share with anyone, not even with his beloved brother.

"Free *her?*" Ian questioned.

"I'm going to rescue Jeremy Richardson from the hell he's endured for the last two years. Then..."

Again, Dare's voice faded, as he thought about last night. Eventually, he strengthened it, thanking heaven that what he had done had been no worse. And perhaps not totally irredeemable.

"And then, God help me," the Earl of Dare finished softly, speaking more to himself than to his brother, "I shall try to rescue his sister from hers."

"Are you sure he's reliable?" Dare asked.

"As long as you pay him enough," Paul Simenon assured him, "the bastard will tell you anything you want to know."

"That's exactly what I'm afraid of," the earl said.

"I don't want him to tell me what he *thinks* I want to know. I want him to tell me the truth."

"He'll tell you what he knows. He has no loyalty to any ideology but his own greed. He'd cut his grandmother's throat for a Louis."

Simenon pulled his cloak closer, hunching his shoulders against the breeze coming off the river. The stench of raw sewage that poured into the Seine rode on the night air, assailing the senses. They were waiting in one of the poorest sections of the city, near the home of the man they had come to meet—a guard at the infamous Conciergerie Prison.

"Come on, you weasel," the Frenchman muttered. "It's too damn cold out here to be waiting for your scurvy hide."

Despite their surroundings, Dare had expressed none of the impatience his agent felt. He had been in Paris for four days, and only today had he had any success in finding a trace of an imprisoned English officer named Richardson.

Although the prison rolls were haphazardly kept in criminal cases, political prisoners were more closely monitored. Their locations were always recorded, so that any official who might want to question such a prisoner could find him in the chaotic maze of the present Parisian prison system. That had not seemed to be the case with Captain Jeremy Richardson, however. And sometime in the past twenty-four hours, Dare had begun to suspect a reason for that, a reason he thought would perhaps be even more terrible than any other alternative.

His agents had connections throughout Bonaparte's regime, even within Fouché's dreaded secret police, and yet not one of them had been able to locate Jeremy

Richardson. Finally, however, in working backward through the records, they had found a faded entry for a J. Richardson. A little more than two years ago, that man had been brought to the Conciergerie. There seemed to have been no further entries for that name, however, so there was a possibility that, once there, he had not been moved.

It was then that Paul Simenon had thought to mention a guard whom Dare's agents had bribed for information in the past. And so an opportunity to talk to a man who might be able to shed some light on this mystery seemed worth a few minutes of waiting, even in a chilled discomfort by the stinking river.

"Here he comes," Simenon said, relief clear in his voice.

Dare turned toward the direction his companion was facing. A figure was moving toward them through the shadows, his gait unsteady. At first the earl thought that might have been caused by the unevenness of the cobblestones. And then, as the man lurched nearer, it became obvious he was staggering because he had been drinking.

No doubt that was also the explanation for his tardiness. Dare would never trust a drunkard to help them rescue the English soldier. He wondered, despite Paul's confidence, if he could trust the information he would give them. Another frustration. And possibly another dead end, Dare acknowledged bitterly.

He could feel his anger building. For four fruitless days, as he had worried about Elizabeth, he had searched for some sign of her brother. For some mention of his name in the endless records. For someone who remembered him.

At Ian's request, the Horse Guards had verified his

informant's information about Richardson before Dare had left London. As far as the War Office was concerned, Major Sinclair had been informed, Captain Richardson was still a prisoner.

A prisoner who had left no trace of his existence except for a dated record of his arrival in Paris, Dare thought. And unless the drunken guard approaching them could provide him with some hard facts about Richardson's subsequent incarceration, Dare didn't know anywhere else to turn.

"Bastard's drunk," Simenon said.

"Maybe it will loosen his tongue," the earl suggested quietly. He had begun to prepare himself for disappointment.

"*Gold* will loosen his tongue. Drink only makes him surly."

The last was uttered under his breath, since the guard was now so near they could smell him. Despite the stench from the river, the odor of his body was powerful. Dare fought the urge to turn his head, concentrating instead on trying to read anything in the man's face, despite the surrounding darkness.

What he could see wasn't reassuring. A broken nose and a low forehead made him appear brutish and stupid. It was hard to tell if the gray tone of his skin was the result of his heredity, his profession, or sheer filth. Given his smell, Dare favored the latter.

"They said you was wanting to ask me something," the man said belligerently, speaking to Dare's companion.

At the first word out of the guard's mouth, Simenon had lifted his nose, nostrils flared, as if seeking fresher air. Except, of course, there was none to be found around them, not between the river and the fetid miasma of the man's unwashed body.

"We need some information about a prisoner," Paul acknowledged.

"And what are you offering for that information, *monsieur?* It's very dangerous for me to be talking about what happens behind them doors. You know that."

"We're offering enough," Paul said shortly.

"And much more later on," Dare added, "*if* what you tell me now is proven to be true."

The small, black eyes, almost hidden beneath the beetled brow, moved to consider the earl as he spoke. Dare knew it wasn't his accent that had attracted their consideration. His command of the language was flawlessly idiomatic, thanks to a succession of French governesses.

"And who are *you?*" the guard asked.

"I am the man who will pay you a great deal of money," Dare said softly. "*If* you tell me the truth."

There was a silence, and then, unexpectedly, the Frenchman turned his head and spat on the ground. Dare wasn't sure whether it was the gesture of contempt it appeared to be or simply another nasty habit.

"What do you want to know, *monsieur?*" the guard asked, his tone less menacing. In fact, it was almost ingratiating, like a lumbering, poorly trained bear, begging for scraps.

"I want to know about a prisoner," Dare said.

"Someone at the Conciergerie?"

"Perhaps. That's what we want you to tell us. His name is Jeremy Richardson."

The porcine eyes considered his face, holding on it

for several seconds before he shook his head. "I can't help you then, *monsieur.*"

He turned and began to amble back along the way he'd come.

"Can't or *won't?*" Paul called after him, his voice angry.

There was no response.

"Fifty Louis," Dare said softly.

The shuffling footsteps slowed, and the guard stood still a moment, facing away from them. Finally he turned and again considered Dare's face. Thankfully, he was far enough away that they could no longer smell his breath when he answered.

"If you know enough about that prisoner to offer me fifty Louis, *monsieur,* then you know enough to make it a hundred," he said mockingly.

"Fifty now and fifty later, *if* the information you give us proves to be true."

Again, the guard considered. Then, almost reluctantly, he walked back until he was once more standing before them. This time Paul visibly recoiled, but the guard didn't seem to notice. He was probably accustomed to that reaction or he was totally uncaring of his effect on his fellow men. And of course, most of those he came in contact with would carry the same stench about them as he himself did.

"Describe him," the guard said to Dare, challengingly.

"*I* have never seen him," the earl said, holding his eyes. "And whether *I* could describe him is unimportant. What I need to know is if *you* can."

The guard's eyes widened a little, and then he laughed. "Blond hair, curling, fine as a woman's. And blue eyes. Blue as yours, *monsieur.*"

Dare's heart jolted. "And?" he forced himself to ask.

"And?" the Frenchman said, shrugging. "And nothing. He's dead."

"Dead?" Simenon echoed. "What the hell—"

"I don't believe you," the earl said, holding the small, dark eyes as if he could compel the man to tell the truth. "We have good reason to believe that is *not* the case. We believe that man is very carefully being kept alive so he can be used."

The guard's mouth pursed as if he were thinking. The expression seemed incongruous within the brutality of his visage, but Dare patiently waited out the process in silence.

"Ah, that's the story, all right," the guard said finally. "The official story, I mean. That he's still alive. I thought *you* wanted the truth, *monsieur*."

"I do," Dare said. "*But*...I also want proof that what you have said *is* the truth."

The man grinned, revealing broken and blackened teeth. "I can't show you his corpse, *monsieur*. It'll be fair rotted by now, even with the lime we throw into the pits."

Implying...? "Do you mean he's been dead a long time?"

The brute laughed again, his lips lifting unpleasantly away from the dark stubs that lined his gums. "Oh, they tried to keep him alive, right enough. We was all instructed to look out for him special. Treat him like we was his mother, you see. But it was too late. He was dead of the fever within a week of when they brought him. What with his wound and all, they should have known that would happen. Prison's no place for a sick man. Not for that one, anyway. Fair, pale young thing. Almost pretty. He might not have lasted long anyway." Again the lips pulled upward in that parody of a smile.

"And when was this? When they brought him to Paris?" the earl asked, ignoring the rest.

"Two years ago. A little more maybe. I remember my youngest had just been born. Another girl," the guard said. This, too, was accompanied by an expulsion of spittle into the dirt near Paul's feet. Simenon moved back agilely, provoking another glimpse of the guard's blackened teeth. "I took his locket for my wife, to sweeten her after the birth. Clutched in his fist when he died, the chain treaded through his fingers. Had a hard time untangling it, I can tell you. He was already gone stiff when we found him."

"Locket?" Dare asked too sharply, regretting instantly that he had displayed his interest so openly.

The man shrugged. "It wasn't gold. Piece of trumpery, but my wife didn't care. There was a little picture—his mother, I'd guess—inside it."

"Do you still have that?"

"The locket? I suppose—"

"The picture," Dare said.

"What's it worth to you?" the man said shrewdly.

"A great deal, if what you are telling me is the truth."

"It's the truth, *monsieur*. But it'll be worth my life if they ever find out I've told you. That's why his name was never stricken. They didn't want anyone to know he's dead. We was told never to change that entry."

"They won't find out you talked to us," Dare assured. "But I need that picture. Failing that, I need the locket."

"You'll pay me for it? Extra I mean?"

"Another fifty for both," Dare offered, and watched the man's eyes widen.

"She won't like it. Not losing the bauble, but I can get her something else. We get to keep whatever's on the bodies when we carry them out."

"What else was on his?" Dare asked softly.

"Not a thing," the guard said. "I thought it was odd at the time. That's why I worked so hard at getting the locket loose—because there was nothing else. Of course, they could have been stolen before, but usually there's something, especially if it's something worthless. Letters. A journal. A lot of soldiers keep those, but there was nothing like that on that one." He paused a moment, before he added musingly, "It was as if somebody else had got to him before we did."

Somebody had, Dare thought. Another kind of scavenger, far crueler and far more predatory than the one standing before him.

Chapter Twelve

Dare usually approached homecoming with eagerness. Lately, that customary anticipation had been mixed with relief if he was coming back from France. Each mission there increased the odds that what he was doing would be discovered, not only intensifying the danger, but bringing nearer the day when his usefulness to his country's war effort would end.

Given Bonnet's interest in his activities, that day might already have arrived, he acknowledged. Which should, of course, have made each homecoming more precious. He had been dreading this one, however, since his meeting with the prison guard who had buried Jeremy Richardson's body.

"Welcome home, my lord," his butler intoned, reaching out to take his hat, gloves and cane as soon as the earl stepped through the door of his London town house.

"Thank you, Watson," Dare said. "Would you ask Mrs. Carstairs to come to me in the library, please?"

"Very good, my lord."

His majordomo's face registered neither surprise nor distress. At least she's still here, Dare thought, drawing the breath he had missed as he waited for Watson's reaction. He had fully expected Elizabeth to try to leave after what had occurred between them the night before he received Ian's message.

That had been more than a week ago, however, and she was still here. Apparently Ned's vigilance had been successful. And Dare hadn't been completely sure when he left for France that his valet wasn't secretly planning to help Elizabeth leave instead.

All the way home Dare had tried to find a reason to postpone this conversation. However, he could think of no excuse not to end, as quickly as possible, the nightmare which Elizabeth had been living for the last two years. What he had to tell her was not a revelation he could anticipate with any possible degree of pleasure, of course, but the sooner he made it, the sooner they could put everything that had happened behind them.

It would be like lancing a long-festering boil and letting the poisons out, he reasoned, as he walked across the library. A painful operation, but a necessary one. Only when he had told her, he knew, could the healing begin. He put his hands on the mantel and looked down into the cheerful flames as he waited.

"I didn't know you had returned, my lord," Elizabeth said.

At the sound of her voice, as calm and controlled as it had always been, he turned and found her again standing on the library stair. Apparently, she had been there all along, silently watching him.

She had a feather duster in one hand, and one of the ancient, leather-bound volumes in the other. After their eyes had met and held a few seconds, she turned and pushed the book back into place on the shelves, as if his arrival had been only the most ordinary interruption of a familiar task.

And undoubtedly it was, Dare realized, his eyes moving over rows of neatly arranged books. Quite a contrast to the last time he had noticed the condition of the shelves in this room. Elizabeth had taken their conversation to heart and was making progress in banishing the chaos that had reigned here for years.

And as for the chaos that reigned between them…

"I have only arrived," Dare said. "As a matter of fact, I dispatched Watson to ask you to meet me, so I suppose I should consider it fortuitous that you are already here."

Her hand hesitated in midair, the volume once more in its proper place, and then she let her arm fall as she turned to look down on him again. Her face was perfectly composed, without emotion, almost like the face of a statue or a painting. There seemed to be no spark of the animation he was accustomed to seeing in her eyes. An animation he had cherished.

"You wanted to see *me*, my lord?" she asked, surprise injected into her voice, as if she could think of no reason for the need of any conversation between the two of them.

"I have news of your brother," Dare said.

Whatever reaction he had expected, it wasn't the one that occurred. Elizabeth dropped the duster, and it clattered off the stair and onto the floor. After a second or two, she reached out blindly for the shelf beside her, fumbling for its solidity as if she groped in some alien darkness. And then, touching its wood, holding on to it for support, she sank down on the top of the stair, her eyes fastened on his face.

She hadn't asked which brother. She didn't pretend

not to know exactly what he meant. She simply waited, eyes too wide in the pale, lovely oval of her face.

A kindness, he told himself again, watching the color drain from her cheeks. She was terrified, but then this was news she had dreaded for more than two years. And it was *not* a kindness to delay it, he reminded himself. Not once he had begun.

"Jeremy is dead," he said. "He succumbed to a fever, which was either the result of his wound or of the conditions under which he was kept."

"Dead?" She repeated the word as if she had never heard it before. Or as if she could not accept that something like death should befall her brother. "Are you certain, my lord?" she asked after a moment, visibly struggling to regather the implacable courage that had seen her through those years.

"I spoke to two men who…saw his body."

At the last second, he amended the raw truth. It would serve no purpose to tell her of the meaningless indignities to which her brother's corpse had been subjected. Jeremy Richardson had been aware of none of them. There was no reason why Elizabeth ever should have to be, either.

"How can you be certain it was Jeremy's body?" she asked.

He had known she would demand proof. Just as he had. And it was for this that Dare had waited the extra day in Paris. Waited for the guard to bring him the locket and the miniature it had contained.

Not proof absolute, perhaps, but with the lack of any other record for Jeremy Richardson during the supposed two years of his long imprisonment—no record of questionings by the officials or of transfer or medical treatments—Dare was himself convinced the man had been telling the truth.

He reached into the small pocket of his waistcoat and pulled from it the slender chain and the locket it held. He walked across the room, his footsteps making no sound on the thick oriental carpets, despite the heavy silence in the room. He held his hand up to her, the locket dangling from his fingers.

"Do you recognized this?" he asked.

He knew by her face that she did, although her eyes were on the small golden heart that swung from his fingertips. After a moment, she touched it, stopping its motion. And then she gathered both the chain and the locket, enclosing them in hers.

"There's a portrait inside," he said.

The guard had thought it was Richardson's mother, but Dare had known as soon as he saw it that his conjecture was wrong. The portrait was of Elizabeth, and if he had had any doubt of that, the sudden trembling of her fingers as she pressed the minute latch would have removed it. As would the smile that touched her lips as she looked down on the miniature her brother had worn next to his heart.

"Your picture," Dare said softly.

Her eyes came up from the portrait to meet his. Tear-washed, anguished, full of emotion she could no longer deny or control, Dare thought them more beautiful than they had ever been before. Seeing what was in them, answering tears burned in his.

He refused to let them form. This was her grief, and as yet he had no right to share it. Whatever rights he might once have had as far as Elizabeth was concerned, he had destroyed the night before he left this house.

"We were nearest in age," she said, looking down once more at the locket, the small, remembering smile playing over her lips again, despite the tears. "We were born only ten months apart. So close we were almost twins. All our lives…"

The words faded, as did the smile. Her chin quivered, and she swallowed, seeking to reimpose the familiar control.

"I am so sorry," Dare said.

She looked up again. "I said too much that night on the stairs. I was afraid I had made you curious."

"I was curious from the first time I saw you," Dare said truthfully. "I couldn't understand…" He hesitated.

"Why I was with Bonnet," she finished for him.

"Now I know," he said.

Her eyes rested on his face, and then her fingers closed around the locket. She brought the hand that held it to rest between her breasts and took a deep, shuddering breath.

"Finally, it's over," she said. "It seemed…" Again the words faltered, but she strengthened her voice and went on. "At times, it seemed as if it would never end. I knew the only way it would was if Jeremy were no longer their prisoner. If the war were over. Or if—"

If he died. Dare understood the reality of those unspoken words. She had lived for two years believing the only way she could be free of Bonnet's control was if the war ended or if her brother died. And at the same time, in order to keep him free from torture, she was forced to provide information to the French that could only have the effect of prolonging Napoleon's hold on Europe. Prolonging her brother's imprisonment. And her own.

"I wish you had confided in me," Dare said.

"Why should I have involved you in my problems? And even if I had, could you have gotten my brother out of that prison? Or out of France? Could you have prevented his death, my lord, if I had told you the truth?"

Could you have prevented his death…? It was only with her question that Dare realized she didn't understand. Not the whole of it. Not the deception. Not the depth of their cruelty.

Could you have prevented his death? Which meant she believed her brother was newly dead. That he had died *after* she had come to Dare's house.

That misunderstanding was his fault, Dare realized. His failure. He hadn't intended to keep the information from her. She had a right to know the truth about what the French had done. Dare had intended to tell her the whole, if for no other reason than to keep her from ever returning to Bonnet. In trying to find the right words, the kindest words, however, Dare knew now he had not said enough.

Or perhaps he had, he realized. What possible purpose could it serve for Elizabeth to know that Jeremy Richardson had been dead almost the entire time she had lived with Bonnet? Or to know that it was even possible he had died before she had come under the gambler's control. *Bonnet's well-used whore* echoed inside his heart.

"I promise you I should have done everything in my power to rescue him," Dare said simply.

That was the truth. It was why he had gone to France. To rescue Jeremy Richardson from prison. To smuggle him out of the country. To restore him to his family. And, most important, to free Richardson's sister from her own terrible imprisonment.

Dare had been two years too late to accomplish anything but the last. For her, two long years of an unimaginable, and ultimately meaningless, sacrifice were ended.

Elizabeth smiled at him, and he found himself wondering if she doubted his ability to effect such a rescue, despite what she must suspect about his involvement in espionage against the French. And then he realized that this slightly tremulous smile was almost the same one she had given him on the stairs. Without artifice or artfulness.

"Thank you, my lord."

"I'm sorry I was too late," Dare said softly. A kindness, he told himself again. Sometimes lies could be.

She nodded, wiping at the tears on her cheeks like a child, using the heels of both hands at the same time.

"I know that this isn't the time…" Dare began, and then he hesitated, unsure how to broach the subject.

"Not the right time to ask what I intend to do now," she said. The smile was still in place, but her eyes were as haunted as they had been from the first.

"I hope you know that you are welcome to stay here as long as you wish," Dare said quickly. "You don't have to decide anything. Not until you're ready. This has been a shock, and it's better not to make decisions under such circumstances."

"Decisions," she repeated softly. He couldn't read her tone. "I suppose I *shall* have to make…decisions."

"There's no hurry."

"And I may live here? In your house?"

"Of course," he said.

"Your housekeeper has already left you, my lord," she challenged, "because I am here."

"There are other housekeepers."

She smiled at him again, and this one was mocking. "And you shall simply hire a succession of them until one decides she won't mind living under the same roof as your whore."

"Don't," he said, his own pain revealed in the single word.

The mocking smile faded, perhaps because she had recognized that pain. Her eyes were, however, as cold as when he had first looked up and found her watching him.

"It's what they all think," she said.

"I don't care what they think."

Her lips moved, tightening almost imperceptibly. "You will," she said.

"No," he denied.

"Ned. Your brothers."

He hesitated, because she was right about that. They had had reservations about the wisdom of what he was doing, and they had cared enough about him to express them. Although he had openly rejected those warnings, he couldn't deny that they had been made. Or at least he hadn't denied it quickly enough.

"I'm right, aren't I?" she asked, still mocking.

"They didn't understand. Neither did I."

"They understood. And so do you. You understood everything that was important the night before you left."

"Don't," he said again, more softly this time.

"You understood exactly what I am. As they do. Nothing has changed."

"Except I know why."

"Why?" she repeated. "And the *why* of what I have done makes a difference to you?"

"Of course," he said. "You had no choice."

She took another breath, visible but no longer shuddering. The movement lifted the hand that enclosed the locket she held against her breasts.

"Of course I had a choice," she said.

"No," he said. "You could have done nothing else."

"You are truly a remarkable man if you believe that, my Lord Dare. But I assure you, a hundred women of your acquaintance would have made another choice. And would condemn mine."

"That doesn't matter," he said again.

"I think it does," she said softly. "Even to you. And I promise it shall always matter to them. To everyone of your acquaintance. To your brothers. To poor Ned. He's afraid of me, you know."

"Afraid?" Dare repeated, puzzled by the word, unable to fit it into the context of this.

"You're all Ned has. And he isn't sure he's willing to share you with anyone else. At least not with someone who might be able to engage your emotions."

There was a long silence.

"I have always believed Ned to be astute," Dare said.

Again their eyes held, without words, because none were necessary.

"Thank you," she said finally. "Whatever else you believe about me, please believe I will always treasure that."

She rose from the library stair, control back in place. She put her fingers on the shelf beside her and using it for balance, stepped down. Dare walked across as he had before and offered his hand. She regarded it a moment, before she looked up at him.

"Did they give you any other proof?" she asked. "Any other identifying mark on my brother's body?"

The second time he had met with the guard, the man had remembered to tell him. Despite his suspicions about the meaning of what he had been told, Dare had chosen not to bring it up. Perhaps this would serve, however, to make her brother's death final. The removal of doubt, if she had any, that the nightmare was over.

"The body they identified as your brother's was missing the smallest finger of its right hand," Dare said.

"They sent it to me," she said. "In a velvet box. To prove they would really do to him what they had threatened."

It was what Dare had imagined when he had heard the guard's story. To listen to her verify it, calmly, almost dispassionately, however, somehow made the horror far more real. And what she had suffered to keep her brother safe more poignant.

"Marry me," Dare said softly.

Her eyes, still on his, dilated with shock.

"Marry me," he repeated, his voice stronger because he knew now, without any doubts, this was what he wanted. To protect her. To shelter her from slander. To keep her safe from any other pain for the rest of her life. For the rest of his.

"No," she said.

"I will demand nothing of you," he promised. "Nothing you choose not to give." He really believed that he was strong enough for that. And that he loved her enough.

"No," she said again. And then slowly she examined his face, her gaze tracing over each individual feature as if she had never seen them before. "And you *are* a remarkable man," she said when her eyes had come back to his.

Still holding his hand, she stepped down the remaining steps of the stair. When she began to pull her fingers away from his, he tightened his hold, and her eyes came back to his face.

"Where will you go?" he asked.

"Home," she said, smiling at him.

"To Kent."

"If my brother will have me." There was no fear in her face, only acceptance. "We live with the consequences of our choices, my lord. All of them."

"And if he won't?" Dare asked, holding her fingers too tightly in his.

"That isn't your concern."

"If I choose to make it my concern?"

"I hope you will not. For two years, I have lived under someone else's control. I have no wish to live under yours."

The dismissal of his proposal was incredibly hurtful. It shattered all the romantic dreams he had been formulating, envisioning how he would take care of her. It had been rejection, unequivocal and without apology, of an offer no one would have expected him to make. Stunned and angered by the coldness of it, Dare freed her fingers and stepped back. He bowed slightly, inclining his upper body almost mockingly.

When he raised his head, her eyes were on his face, and he wondered how much of what he was feeling was exposed there. At whatever his face revealed, her eyes filled again with tears, and she put her fingers gently on his cheek, running her thumb across the full-ness of his bottom lip.

"Don't," she whispered.

And then she turned away and, back straight, head held high, she left him alone.

If he had ever doubted how well Ned Harper knew him, he couldn't after today, Dare thought. His valet hadn't said a word as he had helped him remove his traveling clothes. There had been none of the usual questions about the success or the failure of the mission into France. Perhaps Harper had already read all the answers in his face.

"Thank you, Ned. That will do, I think," he said at last.

The familiar rituals had been completed. His valet had spent more than the normal amount of time fussing with the garments he'd removed, brushing imaginary specks of dust off the lapels of the navy superfine and rubbing his sleeve over the toe of one of the Hessians.

The earl, preoccupied with his own thoughts, finally recognized the delaying tactic. And realized he had prematurely congratulated himself for escaping Ned's questions.

"You didn't succeed then," Harper said.

Was what had happened in France success? Dare wondered. He had gone there prepared to use every one of the formidable resources at his command, including his own skills, his own life if necessary, in order to mount a rescue. And perhaps he had managed one of sorts, but the results had not been what he had hoped. Even if he had not fully known then what his hopes were. Or how strongly they would be tied to what happened in France.

"Her brother was dead," he said simply.

"You were too late then," Ned said.

"They lied to her. All along it had been a lie."

"They didn't have him?"

"He died within a few days of being brought to Paris."

"Then how…"

"I don't know. The guard wasn't sure how it could have been managed. Letters the bastards found on the body, perhaps. Maybe they took them and used them to forge his hand. Whatever they did, she believed she was keeping her brother alive. That her actions here in London had a direct result on his treatment."

"And all along he was dead," Ned said softly, his voice almost pitying. "All that time with Bonnet, and her brother was already dead."

Dare nodded, and finally he looked up from the stickpin he had been twisting mindlessly between his fingers.

"What are you going to do?" Ned asked.

"About Bonnet? Put an end to his activities, of course. I can only guess at the amount of information he has relayed to the French over the last few years. He has to be stopped."

"I didn't mean about the gambler," Harper said. "I knew you'd stop him. I mean about her. What are you going to do about her?"

"She's going back to her family," Dare said, still attempting to hide what he felt, even from someone who knew him as well as Ned. Just as he would have hidden it from Ian. From anyone. As he would hide it the rest of his life.

"And you're going to let her go?"

"I have no right to stop her."

"Right? Are we talking *rights,* my lord?" Ned asked softly. "Given what those bastards have done to her?"

"I have asked her to stay," Dare said, stung by the accusation in Harper's tone.

"And she refused you?"

In every way, Dare thought bitterly. "She values her freedom. After the last two years, I can't fault her for that."

"So you'll do nothing to stop her leaving?"

"What would you have me do, Ned?" the earl asked. "Force her to stay? Threaten her?" he suggested, his voice rising. "I am not Bonnet."

"She doesn't want to go. Whatever she says, she doesn't want to leave."

"She *is* leaving. And there is nothing you or I can do about it. She is a free agent. After two years, she is finally free to make her own choices. I can't stop her."

"And you're not worried about what Bonnet might do?"

"His hold is broken. He can't do anything."

"He can do whatever he damn well pleases if there's no one to stop him," Ned warned.

"I'll have her escorted to her brother's estate. After that, she's his responsibility."

"She turned you down," Harper guessed shrewdly. "That's why you're letting her go. You asked her to stay, and she turned you down and it made you fair furious. The first woman you've really wanted who hasn't fallen at your feet."

"I asked her to marry me," Dare said coldly. His

tone was full of the arrogance he employed in the role he played as the Regent's beloved crony.

"Marry you?" Ned repeated, the repetition incredulous. "You know what she is. You can't make a woman like that your countess."

Dare laughed. "Apparently not," he said, turning away and walking over to the window, his back to Harper. "You may go, Ned," he said tiredly. "There's nothing else for you to do here."

"Nothing but tell you what a bloody fool you are."

"Believe me..." the Earl of Dare said softly, looking down once more on the sweep of lawn below his bedroom windows. "Believe me, Ned, no one can possibly be aware of what a bloody fool I am better than I."

Chapter Thirteen

Marry me, the Earl of Dare had said, and her heart had hesitated, confronted with something she had not even had the courage to dream of, at least not openly. Not consciously. She had fantasized about Dare making another kind of offer, wondering what she would say to that temptation. And even then, she had recognized that her fantasy was as insubstantial as the moonlight which had created it.

He had spoken words this afternoon she had never hoped to hear him say. And when he had, she had rejected them. And rejected him. Coldly and unemotionally.

She had known from his face how much that had hurt. But she also knew, because she had endured some taste of it already, what such a marriage would do to the man he was. To the romantic he was. Despite her unhappiness, her lips tilted at that thought.

He *was* a romantic. He believed that by putting their names in a church registry somewhere he could protect her from society's judgment. And he couldn't, of course, not from the reality of what she had done. Too many men in his circle had seen her at Bonnet's. She could never go out on Dare's arm without provoking outrage within the ton.

He would be forced to "overhear" a hundred crude and suggestive comments. Or worse, to face the deliberate snubs their presence at any function would provoke. Backs would be turned and eyes averted, as if her past might somehow contaminate that select circle, many of whom had committed sins far worse than hers. Theirs were hidden and therefore unexposed to the cruelty Dare would have to face.

She might have borne all that to be his wife. He, however, would never be able to endure it, not without striking back in the only way a man like Dare could strike back—on the field of honor. Not because of his own pride, but because he wouldn't be able to stand the slurs on her behalf. She understood that, because now she understood him.

She hadn't at first. Not when Bonnet had sent her here. Now she knew him, and so she could never marry him. She could never open him up to that kind of torment—an agony of the spirit as terrible as the agony of the body she had given herself to prevent her brother from suffering. It was better to make the break between them now, to make it quickly, brutally even, than to put Dare through that.

Realist that she was, Elizabeth believed that in time he would forget her. The sooner she left him alone to do so, the better it would be, she thought, letting the jonquil silk of the drapery fall to cover the now familiar view of the grounds from the window of her chamber.

She wished she could leave and never have to see him again. If she did, if he asked her again, she was afraid her will might not be strong enough, despite her resolve, not to reach out and grasp the one thing she wanted more than she wanted life itself.

Tonight, she thought. She would leave this house tonight, and in time the Earl of Dare would marry someone suitable. Whatever he claimed about his brothers and his title, he would eventually be forced to. That was the way the world worked. Their world, at least.

But she would need someone to help her with the arrangements for her departure. She doubted Watson would order up the earl's coach on her say-so. And she had no money. Certainly not enough to reach Kent if she did choose to appeal to her brother for shelter.

Someone to help her, she thought again. Maggie might, but she was only a child, with as little influence in the household as Elizabeth herself had. Not Watson, of course. No matter how strongly she appealed to him, he would consult with his master before doing anything. Then suddenly, almost like an answer to prayer, she knew the one person in this household who would be even more eager to help her leave it than she could be to go.

"Dare's coach," Elizabeth said. "Or enough money to see me to my brother's."

Ned Harper's eyes considered her face, and she held her breath, wondering how much he knew. As close as he was to the earl, he probably knew everything. After all, Harper had known her for what she was from the first.

"Why?" he asked.

Looking into those shrewd, dark eyes, she realized that only the truth would serve. "Because I love him," she said.

Nothing of the depth of that love or of its pain was revealed in her face or in her voice. She had had two long years to perfect the art of concealment.

"Then why are you leaving?" he asked.

"To protect him."

Dare's valet laughed, and she was surprised to realize his laughter was amused rather than mocking. "And has the earl asked for your protection?"

"He has asked for my *hand*," she said sharply, trying to goad him into helping her. "Is that what you want for him, Ned? To be married to a whore?"

The word was bitter in her mouth. She could see the flinch of disgust in his face when she said it, but she imagined he had used the term in reference to her, in thought if not in speech.

"I want him to be happy," Ned said.

"I can't give him happiness. If I could…" she began, and knew that was a misstep. No half measures would suffice. No equivocation. "I can't make him happy," she said simply. "We both know that."

"He's a man, not a child. He knows what he wants. He doesn't need you to protect him."

"Will you help me leave this house or not?" she demanded. Arguing was pointless. She knew better than Harper what Dare felt. Knew and had still rejected it.

"He knows why you did what you did," he said rather than answering.

"The why of it doesn't matter," she said softly.

"It does to him. Give him credit for that, at least. He deserves that much of your trust."

"This isn't about *trust*."

"Of course it is. That's all it *is* about. You think he'll take you to bed and imagine Bonnet topping you.

And be sickened by it.'' Then he added the last, his voice almost compassionate. ''And you're afraid eventually he'll be sickened by you, as well.''

The nausea rose in her throat at the accuracy of the image he had drawn. That was exactly what she feared, she realized. A fear that had lived only in the darkest, deepest pit of her soul until Harper had given it life. It was something she had not had the courage to confess, not even to herself, certainly not in the midst of her self-righteous prattle about protecting Dare.

''You don't trust *him* not to be sickened by what you did,'' Ned said. ''Because *you* are.''

''He deserves better than what I am,'' she said softly.

''Maybe he does,'' Ned agreed. ''But *you're* what he wants.''

''Help me leave,'' she begged again, his words battering at her resolve. Both the truth and the temptation of them.

''He doesn't blame you for what happened. They tricked you, and they lied to you. You had no way of knowing what they were up to. He knows that. If there is any man on this earth who would be capable of forgetting the other…'' Harper shrugged, but his eyes held on her face.

''What do you mean?'' Elizabeth asked, her mind going over his words, trying to make sense of them. Trying to understand what he was talking about.

''He may be strong enough to put Bonnet out of his mind. And out of your bed, as well.''

''Not that,'' Elizabeth said. ''Who tricked me? The French? About my brother?''

The questions were rapid, her voice rising with each

one. She realized by what was happening in his face that Harper had unintentionally revealed something he thought she already knew. Except she didn't know. Not anything about tricks or lies.

"Tricked you to work for them by holding your brother," Ned said. There was a flush of color over his cheekbones.

"But that wasn't a lie, Ned. How did they lie to me?" she asked, recognizing the evasion.

Apparently he couldn't think of anything to tell her. The color across his cheeks deepened to crimson. *They tricked you and they lied to you. They tricked you....*

"Tricked me how?" she asked again, her voice very low and again controlled. "If you don't tell me, Ned, I'll ask him."

"There's nothing to tell you," Harper said.

"That was Jeremy's finger," she said with conviction. "I know that."

"Finger?" Ned repeated, his bewilderment obvious.

"They cut off my brother's finger to prove to me he was their prisoner. And it was *his* finger. He had broken it when he was a boy and there was a distinctive crook and a scar. So I know the French took him prisoner. And my oldest brother was notified by the Horse Guards. There was no mistake," she said, trying to think what Ned could have meant. Trying to fathom what she hadn't been told.

Harper said nothing.

"They gave me notes from him," she continued, watching him. There had been the smallest movement of his pupils, the minutest widening when she said *notes*. "Those were in my brother's hand, so I would know that he was still alive…"

Still alive. Still alive. For some reason the words

seemed to echo in her head. And were replaced by Dare's. *He succumbed to a fever, which was either the result of his wound or of the conditions under which he was kept.* The result of his wound? After two years? A long debilitating illness, stemming from his original injury?

If so, why hadn't Jeremy mentioned it? Why hadn't his notes to her contained any mention of illness? He had even commented a few times on his continued good health and had thanked her for keeping him safe.

She had thought those phrases strange. It would have been far more like Jeremy to order her to let the French kill him and be damned than to thank her for what she was doing. She could only assume from them that he hadn't really *known* what she was doing. But now...

"Those notes weren't from my brother," she guessed, and knew from Ned's face that she was right. And when she knew that, the rest of it fell into place. "They forged the notes, making them look as much like his hand as they could. He said his handwriting had been affected by the injury to his arm. But Jeremy was already dead. He had died of his wound, and they made me believe he was alive. That's what you meant. That was the trick," she said. "And the lie."

She articulated the thoughts as they came into her head, giving voice to the horrified realizations which were forming in her mind. And as they did, the memories of the things she had been forced to do during the past two years paraded through her consciousness, the images vivid. And hated.

They had tricked her. And they had lied. They made her believe that what she was doing in Bonnet's hell was keeping her brother alive, while all the time...all the time...

"He was already dead," she whispered again. And again saw the truth reflected in the dark, pitying eyes of the Earl of Dare's valet. "Dare knows?" she asked.

Harper took a breath before he nodded. "He knows the bastards. Better than any man you're like to meet he knows what Fouché and his ilk are capable of."

What they are capable of, she echoed mentally. A cruel and inhuman depravity she could barely conceive, even though she had been its victim.

Slowly, she nodded. Dare had never intended her to find out the truth. Perhaps he understood that the only thing which had made her life bearable these last two years was the thought that what she was doing protected her brother. And kept him safe.

Safe in a grave, she thought bitterly. She had given her body and her soul to Henri Bonnet to protect a man who was already dead. She had betrayed her country for a corpse, rotted long ago in some unmarked plot of French soil. And she had destroyed her own life. Any chance for happiness. Any chance—

"He knows it all, lass," Ned Harper said again.

She looked up, her vision blurred with hot tears she refused to let fall. She wasn't even sure for which of them she was crying.

"You don't need to run away," he said. "Let the earl see to it. Let him take care of everything. Let him take care of you."

She held Ned's eyes a long time, surprised to find that her heart was still beating and her lungs still expanding to accept the air. Even in the face of this depravity, the familiar, unthinking processes of living went inexorably on. And it seemed to her there was something wrong about the fact that they did.

The Earl of Dare returned to his town house surprisingly early that evening. His meeting with his contact at the Horse Guards had been clandestine and hastily arranged after his return from France this afternoon. Though considering all he thought they needed to discuss, it had occupied far less time than he had anticipated when he'd left home.

It seemed that his usefulness to the English cause was at an end. If the French had discovered his activities, his contact said, then his ability to enter and leave France unnoticed would be compromised. He could still maintain his network of agents and collect information for the War Office, but as far as any personal participation was concerned, he had been told in no uncertain terms that it was a risk England could not afford.

Bonaparte and Fouché would not take kindly to what he had done. Every trip into France now carried the threat of capture and imprisonment. Dare knew far too much about the workings of British intelligence to be allowed to fall into enemy hands.

"Torture, you know," the general had said, his voice lowered as if he couldn't bring himself to admit civilized people resorted to such barbarisms. *"And there is not a man alive who can resist that kind of questioning, my lord. Not even you."*

He would, however, take care of Bonnet before he retired from the field, Dare decided grimly. He had tried to put the bastard and what he had done to Elizabeth from his mind. He had known that if he didn't, he would have gone straight to Bonnet's and killed the gambler with his bare hands. He had known he couldn't commit murder, as much as he wanted to, if he were to be of any further use to the War Office or any help to Elizabeth.

He walked over to his dressing table, his fingers beginning to loosen his cravat. He had already removed his coat, wondering idly about Ned. It wasn't like Harper not to wait up for him. Especially since his valet had known with whom he was meeting.

Of course, he was perfectly capable of undressing himself, the earl thought in amusement, unfastening the buttons of his waistcoat. He shrugged out of it and tossed it at the high bed. It slipped off the satin coverlet and fell to the floor, but Dare ignored it. He walked across to the tall windows and, lifting the edge of the drapery, he looked down on the moonlit patch of lawn where he had danced with Elizabeth. A lifetime ago.

He had accomplished what he had set out to do that night. He had freed her from the captivity in which she had lived these past two years, but in doing so, he had imprisoned himself in a far different kind of bondage. One that would never end.

"I *could* hum, my lord," Elizabeth said from behind him, "but perhaps you would prefer the silence."

He turned, and found her standing in the shadows. She was holding his waistcoat, which she had neatly folded. She laid it across the foot of his bed before her eyes came back to his.

He wondered if she had been in the room all along, waiting for him, or if, in his abstraction, he had simply failed to hear the door. And then, when he noticed what she was wearing, those questions faded, leaving only one thought in his head. One question. Which was not the one to which he gave voice.

"Have you come to dance?" he asked, his throat thick with the realization of how much he loved her.

"I suppose that's up to you, my lord," Elizabeth said. "Do you want to dance?" she asked.

"No," he said truthfully.

She smiled at him. Free of artifice and mockery, it was the one he had come to cherish for its rarity.

"Nor do I," she said. "Not tonight."

"Should I assume the presumption of my gift has been forgiven?"

She hesitated a moment, looking down on the rose-and-cream gown. Her fingers touched the bottom of the lace overtunic, and then she looked up to smile at him again. "You should assume only that this is the most beautiful dress I have ever owned, my lord. And I wanted to wear it for you."

There was something underlying her tone. Some emotion he couldn't read. Something...

"And I wanted to thank you again for giving it to me," she continued. She turned, making a slow pirouette, and the narrow skirt flared around her ankles.

Which were bare, Dare realized, as were her feet. Just as it had when he had seen her from his window, dancing through the moonlight, Dare's heart began to hammer in his chest.

"Is that why you're here? To thank me for the dress?" he asked, and held his breath.

The graceful circle stopped, the silk returning to its perfect drape. Her eyes met his. "I have come to say goodbye," she said.

Again, Dare was aware of an undercurrent beneath the calm surface of that commonplace. "You are go-

ing to your brother's?'' he asked, trying to read her
expression and hampered by the shadows in which she
stood. He wondered for the first time if that were deliberate.

"If he'll have me," she said.

It was the same caveat she had made before. Something had changed, however. Dare wasn't sure how he
knew that, but he did. Something had happened. *I've
come to say goodbye.* Perhaps…

"And if he won't, will you come back to me?" he
asked.

There was the smallest movement of her mouth. Her
smile this time was almost secretive, as if she were
amused by the naiveté of his question. "No, my lord,"
she said softly. And then she held out her hand, her
eyes still on his.

He walked across the distance that separated them,
and took her fingers. In contrast to the first time he
had touched her, that night at Bonnet's, it was his hand
that trembled.

"Thank you for your many kindnesses, my lord,"
she said. "They have been far too numerous to enu-
merate, but I shall never forget them. Or forget
you…" Her voice broke on the last, her eyes touched
with moisture.

"Not kindness," he said softly.

"I know," she whispered.

"I love you," Dare said, watching her eyes fill with
tears.

She drew a breath, banishing the small quaver he
had heard in her voice. "I will never forget that either,
my lord. A gift more rare than even this," she said
smiling. The fingers of the hand he did not hold
touched the silk of her gown.

At the finality of her tone, despair gathered like a cold, dark void in the center of his body. *I have come to say goodbye.*

"And I will never forget that once you asked me to marry you," she said. "Even knowing what I have done."

He shook his head, a small negative motion as his fingers tightened over hers. "*You* have done nothing. And as for the rest...it truly doesn't matter."

"I *do* believe you think that, my lord. I assure you, however, that it will matter a great deal to everyone else. And therefore, eventually it will matter to you."

"No," he said simply.

She shook her head, smiling at him again. "I haven't come to argue with you. At least not about that."

She said nothing else for a long moment, and the silence deepened. He felt her fingers begin to tremble within his.

"You have come only to say goodbye?" he asked.

"I have come..." she began and then she hesitated, her eyes searching his face, tracing over it as they had done once before. "I have come to make you an offer, my lord."

"An offer," Dare repeated carefully, his chest tight, aching with love and pain.

"I believe that you desire me," she said.

Dare's brain seemed incapable of formulating an answer, afraid that whatever answer he made would be wrong. So afraid.

"Or am I wrong?" she asked finally when he didn't speak.

"No," he said softly, "you aren't wrong."

"In spite of Bonnet?"

"I love you," he said the words again. If she didn't understand that they alone answered every question she had asked, then there was no point in trying to answer any of them.

"Then…will you make love to me?" she whispered.

Why not be my whore as well? It was only what he had asked her before. Phrased differently, of course. Dressed in a language intended to make this acceptable to both of them.

"No," he said, releasing her hand. At the same time, he stepped back, putting distance between them. A necessary distance, for he was fighting against the clamor of his heart. And against the hot, painful ache of his body.

Her hand fell, and then she put the two of them together under her breasts, one within the other. Their vibration was visible even in the darkness.

"I will marry you, Elizabeth, but I won't make you my whore."

"Because I was his," she said, and it was not a question.

"No," Dare denied, letting her hear the surety, despite his nausea at the thought of the Frenchman. "Whatever Bonnet did has nothing to do with this. Nothing to do with us."

She laughed. Mocking and bitter, the sound jarred in the pleasant darkness. "It has *everything* to do with this."

For the first time, whatever had underlain every statement she had made tonight was obvious. And at last he recognized it for what it was.

"You know," he said.

"My brother was dead. All that time…" Her voice failed, the words choked off by hatred.

"It changes nothing," Dare said.

"It changes *everything*," she said fiercely.

"If you let it, this will destroy you," he warned.

"I am already destroyed."

"No," Dare said.

And then after a long time, she spoke, her voice again soft, the anger controlled.

"When I was a girl, I used to dream of the man I would marry. I dreamed about dancing with him. Kissing him. I was too innocent, I suppose, to have imagined anything else, but I know that if he had been someone like you…" She paused, her eyes on his. "My father sold me to a man old enough to be *his* father. For five years, I belonged to that old man in what our world considered a respectable marriage. And when I was finally free of that, I was forced to give my body to Bonnet. To keep my dead brother safe. And all of it was a lie. Everything in my life has been a lie," she said, her voice almost inaudible. "Everything," she said again, "but you."

"Elizabeth," he said softly.

"They *took* me. Not in love, but in lust, like dogs rutting over a bitch in heat. They made me betray my country. I told them as little as I dared, but all along I knew that what I told them would send other soldiers to their deaths. And so, they took my soul as well."

"No," Dare said. "Whatever—"

"You are the only person in my life who has asked me for nothing," she continued, raising her voice so that it drowned out his. "And the only one to whom I would willingly have given everything. But now there is nothing left of what I once was, my lord. I have nothing to offer you but this. Nothing but the body of Bonnet's well-used whore.''

There was no sound in the dark bedroom. Neither of them moved. Or even breathed, it seemed. For Dare the decision she had asked him to make seemed almost as monstrous as the one the French had forced on her.

She was the only woman he had ever loved. He had offered her his protection and his name. She would accept neither because she believed she was unworthy of them. If he did what she had asked, if he accepted the gift she offered him, would he not value her at the same standard she had applied to herself? But if he didn't…what would she read into his refusal?

Finally, as the silence grew and expanded, stretching unbearably, her hands unclasped and fell to her sides. Then she turned and began to walk across the room toward the door.

''Elizabeth,'' he said.

She stopped, her back to him still, waiting in the shadows. Only when he walked across the room to touch her, his hand closing over her shoulder, did she turn.

She lifted her face for his kiss, and the moonlight revealed the silvered tracks of tears. He touched them with fingers that trembled again. With love. And with need. And with a fervent determination that for tonight at least he would make her what she once had been.

A girl, as innocent as the moonlight, dreaming of the man who would truly, and forever, love her.

Chapter Fourteen

The intricacies of feminine dress were no mystery to the Earl of Dare, and he realized very quickly that he had been correct in his original surmise. Under the cobweb lace and dusk-rose silk, Elizabeth was wearing nothing at all.

"I dreamed of this," he said softly when he had unfastened the last of its tiny buttons, exposing the slim delicacy of her bare back. He pressed a kiss on the side of her neck, just below her ear, where soft blond tendrils clung to scented skin.

Hands on her shoulders, Dare felt the depth of the breath she took when his lips touched her, and so he bent, running his tongue lightly down her spine. As he did, his hands eased the gown off her shoulders and carried it downward with them.

When he had pushed the dress past her hips, he released it. It pooled around her feet in a foam of cream lace and shell-pink silk. As if she, like the mythical Venus, had just stepped out of the dawn-lightened sea. As beautiful, he thought. And to him, as newly born.

Kneeling on one knee behind her, the tips of his

fingers found the small protrusions of her hip bones. As he held them, his tongue touched against the dimples at the base of her spine. He explored them, as if he had all the time in the world, trailing slow, wet heat from one to the other.

He was a little surprised when she moved under his hands, turning to face him. But then Elizabeth was no seventeen-year-old virgin, and he should not expect her to react like one, he reminded himself. He looked up and found she was smiling at him.

"I knew you would be like this," she said softly.

"Like this?" he questioned, returning the smile.

Whatever twisted path had brought them to this place, it seemed they were both prepared to forget the journey and revel, for tonight at least, in this homecoming. Dare leaned forward, a matter of an inch or two, and touched his tongue to her naval, rimming the small, neat depression with moisture.

"Or like this?" he whispered. Then, mouth still open, he dragged hot, wet kisses down her stomach, just as he had when he'd worshipped her back. Except this time…

He heard her gasp. She put her hands on his shoulders, as if her knees had grown too weak to support her weight. Her entire body was vibrating. For a terrifying second, he thought that was fear. Until she breathed a single, telling syllable.

"Yes," she whispered. And, as his tongue moved in response to that permission, that entreaty, she said it again. "Oh, yes."

What he had heard in her voice was not fear, but need. A shivering anticipation, perhaps as great as his own. He looked up once more. This time her eyes were closed, long lashes lying against her cheeks. Her head was tilted a little, as it had been when they danced, exposing the vulnerability of her throat.

That night on the lawn she had surrendered to the music and the moonlight. This was simply another form of surrender. And another dance. An ancient and elegant *pas de deux,* to which they both knew the steps.

Perhaps they had learned them from different partners, but that did not mean that the movements they would share tonight would not be made in a perfect harmony. This was their duet. And theirs alone.

The thread of self-doubt that had remained in Dare's heart, despite his determined avowal that her past made no difference to him, finally dissolved, freeing him to be with her what he had been created to be. Partner. And lover.

"Don't stop," she breathed.

"Your eagerness, madam, will unman me," he warned softly, laughing. Deliberately letting her hear his amusement because he had not expected so frank an admission of her enjoyment.

Her eyelids lifted, revealing eyes that were already passion-dazed, a little distant. They lowered, contemplating his body, and when they rose to his again, he saw within the heated desire an answering amusement. Her laughter was a breath, but it was laughter, and he thanked the gods for this, too. The precious gift of lovers' laughter.

"Unmanned, my lord?" she challenged. "I think I shan't worry about *that,* given such blatant evidence to the contrary."

"Valentine," he said.

Her head tilted, as if considering his name, a Sinclair family tradition. He wondered if she disliked it.

"Or Val, if you prefer," he offered. "My brothers call me Val."

"Your...estranged brothers?" she asked, her smile mocking the fable he had told her.

"My beloved brothers," he acknowledged, his throat tight, knowing how true that was. It was the reason he understood her sacrifice.

"My Lord Dare," she said, touching his face. The gentle mockery in her eyes had been wiped away by the shining love that took its place. "You will always be Dare to me."

"Why will you not—"

Before he could finish, the tips of her fingers were pressed against his lips, blocking the words. "That isn't what tonight is for. Not for questions. Or answers. Tonight is for something else. Something very different."

He shook his head slightly, still holding her eyes.

"Make love to me in the moonlight," she whispered. "Make me forget the rest, at least for tonight."

Make me forget...at least for tonight. And so the Earl of Dare stood and, putting his left arm under her knees and his right around her back, he lifted her easily, her weight nothing to his strength. Her arms automatically settled around his neck, as if they belonged there. As if he had carried her to his bed a thousand times.

When he laid her on its satin coverlet, he stepped back so he could see her. In the moonlight the alabaster skin gleamed, its curves touched with silver, the secret places he would soon know shadowed and dark. Eyes wide in the carved-cameo perfection of her face, she held out her hand to him as she had before.

Invitation. Now, of course, he needed none.

He began to undress, stripping clothing from his body rapidly and methodically. His shirt pulled over his head in one motion. Shoes quickly discarded, followed by his hose and britches. Only when he was wearing nothing but his knit drawers did he look up again. She was lying where he had placed her, propped on one elbow. And she was watching him.

Her eyes had lifted with his. The laughter that had been in them was gone. Only a sensual heat was left, blue flame. Seeing it, he bent and slipped off that last garment. And saw the breath she drew when he straightened.

"You are…" she began, and then she hesitated, her eyes tracing over his nudity. "So beautiful," she whispered, her gaze coming back to his face. "Within *and* without."

Dare laughed, embarrassed, of course, by her assessment, and again surprised by her openness.

"Don't laugh," she commanded softly, her eyes still serious. "It's true. Every part of you is good and clean and fine."

"And every part of you—" he began.

At what was suddenly in her face, those words died, cut off by the almost palpable force of her pain. And he took the single step that separated him from the bed where she waited. There was probably nothing he could *say* that would make her believe him. Far more powerful than the spoken word would be a demonstration of all that he felt about her.

He had one night to change her perception of herself. One night to convince her that to him every part of her was good and clean and fine. And beautiful as well. *Within and without.*

One night. It was the greatest challenge the Earl of

Dare had ever faced. And it carried for him the greatest danger. Because if he failed…

He destroyed the thought, banishing even the possibility of failure. After all, he had only to show her what was truly in his heart. Surely he could not fail at that.

His hands are so knowing, Elizabeth thought, almost drugged by their unhurried movements over her body. Almost mindless with their slow caress.

She had been touched by other men's hands, but those experiences had never been like this. Never of her choice or by her will. And never had anyone sensed her needs almost before she herself recognized them—sensed and met and exceeded the boundaries of every one.

She had begged Dare to make love to her, and through the long hours that was exactly what he had done. And he had required nothing from her in exchange, not even thought. Perhaps the greatest of all the gifts he had given her.

After a while, the cacophony of sensation had become so great it drowned out the lingering echoes of her past. In his arms she achieved what she had come here for. Not absolution, of course. Dare could not grant her that. What she had asked from him was forgetfulness, that cherished gift of the lotus eaters.

His lips found her breast again, closing over the distended nipple, first to nuzzle and then to suckle, hard and strong. An answering pressure started deep in her lower body again.

And it would build, she knew, turning her core to flame. Igniting nerve and sinew. Burning along artery and vein. Sending waves of heat to melt her bones and then reform them, tempered and made stronger by their exposure to this fire.

Under the guidance of his hands and mouth and tongue that had happened so many times tonight she had lost count. This, she now knew, was lovemaking. And she, who had borne the hated touch of other men because she had no choice, delighted in his.

Sure and deliberate, supremely confident, Dare had coaxed from her body sensations she had never experienced before, despite five long years of marriage. Despite...

She jerked her mind away, concentrating instead on the pull and release of his lips as they tantalized her breast. His hand flattened, callused palm down, to slide over her stomach, its destination now known and understood. Her body arched in anticipation, reaction to the mere thought of what he intended.

And then his fingers touched her. Her body was sated, desensitized by too much pleasure, so that she feared she could not again be induced to begin this spiraling journey. Under the demanding tutelage of his fingers, she discovered how wrong she had been.

Dare shifted his weight slightly, his mouth moving to the other breast, his tongue branding her skin as it did. And his fingers continued to caress the center of her need. To rebuild the trembling, unstable tower of ecstasy he had constructed again and again tonight. When he had built it high enough to stretch beyond the bounds of endurance, it would tumble again, sending her reeling into the darkness as her mind retreated, protecting itself from the force of what he could make her feel.

She put her hand on his cheek, applying enough pressure to force him to lift his head. To make him look at her. In the darkness, the sapphire eyes were black, their pupils expanded to capture every shred of the fading moonlight. The only witness to his love-making. Only she and the moonlight.

It lay in a silver path from the window to the bed, but Dare's eyes reflected none of its light. Dark and unfathomable, they examined her face as he continued to touch her.

Eventually, her lips parted, and her breathing began to deepen, becoming sound. Becoming movement. The incremental series of shuddering gasps disturbed its measured regularity as harbingers of the coming ecstasy began to flood her body.

She wanted his mouth over hers as it happened. She wanted his kiss as much as she wanted release. More than she wanted his body now, she wanted his soul. One with hers. And every part good and clean and fine.

"Kiss me," she whispered, as she writhed against the damp, tangled sheets.

There was no hesitation in his response. Dare's head tilted, aligning, and then his tongue met hers, echoing the movement of his caressing fingers.

At its invasion, there was an answering reaction in her lower body. Seeming to sense what was happening there, almost before she had, Dare put his knee between her legs. Mindless with need, she allowed them to fall open.

And he pushed into her body, into the sweet, dark heat he had so lovingly created. This time he held nothing back. Again and again he drove into her, his palms cupped under her hips, lifting her upward into the relentless power of his strokes.

She felt weightless, boneless, her body simply shap-

ing itself to his. No longer having any form of its own.
She was only a receptacle. He pushed deeper and
deeper, filling her. His strength more than she could
bear. *More than she could bear.*

Just as the words of protest moved from her brain
toward her lips, the enormous pressure released in a
flood of sensation. Molten heat spread into every cell
of her body. Filling every corner of her soul with him.
Good and clean and fine.

Again and again she arched, meeting the downward
thrusts of his hips, even after she felt the hot jet of his
seed pour into her body. And like a new fire that
sweeps across a devastated landscape, it burned away
the cold gray ashes of the past.

Dare never knew what had awakened him. Perhaps
a shift in the pattern of the moonlight as the hours
slipped past midnight. Or perhaps the silence. Silence…when there should have been the soft inhala-
tions of the woman sleeping next to him.

Slowly, almost dreading what he would find, he
turned his head. The pillow beside him was empty. It
bore the faint imprint of her head, the shallowest of
indentions. The sheet was turned back, as if someone
had slipped carefully out of bed.

"Elizabeth?" Dare questioned the darkness. And
then he waited, breathing suspended, through its un-
answering silence.

The room seemed blacker and colder than when he
had fallen asleep. But that seemed to have been only
a few minutes ago. If that were true, he thought, then
where was Elizabeth? He threw the sheet off his legs
and stood, hesitating a few seconds beside the bed,
again listening.

All he could hear was the familiar ticking of the clock on the mantel. He fumbled a moment in the darkness, trying to light the lamp, and when he had, he carried it across the room with him, holding it up to illuminate the face of the clock.

It was just past four. Too early for her to have risen. And then he remembered her concern for the sensibilities of his household. Perhaps she had returned to her own room, so that no one would find her with him here in the morning.

Dare set the lamp down on the mantel and walked across to the window. The garden below was empty, eerie in the shadows, the familiar shapes of tree and bushes distorted and sinister.

He turned away, his eyes moving slowly across the chamber. There was nothing out of place, nothing except the scattered items of his clothing lying on the floor beside the bed. Seeing them, his eyes sought the spill of cream lace and rose silk. And found that it was gone.

He walked toward the door to be sure, but there was nothing at all at the place where he had pushed the gown over her hips and let it fall off her body. Nothing on the floor but the subtle play of moonlight from the windows behind him.

I have come to say goodbye. The words echoed in the emptiness, and he realized he should have known. After all, she had told him herself what tonight was all about.

As he had once before, the Earl of Dare hurriedly gathered the scattered items of his clothing and pulled them on, his fingers trembling with a fear he didn't understand. And with a cold sense of foreboding which had grown since he had turned his head and realized that the pillow beside him was empty.

He opened the door to her room without knocking. After all, there were no secrets now between them. Nothing undiscovered except the reason for her departure from his bed. The chamber was empty, the counterpane as smooth and undisturbed as when the maid had left it yesterday. The draperies were pulled back, letting into her room the same spill of moonlight as was in his.

He crossed the thick rug, pulling out the top drawer of the chest that stood between the tall, mullioned windows. Her belongings were still there, a breath of the scent she had worn at Bonnet's drifting upward from them.

He touched the lid of the box that held her cosmetics, running his fingers across the scarred wood. The ruby-wine dress she had been wearing the first night he had seen her was here as well. The lack of light in the room turned its richness dark, the color almost bloodred in the moonlight.

And between those two items, not folded as the dress was, but untidily wadded, as if she had pushed it there to hide it, was the night rail he had torn. He took it out, crushing it in his hands. He remembered the feel of it ripping under his fingers. Heard the sound again in his memory.

I have come to say goodbye. He began to pull out the other drawers, finding that they, too, still held clothing. Determined to make a break with everything in her past, she might have left the gaudy, carnival-colored dresses the gambler had made her wear. Those lay side by side, however, with thin, worn chemises, white and touchingly virginal. He couldn't imagine that she would want to arrive at her brother's house without at least a change of undergarments.

So where the hell had she gone? As he turned away from the chest, he realized that he held the torn rail in his hand. Unable to resist, he raised the fabric to his face, breathing deeply, trying to find some trace of her, some lingering essence of the woman he had made love to all night.

There was no hint of the French perfume. Only the scent of her body was caught in the cloth. A body he now knew so well. Nothing undiscovered or unexplored. Nothing hidden or held in reserve. Nothing that had not generously been opened to him.

And he had made love to Elizabeth in every way his brain could devise, imprinting each sensation on his memory. Afraid that despite everything, she would do what she had said. *I have come to say goodbye.*

He knew now that he had failed to change her mind, failed to convince her that none of it really mattered. Forced to that admission, the Earl of Dare's fingers closed around the torn nightgown, gripping so tightly that they whitened at the tips. Rage at what the bastards had done to her flooded his body, threatening his judgment. And his control.

Perhaps he had failed at proving to her what he felt, but there was one thing at which he wouldn't fail, he vowed. One last thing he would do for Elizabeth.

By the time he had returned to his rooms and finished dressing, the earl's household had begun to stir. As Dare hurried down the stairs, he ordered the first footman he encountered to have his horse saddled and brought to the front door. Not his usual mode of transportation in London, but riding would be faster than waiting for the carriage.

As the servant disappeared on his errand, Dare strode to the library where he kept his father's dueling pistols. When he entered the room, his eyes automatically found the library stair. It was empty, of course, but all the memories were still here. They would always haunt this room.

At the word haunt, Dare felt again that cold, unexplained frisson of dread. He stood a moment in the doorway, almost riveted by the power of a thought that was too devastating to give expression to, not even mentally.

"You know that she's gone?"

Shocked at the voice from the darkness, Dare whirled, his eyes finding the speaker. Ned Harper was sitting in one of the wing chairs before the fireplace. There was no fire, the ashes in the grate cold and gray and dead.

There was a nearly empty decanter on the table beside the valet. He held a glass of brandy in his hand. As Dare watched, Ned lifted it to his mouth and tossed down the contents in one long draught. He wiped his lips with the back of his hand, and then his eyes lifted, almost challengingly, to meet his master's. They seemed as cold and as dead as the ashes.

"What have you done?" Dare asked, sick with fear.

He had told himself that Elizabeth had gone to her brother's. Despite the fact that her clothing had been left upstairs, it was the only thing that made sense. It was what she told him she intended to do, and he could think of nowhere else where she might find refuge.

"What she wanted me to do," Ned said, holding his eyes.

"What she *wanted?*" Dare asked carefully, trying to read his valet's voice.

"She wanted to go."

"But you must have known, Ned, that's not what *I* wanted," Dare said softly.

His valet's lips pursed slightly, and then he put the glass down on the table beside him, and picked up the decanter and attempted to refill the tumbler. His hand was so unsteady that he missed the rim on his first attempt, and for a few seconds the liquid ran onto the table instead of into the tumbler.

"What have you done?" Dare asked again.

"You can't marry a whore. She understood the reality of that. And she'll never agree to be your mistress. I don't think either of you could live with that."

Ned fell silent as if he had finished everything he intended to say on the subject. He looked down into the brandy in his glass, but he made no effort to raise it to his mouth.

"So you helped her go to her brother's?" Dare questioned, his heart racing with a fear he didn't want to acknowledge.

The smell of the liquor was too strong in the room. What Harper had spilled was trickling off the table and onto the floor. Dare wondered how long Ned had been drinking, sitting here in the darkness. Since he had helped Elizabeth leave? Or since she had come to Dare's bedroom at the beginning of the night?

"Where is she?" he asked softly, sensing from the quality of Harper's silence that there was more to this.

"She didn't want you to know," the valet said.

Without looking up, he raised the brandy and drank

it down, provoking a fit of coughing. Dare turned away in disgust and walked to the rosewood case that held the dueling pistols. He opened the lid, looking down on the beautifully deadly pair, that should have been nestled together like lovers in the black velvet lining of the case. Only one of the Mantons rested in its cunningly designed compartment.

Dare's heart stopped, and it took too long for blood to uncongeal and flow through his veins again, allowing him to move. When it had, Dare walked back across the room, his movements more controlled than they had ever been in his life. Because he knew if he didn't control them...

As he approached, Harper's eyes widened at what was in his face. Dare didn't speak until he had locked his fingers into Ned's shirt, lifting him out of his chair. The glass fell and shattered on the hearth. Neither of them looked at it.

"What have you done?" Dare demanded.

"Only what she asked me to do," Ned said defiantly.

"What was that, you drunken bastard?"

"I loaded the pistol. She asked me to. You're the one who talked about her bloody right to do what she wanted now."

"Not the right to kill herself," Dare said, shaking Harper, his fury so great he was almost mindless with the force of it.

"Kill herself?" Ned repeated. "That's not—" he began to deny, and then he started to laugh, still dangling from Dare's hold. "You don't know her, do you? Despite all you know about her now, you still don't understand her. Not even yet."

The words stopped the earl, the blind rage fading

as they began to sink in. "Then...where the hell is she?" Dare asked again. And this time, finally, he was answered.

"She's gone to kill Bonnet," Harper said.

Chapter Fifteen

"Elizabeth!" Henri Bonnet said. His eyes, lifting from his cards to her face, were as full of shock as his voice.

Given his skills, the gambler would recover his poise quickly enough that the gentleman playing in his private salon would probably never be aware that his first unguarded exclamation hadn't been one of pleasure. She knew, however, that she was the last person Bonnet expected to see in this room tonight.

After all, she was supposed to be watching and reporting on the activities of the Earl of Dare. And until yesterday, dutifully she had been. She had not told the entire truth of those, of course, but she had given Bonnet a version she believed skirted it near enough to keep the French satisfied. During the past few weeks, she had walked a nerve-rackingly fine line, careful to reveal nothing that would endanger Dare and yet trying to provide enough information to keep Jeremy safe.

Jeremy, she thought. His name was a raw and open wound in her heart. It had been since she had learned about his death. And the only time she hadn't been acutely aware of that loss and that pain...

But the hours she had just spent in Dare's arms were something else she couldn't allow herself to think about. She couldn't afford to indulge in those memories, as precious as they were, because they would weaken her. They were the only thing she feared might break her resolve.

"But how wonderful to see you, my dear," the gambler said, his tone modified now to signify pleasure. Bonnet had even risen from his chair and was bowing to her. When he straightened, his welcoming smile was firmly in place. "I believe you already know everyone here," the Frenchman said, his hand sweeping the table.

Several of the players had turned to face the door when the gambler had first spoken her name. Now they were all staring at her. As a matter of intellectual curiosity and nothing else, Elizabeth wondered what they saw.

The wrinkled gown, of course. And she could only imagine what her hair was like. She had not even glanced into a mirror on her way out of the earl's town house.

Harper had promised that a coach would be waiting at the front door. Lying awake, she had heard the clock strike four, the hour they agreed upon for her departure. So she had stolen from Dare's bed and in the darkness slipped on the dress he had given her, struggling to refasten the buttons up the back even as she was hurrying down the stairs.

"We've missed you, my dear," one of Bonnet's most frequent patrons, the Viscount Haddinton, said with a smile. "May we hope you have come to reclaim your place at the faro table?"

She considered his round face, a little flushed with the wine he had drunk. Given the drink and the hour, his eyes were slightly bloodshot, but they were also kind. They always had been, she remembered, but she didn't respond to his question.

She had smiled at men here for hundreds of nights, whether or not she felt like smiling. Whether their eyes were kind or leering. Whether they behaved to her as gentlemen or as cads. Tonight, she no longer had to do that. For the first time in two years she was not under Bonnet's control. She was no longer his puppet because there were no strings left by which he could direct her will.

And with that thought, her gaze returned to the Frenchman's face. He was still smiling at her benignly, as if he were some proud schoolmaster whose prize pupil was giving a good account of himself.

"No, Lord Haddinton," she said softly, walking toward the table, her eyes holding Bonnet's. "I haven't come to deal faro. I've come to do murder."

The words fell into the relaxed atmosphere of the room like a killing frost touches summer's last flowers, turning them black and dead in an instant. The coldness spread, as one by one, depending on their degree of inebriation, the men at the table began to comprehend what she had said.

Before the first one had, however, the pistol she had stolen from the Earl of Dare, which she held hidden in the folds of her skirt, was pointed at the gambler's heart. Stunned, no one said a word, not even Bonnet, but his eyes had widened enough that there was a rim of white completely encircling the wildly dilated eyes.

"You lied to me," she said, the accusation very calm, her words unhurried.

Time stood still. It seemed as if she were standing alone in a vast, noiseless vacuum. There was not even a breath of sound in the room. No movement. And not a shred of doubt or fear in her heart concerning what she was about to do.

"Elizabeth..." the Frenchman began, and then his words faltered as she straightened her arm to its full length, bringing the muzzle of the pistol a few inches closer to his body. At this distance it would be obvious to all of them that she couldn't miss.

"For two years, you used me, making me believe that what I let you do would keep my brother safe. And keep him alive."

"I swear to you—" Bonnet began.

"Don't," she said, her voice very soft. Deliberately she lowered the long barrel of the Manton until it no longer pointed at the gambler's chest. His protests died again, as he recognized her new target, one far more appropriate if she truly wanted revenge for what he had done to her. "Don't lie to me any more, Henri," she commanded. "I don't ever want to hear you lie to me again."

"I'm sure there has been some mistake," one of the players began. "This is probably a misunderstanding that can quickly be—"

"The French employ Bonnet as a spy," Elizabeth interrupted, her voice flat, but the force of what she said had stopped the man in midsentence. "For years he has listened to your careless, drunken conversations at these very tables and reported to his superiors any information contained within them that might help Bonaparte's efforts against our forces."

There was a shocked murmur from someone at the table, but Elizabeth's gaze never wavered from Bonnet's blanched and sweating features.

"And for the last two years," she continued, willing herself to make this confession, if only to help them understand what she was about to do, "I have helped him spy on you. I did that to save my brother's life and to keep him from torture. And yet all along…"

Fury closed her throat, blocking the explanation she longed to make. The murmur from the table began again. Unconsciously, perhaps feeling the pressure of their anger as well as her own, her finger tightened over the trigger.

"No," Henri breathed, watching her, aware, even if she was not, of how close to death he was.

"Why not?" she asked softly, and now, finally, she did smile at him. "Tell me, Henri, why I *shouldn't* kill you. And remember, when the first lie comes out of your mouth, I'm going to shoot."

There was a long silence. The Frenchman swallowed once, the movement strong enough to be visible.

"You can't do this, my dear," Viscount Haddinton said reasonably. "If what you say is true, then you must let the authorities handle the matter. If you shoot this man, no matter how valid you believe your reasons to be—"

"Everything she has said is true," the Earl of Dare interrupted from behind her. "If ever a man deserved to be shot, it is Henri Bonnet."

In response to that beloved voice, there was within Elizabeth the strongest inclination to turn. Just to look at him again. Just to see his face one last time.

She controlled the impulse, however, with a will

grown strong by conquering every expression of emotion for the past two years. She had come here tonight with only one purpose. One goal. And no hope left in her heart for anything other than its accomplishment.

So she kept her eyes locked on the gambler's face, even as his had fastened hopefully on Dare's. She was sickened to see them lighten with expectancy.

"I assure you, my Lord Dare, there is not a word of truth in anything this woman has told you," Bonnet said.

"And is there truth in what Jeremy Richardson's guards have told me, *monsieur?*" Dare asked. "Is it true that his death was carefully concealed and never reported to the English authorities, as it should have been? Even his gaolers knew there was a double game being played. And in playing it, you and Fouché used an innocent woman as your pawn. For that alone, you deserve to die."

She had been afraid Dare would try to stop her, and she was relieved that he wasn't attempting to convince her, as Lord Haddinton had, to let the government deal with Bonnet. The problem with that solution was, of course, that she was as guilty as the gambler.

Guilty of betraying her country in order to save her brother's life. And Jeremy would have been the first to condemn her, no matter how much care she had taken over the information she passed on. She had always changed details before she repeated anything to Bonnet, so that when the French attempted to use the material she had supplied, it would prove worthless.

Or so she hoped. There was, however, no guarantee of that. No guarantee that the lives of other English soldiers had not been lost because of what she had done to protect her brother's. Therefore, it was better that it end like this. Quickly and finally. And if this was not the ending to her life she had once dreamed of, she had at least had those precious hours with Dare tonight.

"My hatred for Bonaparte and his regime is well-known, my lord," Bonnet said, his eyes still on the earl. "My family lost everything in the Revolution. We became exiles from our own land. Why would you believe I support the very people who cost me so much?

"Because Fouché has promised that the Emperor will restore those lands and titles to you. As soon as they defeat the British," Elizabeth said. "*That's* why it was so important to you to help them."

"Ridiculous," Bonnet snapped, his eyes coming back to Elizabeth's face. "Even if that *were* true, and it's not, of course, by your own words you condemn yourself of a thing far worse than that of which you accuse me. If what you say were true, then you would be a traitor to your own country. It isn't too late to recant these absurd charges, Elizabeth. Tell them the truth, and all will be forgotten. And forgiven," the gambler added softly, his voice unctuous and falsely kind, as if he had only her welfare at heart.

"Nothing I did for you was done through my free will," she said, clearly reading the warning in his words and ignoring it. He was powerless to influence her actions now. Jeremy was dead, and he couldn't frighten her with threats to her own safety.

"No one could force a true patriot to reveal her country's secrets to the enemy. Be very careful what you condemn yourself to, my dear, in trying to falsely tar *my* name," Bonnet said.

"If you threatened to torture my brother," Dare said, "I, too, might tell you whatever you wanted to hear."

"That accusation is a fabrication. It's obvious Elizabeth is out for revenge because I've replaced her with someone who is not only more pleasing to me personally, but who is also more popular with my patrons. This tale is the creation of a woman scorned, gentlemen," Bonnet said, turning to address his patrons. And then his eyes came back to Dare's. "I can't believe you are foolish enough to listen to this, my lord. The woman's demented."

"I listen because I have personally verified what she is saying to be the truth. And I assure you, *monsieur,* I am not demented," Dare said sardonically. "I have proof. Proof which I brought with me from Paris. Would you care to see it? Or perhaps these gentlemen would."

Again, there was a whisper of sound, consternation or shock, from the men gathered around the gambler's table. Bonnet, however, said nothing, and his eyes had lost all pretense at affability.

"If she shoots me," the Frenchman said, "it will be exactly what she claimed. It will be murder, Lord Dare. A cold-blooded murder, which I believe is still against the laws of your country. Considering her confession of treason, which these gentlemen have witnessed, the courts may not be as forgiving as you," Bonnet warned, his eyes cold.

"When they hear the facts, Bonnet, the justices will certainly consider that you were deserving of your fate. As will they," Dare said, his eyes circling the gambler's patrons.

"And what will happen to her *before* she comes to

trial? Or do you believe you will be able to protect her from harm while she is in prison awaiting that judgment? I have heard shocking stories about what can happen to a beautiful woman in your London hell-holes.''

Elizabeth listened to the sudden stillness behind her. Dare would try to protect her, of course, because of what he was, because of his nature. He would try to stop her from killing Bonnet because he would be afraid that the Frenchman was right about what would happen to her in prison.

As soon as that realization formed, she raised the pistol so that the muzzle again pointed at Bonnet's black heart. One shot. One chance to put an end to this before Dare could stop her.

One squeeze of the trigger, she thought, fighting to hold the gun steady, despite her growing anxiety to get this over. Then there would be nothing Dare could do.

Her finger tightened, but before it could complete the motion, Dare appeared in her peripheral vision. She had not heard him move, had not even been aware that he was so close.

Hurriedly, because she knew what he intended, her finger completed the motion. She was surprised at how much force it took to pull the trigger back and make the gun fire. When it did, the shot was far louder than she had expected. It echoed in the enclosed space, assaulting her ears.

And as the smoke cleared, she realized with despair that she hadn't been quick enough. Dare's hand had closed over the barrel just as she fired, wrenching it to the side.

The gambler was still standing beside the table. He

was looking down, his fingers touching his chest, as if he expected to see or to feel blood pouring from the hole her bullet had made in his heart. The ball had plowed instead into the plaster of the wall behind him.

"Damn you," she said vehemently, struggling to pull her arm away from Dare's grip. "Damn you."

Instead, using his other hand, the earl wrested the pistol from her and tossed it on the table. Several of the men sitting there recoiled as the weapon hit, sliding a few inches on the surface. Then, Dare's eyes focused on the Frenchman, and he removed the Manton's mate from the pocket of his cloak.

"You have insulted Mrs. Carstairs' honor, Monsieur Bonnet. I demand satisfaction."

The movement of the gambler's fingers over his unmarred shirt front was arrested. His eyes lifted first to the gun and then to the earl's face. They held on it a long, slow heartbeat before he began to laugh. The sound, almost maniacal, rang through the room, echoing as the pistol shot had done.

Considering all she had endured at Bonnet's hands, this was the final obscenity, Elizabeth realized as she listened to it. He was laughing at the idea that she had any honor. Mocking her brother's death. And her sacrifice. Mocking everything that had happened to her.

She started forward, trying to attack the Frenchman with her bare hands. Dare was quicker. He grasped her arm again, pulling her back and putting her firmly behind him. When he had, he didn't let go, his fingers biting into the flesh of her forearm as he held her there by sheer, physical force.

"The choice of weapons is yours, *monsieur*," the earl said to Bonnet, ignoring Elizabeth's almost inarticulate protests of rage as she continued to struggle.

"And we will do it now, I think. With this many witnesses we have no need to proceed with the formality of naming seconds or making some future appointment. Here. And now," Dare said softly.

"No," Elizabeth said again. She stopped trying to twist out of his hold, but her fingers still pried at Dare's, almost unconsciously. "I won't let you," she said, her voice low and urgent.

"You don't really intend us to fight a duel over a whore, do you, my lord?" Bonnet asked, his voice silken. His mouth was arranged in a sneer, but his face was still white and strained.

"Be very careful what you say about Mrs. Carstairs," Dare warned.

"I shouldn't say she is a whore? But I assure you, my lord, I have it on the very best authority. My own. A tasty piece, especially for an Englishwoman, but hardly worth fighting over. Your pardon, gentlemen," he said, his smile to his patrons mocking. "No offense, of course. It's just that most of your women are so cold. And fat. And they bray like jackasses when they laugh. Of course, I don't suppose you would notice, since most of you do the same."

"Now see here, Bonnet," Lord Haddinton said, getting heavily to his feet.

"Don't interfere," Dare ordered, his eyes on Bonnet. "That's what he wants. To cause a diversion which will provide him an opportunity to escape."

Haddinton subsided, sinking wordlessly back into his chair. In the midst of the distraction the viscount's protest had provided, Elizabeth again tried to pull her arm from Dare's hold.

He glanced at her, but he didn't loosen the pressure of his fingers. She realized there was not a trace of fear in his eyes. There was amusement there instead. The hint of a smile that had played around his lips as he looked at her had disappeared, however, when he turned back to face the gambler.

"Weapons?" he repeated.

"I am not going to fight you over the *supposed* honor of a woman who has been my mistress for over two years," Bonnet said.

He pulled a linen handkerchief from his pocket, dabbing at his sweating forehead. He seemed braver now that Elizabeth wasn't holding a loaded pistol pointing at his lower body.

"Then I shall shoot you myself," Dare said pleasantly. "As a peer, I would have certain advantages in the courts that Elizabeth might lack. And given the fact that I can *prove* you are a French spy, Bonnet, I might even be awarded a medal for valorous service to the Crown. I am, after all, a dear, personal friend of Prinny's."

This time the smile was allowed to form. It was not the one Elizabeth had so briefly seen. This was as mocking as the gambler's laughter had been. And it taunted Bonnet.

"I won't let you do this," Elizabeth said softly, the words intended for Dare's ears alone. "He's right. I have no honor for you to defend."

"Please allow me to beg humbly to differ with your opinion of your honor, Mrs. Carstairs," the Earl of Dare said politely, his gaze still on the Frenchman.

"Can't fight a duel over a whore, Dare," old Lord Merritt called from the far side of the table. "Ain't done, you know. Bed the chit, if you will, and shoot the Frenchie for the spying bastard he is, but don't make mock of affairs of honor, my boy."

"I assure you, sir, I mean no disrespect. Since I intend to make Mrs. Carstairs my wife, however, I believe I have the right to demand satisfaction from a man who has just insulted her. Your choice of weapons, Bonnet. Or I can shoot you down like the cur you are."

"Your *wife?*" Merrit said, his voice rising incredulously. "A peer can't marry a gal from a gaming hell."

"You can't be serious, Dare," Haddinton said. "I mean, after all, everyone knows…" Slowly his voice trailed away as he realized it might not be wise to remind Dare of exactly what everyone knew.

"Mrs. Carstairs has explained that for the past two years she was trying to protect her brother, who was a prisoner of the French. Whatever she was forced to do in that period of time is on Bonnet's head. *Not* on hers. There should be no stain attached to her name because of it. Or to her reputation."

"But still…" Haddinton began hesitantly, his eyes going from Dare's face to Elizabeth's.

"He is *not* going to marry me, Lord Haddinton," she said quickly, with as much surety as she could put into her denial. "Lord Dare is a gentleman whose chivalry has momentarily overcome his common sense. Send for the constables and have Monsieur Bonnet arrested. It will save the earl from embarrassment."

"If you do, Haddinton," Dare warned, "I shall call you out next. And then, in order, any other man who interferes. Bonnet is mine. All I want from you gentlemen is to get out of the way and give us room to fight."

"Swords," Bonnet said.

The word dropped into the conversation like a stone. Every eye focused on the Frenchman's face.

"He's very skilled," Elizabeth warned, cold with horror.

The thought that she might be responsible for Dare being hurt or even killed pushed her heart into her throat. She had not been afraid for herself, but she had never wanted this. She had never intended to endanger Dare by her actions. Nothing was worth that—not even revenge for Jeremy's death.

"Call the constables and let them take care of Bonnet," she begged. "You have powerful friends. There is no need for this. No need to put yourself into danger."

"If I didn't know you better, Mrs. Carstairs, I would believe that's fear I hear in your voice," Dare said softly, turning again to smile at her. "Are you afraid for *me,* Elizabeth? If so, I can't tell you how flattered I am."

"Don't fight him," she pleaded, ignoring the teasing smile, as well as the memories, which had clearly been in his eyes, too, before he turned his attention again to the Frenchman.

"This is the only way," Dare said, watching Bonnet, the pistol still leveled at his heart. "All I ask from you, my darling, is your trust. I asked you for that once before, and you refused. You didn't know me then. Will you trust me now, Elizabeth?"

"It isn't about trust," she said, her voice sharp with fear.

And in her head, like an echo, she heard Ned's answer when she had made that same claim before. *Of course it is. That's all it is about. You don't trust him not to be sickened by what you did. Because you are.*

"Of course it's about trust," Dare said. "Do you trust me to take care of you? I think that's the *only* question that matters now."

"I'm not worth—"

She stopped because he had turned to look at her again, and because of what was in his eyes.

"I tried very hard to show you last night how *I* value you," Dare said, his voice so low she strained to hear the words. "Did I fail in that?"

He hadn't, of course. What he felt about her had been branded forever on her body. And on her soul. And so, slowly, still holding his eyes, she shook her head.

He drew a breath, releasing her arm, before he turned again to the Frenchman. "You must provide the swords, *monsieur*. I trust you have a pair."

"My father's," Bonnet said, smiling. "He was considered to be something of an expert."

Dare laughed. "And no doubt he taught you all he knew," he suggested mockingly, unfastening his cloak and handing it to Elizabeth. His hand, making accidental contact with hers, was warm and steady, as were his eyes. *Trust me...*

"I was afraid of that," Dare continued, the laughter still coloring his tone. "In that case, Monsieur Bonnet, let us test how well you learned your father's lessons."

They were so evenly matched it had been obvious to Dare from the first engagement that he was in the fight of his life. Despite the fact that this heady feeling of living so keenly balanced on the edge of death had always been like a drug to him, he was too aware of the white-faced woman who stood across the room, holding his cloak. Holding it as if it were something infinitely precious—a holy relic or her own child.

He had asked Elizabeth to trust him, he remembered, parrying a feint from the Frenchman. He knew now, however, that the longer this went on, the more likely it was Bonnet would find a way past his defenses.

The gambler was fighting with a brilliantly reckless disregard for his own safety. After all, what did he have to lose? Bonnet's only hope was to kill or disable Dare and then to fight his way out of his own establishment and disappear into the dark streets of the English capital.

Bonnet had surely made arrangements years ago for just such a contingency as this, and there was no one among the other Englishmen in this room whom Dare judged capable of preventing the gambler's escape. He was beginning to doubt he was.

It had been a long time since the sword was considered a necessary personal accessory for a London gentleman. Dare had been trained in its use, of course, and his forays into Paris had kept his skills well-honed. Bonnet, however, had every right to brag about his abilities. He had been trained in the Italian school, and his counterattacks were ruthless. Dare had all he could do to defend himself, even when he was on attack.

There was no sound in the room except for their breathing, gasping now. And the click and hiss of the swords as they met and slid, blade across blade, metal against metal. They had both removed their shoes, of course, so that their feet made no noise as they moved again and again through the classic sequences of feint and parry and riposte.

Dare's shirt was drenched with sweat, but then so was the Frenchman's. Neither had yet scored any disabling blow. He had gotten in under the gambler's guard once, and Bonnet bore a long slash along the side of his neck as witness to that success.

Dare had had two pricks from the razor-sharp point of Bonnet's *épée*. Both of them were bleeding, the one on his upper chest rather more than he would like, the blood pumped out by the heavy exertion the duel made on his heart. Luckily neither wound was in a position where the blood would interfere with his grip.

But he was tiring. He could feel the growing strain on the muscles of his legs, and he knew that if the duel were stopped now, his arms would tremble with fatigue. Of course, the fighting wouldn't stop. There was no rest in a contest such as this. It would go on until one of them was dead or unable to fight any longer. And Dare did not intend to be that one.

He fought the urge to look to where Elizabeth was standing. He could not afford even one second's inattention. He knew that rationally, but as the tiredness seeped into his brain as well as his body, he didn't know it so well in his heart. And at this stage of a duel, heart was always where it mattered.

Because this was not only about skill, Dare told himself, driving Bonnet back with a series of feints, the classic *coup d'arrêt*. It was about Ian, he thought, thrusting again and again at Bonnet, his sword flashing like lightning under the lights of the chandeliers. About Sebastian. And poor Jeremy Richardson. About all the English soldiers who had suffered and died because of information this bastard had provided.

Most of all, of course, it was about Elizabeth. A helpless pawn in a game put into effect by this man.

He could see the surprise in Bonnet's eyes at the fury of his attack. Now, Dare thought. Finish him now, before exhaustion and blood loss make victory impossible.

He had driven the Frenchman to the far end of the room, near where Elizabeth and the others were standing. Thinking of her, his anger fueled his determination that it was now or never. Now or—

Bonnet's free hand had grasped the back of a chair and toppled it, so that it fell onto its side between them. Dare was forced to leap back, and when the Frenchman came over the top of the chair, he held in his left hand the earl's cloak, which he had apparently snatched from Elizabeth's hold in the split second of distraction the falling chair provided.

The hilt of the gambler's sword was held high as he jumped down from the chair, its tip pointing straight at the earl's face. Dare parried, and Bonnet counterparried, his movements swift and sure. And at the same time he threw the cloak at the earl's head.

The heavy cloth fell over Dare like a net, momentarily blinding him. Frantically, he clawed at the fabric, trying to pull it away from his face and trying to judge what Bonnet was doing by the sound of his breathing.

The Frenchman's sword slashed into his left forearm, around which he had finally managed to wrap the coat, freeing his head just in time to see the thrust coming. The gambler's blade cut deeply, but not so deeply as it would have without the unintended protection of the heavy cloth.

Dare threw the cloak off, lunging toward his opponent, who stumbled in surprise against the chair. Bonnet recovered his balance quickly enough to keep his blade up and to parry, but for once he didn't follow up. The earl renewed his attack, driving the gambler back and around the chair, trying desperately to get past his guard. Almost for the first time, he felt that he had the advantage.

Then Bonnet reached out with his free hand and grabbed Elizabeth by her hair. She had not taken time to put it up when she left Dare's bed. His fingers tangled like talons in the fair strands, the Frenchman dragged her forward and threw her toward Dare just as the point of the earl's sword, fully extended, stretched out to reach the gambler's heart.

With an incredible effort, will more than strength, Dare pulled his blade away from Elizabeth, catching her in his left arm as she careened helplessly into him. Behind her came the Frenchman, his sword moving so quickly it seemed alive. Dare parried, once and then again, pushing Elizabeth to the side and out of his way as he did.

He heard her fall against something, but his entire concentration was again focused on the Frenchman. Slashing and thrusting, they went at each other again, blades speaking the ancient language of hand-to-hand combat. Dare was no longer aware of his fatigue or of his wounds.

He was so enraged that Bonnet would dare to do what he had done that he fought as recklessly as the Frenchman now, reacting almost without thought to the classic movements. The gambler's attempt to use Elizabeth had made a mockery of the principles of the duel. Dare should have known, however, that Bonnet was totally without honor. He had already proven that.

Back and forth across the floor the duelers attacked one another, one seeming to have the advantage for a few seconds and then the other. There was no other movement in the room, and no other sound. He could not lose, Dare told himself again and again. Not to this bastard.

And when the opportunity came, it was as unexpected as Bonnet's tricks had been. The blood from the wound in the gambler's neck had heavily stained the left side of his shirt. It mingled with the sweat, leaving a bloom of color down the sleeve and across the front.

Apparently, it had also been running down his arm and had finally reached the hand that held his sword. In the middle of an expulsion, Bonnet's grip on its hilt slipped, and the blade skittered unexpectedly off Dare's. The earl, following his training, or his instinct perhaps, rather than any conscious thought, disengaged, and thrust, straight and true, driving the point of his sword between the Frenchman's ribs, like a lover's stroke, to find his heart.

Impaled on the blade, the Frenchman's motion was halted. His eyes widened, and a trickle of blood escaped the corner of his open mouth. Ruthlessly, Dare pulled his blade back, allowing the gambler to fall forward like a downed tree.

The silence in the room lasted through several long seconds. Finally, panting and trembling, Dare turned, his eyes seeking Elizabeth. He found her standing behind him, the still-loaded Manton, the one he had brought into the salon, held steady in both hands, its muzzle pointed toward the last place where the gambler had been before Dare's sword found his heart.

"*Not* that I didn't trust you, my lord," she said softly.

For a long moment, no one reacted. And then Dare

began to laugh. He allowed the sword that had belonged to the Frenchman's father to fall, and he opened his arms to her.

Slowly Elizabeth lowered the pistol. And then, moving very deliberately, she put it down on the table before she walked into them. Dare crushed her against his chest, ivory lace pressed tightly against the sweat-soaked, bloodstained shirt he wore.

His throat too thick with emotion to tell her what he felt, instead he pressed his lips into the tangled disorder of her hair. He closed his eyes, savoring the feel and the scent of her.

"I'll buy you another dress," he whispered.

"Indeed you will, my lord," she said, leaning back to look up into his eyes. She touched his face with her fingers, and he turned his head to bring his mouth in contact with them before he lifted his head to look across the room.

"Someone should call the constables now, gentlemen. If they wish to question me about the events of this morning, inform them I shall be glad to receive their call. Next week," he added, looking down into Elizabeth's face again. "This week I shall be unavoidably unavailable in Scotland. Gretna Green to be precise."

"Dare..." Elizabeth began.

"Trust me one last time, my darling," he said softly. "I should hate to have to carry you kicking and screaming from the room. We might never live down the scandal."

"Dare—" she said again.

Whatever else she intended to say, he stopped by the simple expedient of putting his mouth over hers. The message his lips conveyed must have been effective. At least kicking and screaming was never included in the tale whenever anyone recounted the deliciously scandalous affair of the Countess of Dare's elopement.

Epilogue

"Come back to bed," Dare suggested lazily. "Even in June, the climate here is hardly suited to what you're wearing."

Since she was wearing only Dare's cloak and nothing at all under it, Elizabeth turned away from the window willingly. She had been looking down on the panorama of the Scottish Lowlands, which were spread out before her in the dawn. Mist lingered like smoke over the dales, and the rising sun painted the low hills with a rim of gold.

Propped on one elbow, her husband was watching her from the bed where she had believed she'd left him sleeping. His hair was still disordered from the touch of her fingers last night, and his eyes, incredibly blue in the morning light, were alight with amusement.

Her *husband,* she thought again, still amazed she had let him talk her into this. Of course, from the very first she had found it very difficult to refuse Dare anything. Not, she acknowledged ruefully, that she had been much inclined to refuse by the time they reached the border, despite all her previous qualms.

Dare had overridden every objection she had tried

to make, often stopping her quite logical arguments simply by putting his lips over hers. And finally, at some point on that flying journey to the border, which they had made in the earl's well-sprung coach, she had stopped protesting. After all, he was offering her everything she had ever dreamed of and refusing to take no for an answer.

Other than the fact that the ceremony was performed "over the anvil," their wedding had been completely, and for Dare uncharacteristically, unromantic. The honeymoon, however, she decided in satisfaction, her eyes still on Dare's face, had more than made up for that.

"And are you planning to lie abed all day today as well, my lord?" she asked.

"I am, Lady Dare. *If* you'll deign to join me," Dare said

"Lazy bones," she accused.

But she walked across the room toward him, bare feet flinching a little from the cold roughness of the stone floor. Dare lifted the covers invitingly, revealing an enticing glimpse of a broad, hair-roughened chest, with whose contours she was by now very intimately acquainted. She threw the cloak on the foot of the bed, and shivering, she slipped in beside him, snuggling against the strong warmth of his body.

He pulled her close, his hands soothing the chill-bumped skin of her back as his lips brushed over her forehead. She could feel the pleasant abrasion of his whiskers on the tip of her nose as his hands slid lower, cupping her bottom.

"There's someone I think you should meet," he said, his mouth so close to her ear that she could feel the warmth of his breath feathering over the fine hair at her temple.

The freedom from anxiety she had enjoyed in his arms the past few days evaporated as suddenly as water thrown on a hot griddle. Her tranquillity had apparently been extremely vulnerable to the thought of facing anything that existed outside this room.

Of course, she had known that they couldn't hide in the wilds of Scotland for the rest of their lives. *And why not?* her heart questioned irrationally, and was ignored.

"And who is that?" she asked, fighting to keep all of that inward trepidation out of her voice.

"My brother Ian."

"The one who will never forgive you if you manage to get yourself killed?" She injected a teasing note into the question, despite the cold dread that had settled in her stomach.

"Of course. My youngest brother, Sebastian, the hellion of the Sinclairs, is still fighting in Spain."

The chill that had begun in her stomach expanded to jolt the rhythm of her heart before she gathered her courage to question what she had recognized as the vital part of that statement. "Still?"

"Ian was invalided out after Salamanca. His injuries were severe enough that he has not yet fully recovered."

"But...that was almost a year ago."

And one of the battles the British army had fought within the period she had worked for Bonnet. During the time when she had supplied information to the French. She knew Dare was aware of that, but he didn't mention it, of course. And neither did she.

"Don't remind Ian of that, whatever you do," Dare

said. "He is impatient enough with his convalescence. I take pains *not* to remind him of how long it's been."

"Perhaps…" she began and then stopped.

How could she possibly explain to Dare that she couldn't do this? She knew what a coward her reluctance to meet his brother made her. Coward she was, nonetheless.

She had confessed to the men at Bonnet's, feeling an almost virtuous relief to finally say the words aloud. But none of them had been personally involved. And the thought of having to face a man who had suffered for over a year, very possibly because of something she herself had told Bonnet…

At her hesitation, Dare had leaned back, looking at her face. "I think you'll like Ian," he said, pretending to be unaware that anything was wrong. "I hope you will. And I know he shall like you."

I know he shall like you. The words repeated over and over in her head, as Dare's lips began to trace over hers. Even as he trailed kisses down her throat and across her breasts, their nipples pebbled with the cold and with her unceasing desire for his caress.

Eventually, he pushed her down onto her back, as he had done dozens of times during the three days they had spent secluded in this room. His body moved with a dear familiarity over hers, his hands touching her with a tenderness that still had the power to render her speechless with need and love.

In the back of her mind, however, apprehension at having to face Ian Sinclair and confess to him what she had done darkened not only the crisp, shining beauty of the breaking day, but haunted the easy fulfillment she had always found in Dare's arms. This time the edge of pleasure he took her to was bittersweet because she knew that no matter how cleverly Dare had couched his request, he had one more task for her to accomplish. One more step he felt she had to take in their relationship. Perhaps the most difficult one of all.

Trust me…

"I hope you will wish us happy," Dare said to his brother, "but if you will not, then I hope you will one day be able to forgive me for choosing Elizabeth over your approval, however much I value it. And you know I do. But…I could more easily give up food, air and water than Elizabeth," he said softly, his eyes finding hers.

Which she discovered were filling, embarrassingly, with hot tears. She turned away, breaking the almost physical contact between them, to look into the hazel eyes of her new brother-in-law.

Ian Sinclair had probably never had the startling masculine beauty his older brother had been blessed with. Although their features, taken individually, were almost identical, Ian's were somehow less clearly defined. The jaw line less distinctly molded, the eyes fine and clear, but not sapphire, of course. His nose was strong and straight, and the lips certainly well-shaped, but neither so finely made as her husband's.

Or perhaps, Elizabeth admitted, it was simply that she no longer saw Dare with any sort of objectivity. After all, the eyes of love were frequently as blurred as her own had been only seconds before.

And Ian Sinclair's features, however handsome, had certainly been tempered by the hardships of war. And by injury and pain. That was somehow obvious, although she had not known him before. The lines of suffering were etched in his face. His eyes were friendly, seeming to belie the possibility that his life had held any hint of anguish.

"And why should you believe I would *not* wish you happy?" Ian said, smiling at her. "Perhaps I should make that wish for Elizabeth instead. Are you sure you haven't made a bad bargain in taking my brother to husband?" Ian asked, his smile widening into laughter as the earl made a boyishly rude noise.

"Perfectly sure," she said softly, offering him her hand.

He hadn't risen when they entered the room, and she found she liked him more for the fact that he made no explanation or apology for that failure in manners, ignoring it instead. As she and Dare both had.

The day was rainy and cold, especially considering the time of year. And after the trip from the north, she had been very glad to be ushered inside to Ian's fire by his housekeeper. Although she suspected the unseasonable weather might be the cause of her brother-in-law's indisposition, no one had mentioned the subject.

Ian took her hand, but he didn't kiss it. He held her eyes instead, seeming to look more deeply into them than she might have wished, before he squeezed her fingers gently and then released them.

"Welcome to the Sinclair family, Elizabeth. Bounders and scoundrels all, I assure you, but we *do* take care of our own. If you ever have need of—"

"She won't," Dare interrupted. "Get your own woman, and stop flirting with mine."

Ian laughed, but his eyes were now examining his brother's face, Elizabeth realized, almost as intently as they had hers.

"I simply thought Elizabeth should know that she can call on me if you get yourself killed on one of your escapades in Paris."

"You may both rest easy on that account. I have been told in no uncertain terms that those missions are at an end," Dare said with regret. "It seems my identity has become known to our enemies."

"Andre?" Ian asked, his voice serious.

"Perhaps. Of course, there are probably a hundred French agents working within England right now."

Elizabeth's breathing faltered at those words. French agents. Which was, she supposed, exactly what she had been until a few days ago.

"My identity could have been discovered in any number of ways," Dare continued. "Bonnet certainly knew something about me before I showed up at his hell. At least enough to know how I would react to his treatment of Elizabeth. We may never know for sure how much he knew about me or how he had discovered it, but others may have that information as well. And according to the War Office, I know too much to be allowed to fall into French hands."

"I can't say I'm not relieved," Ian said quietly. "I would imagine your wife to be, also."

Ian's eyes had come back to her face. Now, she thought. Now is the time to tell him.

"Are you relieved, Elizabeth?" Dare asked, smiling. "I had thought wives delighted in a few days' freedom from their husbands."

"I should suppose that would be dependent on the manner of husband one has," she said almost absently, holding his brother's eyes. And then, speaking directly to Ian, she said softly, "I have something to tell you."

The atmosphere in the room changed subtly, as Elizabeth held her breath, waiting for his response.

"There is *nothing* you need to tell me," Ian said. "Nothing beyond the fact that you are now my sister."

"This isn't what you think," she said.

She supposed he was referring to the years she had spent in the gaming hell. Perhaps rumors of his brother's terrible misalliance had traveled even here. There were those who would delight in sharing the news of her unsuitability with Dare's family. Or perhaps Dare himself had told his brother.

Ian smiled at her. "Whatever it is, you owe me no explanation. Not about anything."

"And if this is an explanation I *wish* to give you?" she suggested, her voice very low.

Ian's eyes left hers, seeking Dare's. She didn't turn to follow them, so that she wasn't sure what silent communication her husband had conveyed in that exchange of glances.

When her brother-in-law's eyes came back to her face, however, they had not changed. They contained only compassion.

"Then I will listen to what you wish to tell me, of course. As long as *you* understand that whatever it is will make not a particle of difference in our relationship. Now or in the future," Ian said.

"You can't know that."

"Believe me, I can," Ian said.

She waited a moment, thinking about that promise, but in the end, it changed nothing. He couldn't know how he would feel. Nor would she. Not until she had told him.

"I have done things..." Her voice faltered, but his

eyes didn't change. Steadfastly, they held on hers, waiting. "Terrible things," she said finally, unwilling to try to mitigate her guilt. "I repeated information overheard at Bonnet's which I knew would eventually be conveyed to French commanders in the field. Information that might provide them with an advantage when they faced our troops. Information that almost certainly resulted in death and injury."

And now she waited, expecting the hazel eyes to change. Anticipating that they would reflect the judgment she had long ago made of her own actions.

"And did you do that because you wish to put the French at an advantage?" Ian asked.

Of all the questions she had been prepared to answer, this was not one she had expected. Had he asked if she had passed the information of her own free will, she would have told him the truth. She had made that choice to keep her brother alive, and she would not have lied about it, just as she would not now soften the effect of what she had done by explaining how she had tried to make that information useless.

That had not been his question, however. And when she repeated the one he had asked in her mind, she realized that there was really only one answer.

"No," she said softly.

"Good," Ian said. "I would never have believed you *wished* to harm anyone. I must confess, however, that you made me afraid. Now, I find there is nothing in your confession that is so terrible, after all."

"Perhaps you didn't understand," she said.

"There is nothing damaged about my understanding, Elizabeth, I assure you," he said smiling. "No matter what Dare may try to tell you," he said, smiling at his brother. "This, however," he said, putting his hand down flat on his right thigh, "is quite another story. This damnable weather has make a crock of me again, I'm afraid. Will you give me your arm into dinner? Although Dare tries to help, he never manages to do it to suit me."

Left with nothing to say, not even given the opportunity to offer him her apology, she turned to look at her husband, who was smiling at her with what appeared to be a great deal of smug satisfaction. *Trust me...*

"How very strange," Elizabeth said, turning back and offering her arm to her new brother-in-law. "He always manages to suit me very well."

* * * * *

Gayle Wilson's latest Intrigue,
HER PRIVATE BODYGUARD,
a continuation of her popular
MEN OF MYSTERY
series, is currently available.

The next MEN OF MYSTERY *novel,*
RENEGADE HEART,
will be on the shelves in August.

Please watch for Gayle's novella
MY DARLING ECHO
in the upcoming Harlequin anthology
BRIDE BY ARRANGEMENT,
which will be out in the same month.

Discover the joys of
nineteenth-century America with
four brand-new Westerns from
Harlequin Historicals.

On sale July 2000

THE BLUSHING BRIDE
by **Judith Stacy**
(California)

and

JAKE'S ANGEL
by **Nicole Foster**
(New Mexico)

On sale August 2000

THE PAPER MARRIAGE
by **Bronwyn Williams**
(North Carolina)

and

PRAIRIE BRIDE
by **Julianne McLean**
(Kansas)

Harlequin Historicals
The way the past *should* have been.

HARLEQUIN®
Makes any time special ™

Harlequin® Historical

PRESENTS

THE SIRENS OF THE SEA

The brand-new series from bestselling author

Ruth Langan

Join the spirited Lambert sisters in their
search for adventure—and love!

On sale August 2000
THE SEA WITCH
When dashing Captain Riordan Spencer arrives in
Land's End, Ambrosia Lambert may have
met her perfect match!

On sale January 2001
THE SEA NYMPH
Middle sister Bethany must choose between a
scandalous highwayman and the very proper
Earl of Alsmeeth.

In Summer 2001
Look for youngest sister Darcy's story,
THE SEA SPRITE

Harlequin Historical
The way the past *should* have been!

HARLEQUIN®
Makes any time special ™

Take a romp through
Merrie Olde England
with four adventurous tales
from Harlequin Historicals.

In July 2000 look for

MALCOLM'S HONOR
by **Jillian Hart**
(England, 1280s)

LADY OF LYONSBRIDGE
by **Ana Seymour**
(England, 1190s)

In August 2000 look for

THE SEA WITCH
by **Ruth Langan**
(England, 1600s)

PRINCE OF HEARTS
by **Katy Cooper**
(England, 1520s)

Harlequin Historicals
The way the past *should* have been!